THE
MOONCHILD

BY KENNETH McKENNEY

 Simon and Schuster : New York

DESIGNED BY IRVING PERKINS
MANUFACTURED IN THE UNITED STATES OF AMERICA
1 2 3 4 5 6 7 8 9 10
LIBRARY OF CONGRESS CATALOGING IN PUBLICATION DATA

MCKENNEY, KENNETH, DATE.
    THE MOONCHILD.

    I. TITLE.
PZ4.M1559MO 1978 [PR6063.A2429] 823 77-13170
ISBN 0-671-22887-0

Epigraph on page vii from "East Coker" in *Four Quartets* by T. S.
Eliot, copyright 1943 by T. S. Eliot; copyright 1971 by Esme Valerie
Eliot. Reprinted by permission of Harcourt Brace Jovanovich, Inc.

for Groundhog and Miss Mouse
without whose help this would have
been completed much sooner

Home is where one starts from. As we grow older
The world becomes stranger, the pattern more complicated
Of dead and living.

—T. S. ELIOT
"East Coker," *Four Quartets*

PART I

THE DEATH

CHAPTER ONE

Everywhere the cold was bleak and penetrating. Snow flattened the Bavarian landscape, branches and hedgerows were
hung with stalactites of clear ice. Even the air seemed frozen.
Although it was noon the light was feeble and gray, and from
where he stood in the high-paneled, late-nineteenth-century
bedroom, Edmund Blackstone could only just make out the line
of blackish pines two hundred yards from the hotel. Above them
hung low, heavy cloud. The scene was without color, monochrome, like a black-and-white lithograph.

As Edmund Blackstone watched, a small ripple of wind shook
the landscape, thin snow was lifted and whirled over flattened
hillocks, stiffened pine tree branches shook and cracked sharply
as icicles snapped and clattered to the snow beneath. The
sounds they made were crisp and carried clearly over the win-
tered countryside.

"How bleak," Edmund Blackstone said in his light English
voice. "How very unlike Christmas."

As if in response the wind eddied again, thin powder snow
whirled sluggishly. From the pine trees came a further succession
of cracks as more icicles fell and their breaking sounded shotlike
in the frozen air.

Edmund Blackstone shivered delicately and rubbed his hands
together. In a little while he would go downstairs to the wood-

paneled drawing room, curtained in crimson, where a log fire burned hungrily in the grate and where, he knew, he would find his wife, Anna, her face creased with concern. But for the moment he remained, rubbing his hands softly, reviving a little warmth, absorbing the soft, white-blanketed detail of the bleak landscape, remembering how it appeared in the summer, without snow or ice or chilling wind.

Edmund and Anna Blackstone and their son, Simon, had seen it in the summer of two years earlier: then the grasses were sprinkled with the vivid colors of wildflowers and the air had been full of birds. It was a different landscape, in a different time, and the worry which absorbed them now had not begun.

Edmund Blackstone peered into the gray, obscure sky to where he knew the mountains were, those high ragged peaks, now invisible, which in the summer were firm brown landmarks where he and Anna and Simon had often climbed. He wished he could see them now; he needed their solemn strength.

He wished, not for the first time, to be back in those happy days when Simon had been active and well, a healthy golden-haired child running on a green hillside. The memory was painful. Edmund Blackstone closed his eyes at the thought only to open them once more to the cold gray landscape and the shuddering wind.

Edmund sighed and turned from the scene, knowing nothing would bring back the simple happiness they had shared walking the springing grasses, wearing lederhosen, breathing thin clear air, watching the coaches travel the valley below, hearing crisp, delayed sounds of cowbells rising in the sunlight. It had been a lovely time—simple, joyful, contained.

Now Edmund walked slowly, almost reluctantly, from the bedroom, each solemn step carrying him toward his wife's sadness and concern. He went down the broad carpeted stairs to the floor below and entered the drawing room where the fire blazed in the grate and Anna sat, hunched and withdrawn. She turned toward him.

Edmund Blackstone smiled and went to her. In spite of the strain her face was handsome, and the sight gave him a small moment of pleasure. It was always the same; each time he saw her anew it pleased him to see how lovely she was, how splendid her brow and the way her dark hair fell to each side of it, how rich was her mouth. Anna returned Edmund's smile, her own small, still, stiff with worry.

"Is there any news?" Edmund asked.

Anna shook her head. "Edith is with him now and the doctor said he would be back at one, but there is no change. He is still the same." Anna whispered the words as if speaking in the presence of the sick child himself.

"Poor Simon," Edmund muttered.

"The doctor maintains it is fever."

"I am afraid he does not really know what it is." Edmund extended his hands to the warmth. "No more than we."

"It is taking so long."

Edmund Blackstone nodded. "That is the damnable part of it, waiting, not knowing," he said.

They had come to the hotel a fortnight earlier with Miss Edith Harris, Simon's governess, to spend a winter in the mountains, returning to this part of Bavaria to see if the magic they had known in the summer had its counterpart in a winter landscape. But before they had fully arrived in the carriage which brought them up the narrow, winding, icy road from the station to the hotel, Simon had shown signs of the illness which for the past thirteen days had racked his seven-year-old body.

During that time he had barely eaten, had lain limp, flushed, feverish, the heat of his whole being contrasting with the cold winter air. He had drunk little and, almost from the beginning, had failed to recognize those about him who mopped his brow, who held his hand and prayed as his little body gasped for breath and groaned in agony.

Once he had opened his eyes and stared at Miss Harris, the governess, and said in a clear voice, "I am going home soon, aren't I?" Miss Harris had nodded quickly and turned her face away.

On one other occasion, while his mother had been beside the bed, Simon had looked up at her in the same calm way and asked, "When is my birthday? Is it not soon?" His voice had sounded healthy, unfevered.

"Why, yes," Anna had replied uncertainly.

"When is it, Mummy?"

"In less than a month now."

"Will I be home by then?" Simon's voice had persisted. "Will I be home for my birthday?"

"I do not know," Anna replied. "You shall have to get better first, my darling."

Simon then nodded, twisted his head on the pillow and had not spoken a further word for the remainder of his illness.

Early in the child's condition the village doctor had been called, a thin little Bavarian, who it was rumored had studied in Vienna as a contemporary of Freud, and who from the beginning had admitted to himself that he did not understand the true nature of the child's illness. There seemed to be no development to the disease, no sign of a crisis, no turning point from which either survival or death could be predicted. Instead the boy's condition remained constant: high fever, isolation from the world about him, continuing torment of the frail, tortured body.

However there *was* a further aspect of Simon's illness which puzzled the doctor even more, for in spite of the demands of the disease and although Simon had taken little food or drink, there was no apparent wasting of the child's body. There was no obvious loss of weight, the flesh remained stable and the firm skin retained its normal elasticity, there did not appear to be any destruction of tissue—signs the doctor would have expected almost from the onset of the condition. This anomaly puzzled him deeply; he could not imagine what force kept the child whole.

After the first week he remarked obliquely on this phenomenon to Edmund Blackstone. "There is one encouraging aspect of your son's illness," he began warily. "There is no sign of his succumbing to the fever." He cleared his throat and glanced at Edmund's remote English face, awaiting the effect of his words.

"What do you mean, exactly?" Edmund asked.

"It is a most optimistic sign."

"Of what?"

"Of his survival, of course. He must possess an extremely healthy little body."

"Not at the moment," Edmund remarked dryly. "What *is* he suffering from?"

The doctor cleared his throat once more. "A fever, naturally," he began. "But of precisely what nature it is difficult to diagnose. Fever is not common in Bavaria at this time of the year," he added as if to explain his uncertainty.

"But you do have sufficient experience of it?" Edmund inquired, raising his pale eyebrows. "After all, Doctor, we are almost into the twentieth century. Surely medical science is not confounded by so simple a condition as fever?"

"Fevers are not always simple, Mr. Blackstone," the doctor replied, his voice displaying a little more concern. "We still have a great deal to learn about them, twentieth century or not."

"And of my son's?"

"There is nothing more I can tell you at the moment." The doctor picked up his bag, preparing to depart. "Except that I am most pleased with the way his body is maintaining its strength. As I say, there is no sign of deterioration at all."

Edmund Blackstone nodded slowly and then said, "Forgive me for suggesting this, Doctor, but would a second opinion be valuable at this stage?"

The little doctor smiled briefly. "I am not offended by what you suggest," he said. "Already I have sent a telegraph to Professor Walter Albricht in München—Munich. He is a world authority on fevers. I have, in fact, asked his advice and expect a reply any day now." With that he nodded and in quick, short steps left the room.

That conversation had occurred eight days earlier and although Edmund had asked on almost every occasion since what the response from Professor Albricht had been, the doctor assured him there had been no reply. He apologized for the delay, he was certain the professor was in residence at the university, and he could only conclude that the professor was as puzzled as he by the child's symptoms and must be researching the case with extreme care. Edmund Blackstone did not press the matter further; the concern he read in the little doctor's eyes spoke of more than Edmund wished to know; it contained a fear Edmund felt no desire to probe or uncover. He had made no mention of the conversation or the telegram to Anna.

Now as he stood beside her in the wood-paneled drawing room with its crimson drapes, Anna looked up suddenly. "What time is it now?" she asked.

Edmund Blackstone took a gold timepiece engraved with the Queen's image from his waistcoat and looked at it carefully. "Twelve-thirty," he replied, closing the watchfront.

"We should never have come," Anna said abruptly. "There's been nothing but cold and misery here."

"Who could have known that?" Edmund comforted. "Often the Christmases are beautiful, with sunshine and quite hot days."

"Christmas?" interrupted Anna. "Is it Christmas already?"

"The day after tomorrow."

"I had not realized." Anna sighed heavily and reached for her husband's hand. She took it, not looking at him; her eyes returned to the moving flames. When she spoke again her voice was small, remote, distant. "Do you think he will die, Edmund?" she asked.

Edmund Blackstone hesitated. "We must always keep that possibility in mind," he said finally.

"But what do you *think?*"

"I . . . don't know."

"Then you must believe . . . ?"

"No." Edmund Blackstone shook his head. He released his wife's hand and moved a little distance from her as if to remain objective, as if to examine all the facts in perspective. "No, I just do not know, that's all. We can only hope and pray for the best."

Anna examined the neat, blond, dapper man of thirty-four; hair brushed straight back, carefully suited, medium build, one of many such well-bred, faintly delicate faces to be seen in or out of England in this late nineteenth century—one of those faces which, wherever it might be seen, was categorized as unmistakably English. There was a closeness about him, a remove, that even after eight years of marriage she had never penetrated and somehow knew she never would. Although she was a year older than her husband she felt more youthful than he, less restricted somehow, less conditioned in character and attitude by time and the progress of manners. As she watched him now, the closed timepiece in his hand, his neat back straight, everything about him was perfect.

Anna sighed, nodded, and did not reply. There was comfort in his reliability.

Anna had met her husband one late midsummer afternoon nine years earlier at Ascot. There, in the slanting sunlight which turned the oak leaves a clear lime green, she had seen him standing between tables on the grass, amongst the champagne and the silver, the servants and the horses, talking to a friend of her brother's about a new fossil he had discovered in Devon. Edmund's mixture of neatness and maturity, the slightly pompous way he spoke and the completeness of his mannerisms were immediately acceptable to her. He was so molded, so framed, she felt she had known him all her life. Later, after they had been introduced, he talked with her awhile but she was both surprised and strangely delighted when, a week later, he sent his card and asked if he might call.

Edmund courted Anna for a year with all the formality required, with a sense of timelessness and inevitability. When they were finally married in Winchester Cathedral, where an uncle of Edmund's had once been Dean, it was almost as if the service had been planned from the moment they were born and its consummation no more than another marked signpost in their extremely ordered courses. They settled in Tonbridge in a house overlooking the river where the order of their pleasant but passionless days remained unaltered. Simon was born, the seasons turned, Edmund continued his studies. Nothing, it seemed, could ever alter the balance of their progress.

"We are doing our best for him." Anna blinked as she heard Edmund continue. "That I do believe."

"Our best?" Anna's head came up in question. "Here, in this dreadfully cold village with a doctor who gives me no confidence at all?" She closed her eyes in despair. "Even you say he does not really know what Simon is suffering from."

"I have more confidence in him than may appear," Edmund said, changing his mind about informing Anna of the telegram to Munich. "As a matter of fact he's been in touch with an associate. There's a professor something-or-other in Munich who's a world authority on fever. The doctor here has asked advice on Simon's condition and I shouldn't be surprised if he's had an answer by now."

"When did you know this?"

"A few days ago."

"Why did you not tell me?"

"I did not want to raise any false hopes," Edmund said. "There was no reason to worry you further at the time."

"And now?"

"Now I feel you need to know exactly how much *is* being done," Edmund assured her. "We aren't all that remote from the best medical minds up here in the mountains."

"Then why has he not heard from Munich before this?"

"I expect the professor's checking something or other," Edmund replied confidently. "There'll be some miraculous formula on the way any day now."

Anna returned her gaze to the fireplace; there was a comforting assurance in the flames, they lived and moved, danced and progressed. There was no purpose in questioning Edmund further. He would only retreat behind his slight, confident façade, trying to help from that remove. Also, she had something of her own in mind, something she had not been able to mention to Edmund before and, even now, knew she would remain silent about. Because even to herself she denied it, put it out of her mind as if it had been a bad dream, something which would dissolve, disappear in the light of reason.

No, she thought, as she stared at the fire: that heap of rags, that bony old hand reaching for the hem of her dress, those old woman's eyes burning out of the dirty whiteness of the face were not real, did not make sense, could not possibly be taken seriously. Yet the words were as vivid as the day they had been spoken at the railway station of this small Bavarian village.

"I know," the old woman had said in her broken, reedy voice. "Your son . . . I know."

"What?" Anna had stopped, turned, peered down at the crone. "What did you say?"

"Your son . . . the child."

"What about my son?" Anna had glanced across the station to where Simon and Edmund stood, their luggage about them, waiting for the porter to come from the other side of the platform with his trolley. They were laughing, and even in the flat gray winter light Simon's hair glowed golden and vital. As he laughed, his breath plumed with cold; he looked beautiful and eternal, vivid and indestructible; it seemed at that moment he would live forever. "What about him?" Anna asked the crone quickly, fiercely defending the child.

"He is . . ." the crone began, then stopped speaking. Her eyes searched Anna's face, and, perhaps seeing too much, she ceased. Her tongue stilled, the glow in her eyes faded and she whispered only a single further word. "Nothing . . ."

"What did you say?"

The old woman's head returned to her rags and Anna could get no more from her. Anna stood a moment longer bent over the crone, a little confused by the words and their sudden dying, a little frightened that this collection of spent humanity should dare to, could be able to, touch her or her husband or their lovely child. Then, abruptly, she gathered her skirts and moved to join Edmund and Simon, laughing as they waited for the luggage to be collected.

Since then she had tried to put the old woman out of mind, but the image constantly drifted back, curled in and out of her memory as the days progressed and Simon's condition remained critical, unchanged. Again and again she saw the dirty bundle of rags and the old woman's burning eyes; the reedy voice sounded and the words became more and more profound.

"I know," the old woman had said, and Anna wondered what she knew. Had she seen Simon two years earlier, had she spoken to him then? And her final "Nothing" trailing away to nothing itself, chilled with its finality.

Anna lifted her hands and, placing her long fingers to her temples, rubbed gently as if the action might erase the mystery. She wished she were able to talk to Edmund about the crone and the words she had heard. She wished Edmund had been there when the old woman had spoken, but she knew, instinctively, in that case the creature would have said nothing at all. She sighed and turned once again to her husband; she loved him, that much was simple, but at times approaching him was not easy.

Edmund smiled. "The doctor will be here any moment now," he said reassuringly.

As if waiting for such a signal the door was opened by the landlord of the hotel. A tall, florid man, he was dressed in a green Bavarian hunting suit. There was snow on his boots. In his hand he carried a green trilby with a bright red pheasant's feather sewn into the band. But in spite of his colorfulness his usually genial face was solemn, set for the occasion.

"The doctor is here," he said in German. "He is with the boy."

"Thank you," Edmund replied in the same language. "I will join them in a moment."

"I think he would like you to remain here." The landlord appeared momentarily embarrassed. "That is what he asked me to tell you."

"Very well then." Edmund glanced at Anna. "We await his pleasure."

The landlord nodded, his duty done, and left the room. He closed the door silently behind him, moving as if from the sickroom itself.

"Edmund?" Anna asked immediately they were alone. "What was the significance of that?"

"I'm not sure. Perhaps he has something new he wants to apply. He must have heard from Munich."

"Strange he does not want us there."

"It may be easier for him to work alone," Edmund assured her. "Without anyone at his elbow."

"Edith's there..." Anna began, but again as if awaiting its cue, the door opened and Miss Edith Harris came quietly, almost furtively, into the room, one hand holding her skirts above the flooring, her round flat country face shadowed by gloom. "Ah, Edith," Anna asked, "what is going on?"

"The doctor's with him now, ma'am," Miss Harris said quickly. Her accent was broad northern. "He says to wait here, if you don't mind."

"We already have that information." Anna's voice lifted. "How does Simon seem?"

"There's no change, I'm afraid, ma'am." Miss Harris bit her lip. "He's just the same, really."

Anna nodded; the fear on the governess's face enabled her to control her own. "Come and sit by the fire," she said gently and moved to make room for the girl.

Once more the drawing room was still, silent save for the occasional crackle of the fire, motionless as all three waited for the doctor to descend and inform them if he had heard from Munich and what was to be done for the fevered child lying in the room above.

It was a long time before the little Bavarian doctor came downstairs. When finally he entered the drawing room with a firm step, his face was a little flushed and there were small beads of sweat on his forehead. He looked as if he had been laboring but his voice was clear and confident as he said, "Good afternoon. I think I have better news for you."

"What?" Anna rose to her feet uncertainly.

"I have heard from München—Munich." The doctor paused and looked from face to face. "You know about Professor Albricht, I take it?"

Anna nodded impatiently. "What did he say?"

"He has gone into the matter most carefully," continued the doctor. "He studied all the symptoms I forwarded, and, I believe, he has returned me some very sound advice."

"Which is . . . ?" broke in Edmund.

"He suggested . . ." The doctor paused, a knowing smile on his lips. "He suggested that we employ the tried and tested method of cold baths."

"*Cold baths?*" Edmund was astounded. "In this climate?"

"That is exactly why I hesitated to use the method myself," the doctor replied. "But Professor Albricht assures me it will produce excellent results, and after all he is one of the world authorities on this type of disease."

"What type of disease?" Edmund asked harshly. "To my knowledge you've not even diagnosed it yet."

"It is obviously some sort of enteric fever," the doctor said calmly. "The professor agrees with me on that."

"But—cold baths," Anna interjected. "That's medieval."

"I agree," said Edmund. "What is more I positively forbid it."

"Thank God for that," accorded Anna. "I shudder to think what effect anything so drastic might have."

"That is precisely why cold baths are used." The doctor did not appear quite so confident; his smile had been replaced by a slight frown. "The shock effect can be miraculous. Reduction of temperature in some cases has been instant."

"I can imagine," said Edmund dryly. "But under no circumstances. I insist."

The little doctor hesitated; he licked his lips. "In that case," he began, his voice unusually controlled, "I have to inform you that I have already administered the first of such treatments."

"What?" Edmund's pale face flushed with anger. "Without consulting me?"

"It is not usual to consult laymen on matters of treatment," the doctor replied defensively. "Certainly not when the treatment is recommended by so eminent a figure as Professor Albricht."

Even as he spoke the doctor realized he had lost his audience. Before he had completed his explanation, both the Blackstones had begun to leave the room, closely followed by Miss Harris.

"There's no need for concern," the little doctor called after them in his thick accent. "I assure you, the treatment has been most successful."

Only Miss Harris took any notice of his remark, without even clearly understanding all that had been implied. She paused by the open door long enough to turn and say in her north-country accent, "Oh, what have you done, you silly foreign man?" Then she too was gone.

Upstairs Edmund and Anna found Simon lying still and seemingly serene in his bed. Some of the flush had gone from the child's face and his breathing was more even than it had been for days. Edmund placed a hand on his son's forehead; it felt cooler, less fevered.

"What is it?" asked Anna quickly. "How is he?"

"He does seem a little better," Edmund admitted. "At least his temperature appears to be going down."

"Thank God for that."

Miss Harris gave a little choking gasp of relief.

"Not that I approve, mind you," Edmund went on. "Far too drastic a treatment for anyone in this weather, let alone a child. But I must say there does seem to be some improvement."

"Simon?" Anna knelt beside the bed and took one of the child's hands in her own. "Dear, dear Simon, are you really going to be well again?"

"It looks like it, ma'am, doesn't it?" Miss Harris came closer. "He looks more like himself than he did."

Anna nodded. "Yes, he'll be all right now," she said. Suddenly the pain and tension of the past thirteen days broke within her and she put her head on the bed and sobbed. Huge gasping sobs racked her; tears spilled onto the sheet. "You will be all right now, Simon, won't you?" she gasped. "You'll get better now."

Edmund let Anna cry until her sobbing began to subside, until she began to regain control. He stood beside her looking down at the sleeping, almost calm, face of his son and knew a profound relief. He felt simplified, as if a great burden had been taken from him. Then he placed a hand on his wife's shoulder and helped her to her feet.

"Come along," he said softly. "Let him sleep peacefully while he can."

Anna nodded and pressed a handkerchief to her lips.

Edmund glanced at Miss Harris and saw her wipe a tear from her cheek. "Would you mind staying a little, Edith?" he asked.

"Of course not, sir." Miss Harris took the chair beside the

bed. "I'll be happy to." She brushed at a further tear. "Oh, isn't it wonderful to see him like this."

"Yes." Edmund took his wife's arm. "Yes, thank God, he does seem to be on the mend."

Together Edmund and Anna went down the broad carpeted stairs to the drawing room. At the bottom of the stairs Anna paused and put her head on Edmund's shoulder and murmured, "Oh, Edmund . . . the relief . . . the relief." Edmund tightened his arm about her. "Yes," he whispered. "It is enormous." They both realized in that moment just how oppressive the weight of Simon's illness had been, just how grateful they were, greedy for any hope, however slender.

When they entered the drawing room they found the landlord standing, his back to the fire, awaiting them, smiling. "Ah," he said, "there is some better news, I am told."

"Yes," replied Edmund. "The doctor . . ." He paused and looked around for the little Bavarian. "Is he still here?"

"He had to go," the landlord said. "There was another appointment."

"Pity. I feel I owe him some sort of apology."

"So do I," murmured Anna.

The landlord raised his eyebrows and looked from face to face. He saw the relief in each, the lifting concern, the gratitude. "Do not be too concerned," he assured them. "The doctor was in a very good mood when he left."

"He'll be back in the morning," Edmund said. "I shall speak to him then." He patted Anna's arm comfortingly. "For the first time in many days," he added, "I look forward to a hearty meal."

"Like the condemned man?" joked the landlord.

"On the contrary," replied Edmund coolly. "Like one reprieved."

That evening the Blackstones dined in the hall where antlers lined white walls, proverbs were inscribed in runic letters beneath the noble heads, heavy oaken beams bound the ceiling. They took a corner table and ate heartily of goulash soup and *Schweinbraten*, sauerkraut and dumplings; they drank crisp, young Riesling, and later, with his coffee and cigar, Edmund took cognac. The meal was delicious, wholesome, filling, it contented them as little else had for days. It left Edmund in an expansive mood, and as he twirled his cigar and watched the smoke rise, as he lifted his glass and admired the fine pale cognac, he began to forgive Bavaria for the days of inflicted pain.

It was an easy concession to make. Edmund loved all things German. As a young man he had spent a year in Berlin learning, together with the language, the manly art of boxing; each day as he walked the city to either the gymnasium or his tutelage he had grown more and more fond of the country, its people, trees, buildings, monuments. In the early years of his marriage he had taught Anna a little of the language, and later, when it suited him, he would instruct Simon also.

Edmund Blackstone had never known employment, had never been required to work; his father was an importer of German wines, and although Edmund took a passing interest in the business, he knew it would never absorb him. Fortunately it did not need to; his father had settled on him a liberal allowance.

So as not to appear completely idle, Edmund had taken to the study of paleontology and had already established a minor reputation for his classification of the lesser-known trilobites of the Ordovician. He had read a paper before the Royal Society and had been asked to lecture on several occasions to graduate classes at Cambridge.

"I enjoy nothing more than walking a hillside and tapping open a rock," he was apt to say. "There is a peculiar pleasure in knowing that it is your hand, and yours alone, which has caused that rock to part company for the first and only time." He would smile then and add, "It is an intensely personal deed."

Already at thirty-four Edmund had an air of middle age about him. It would only be a matter of time, he felt sure, before he became an established figure in the relatively young science of paleontology. It occurred to him he might even be offered a chair in some university. He hoped this would be the case. There was nothing he would like more, for the rest of his life, than to work with his fossils, to collect, examine, classify and record those which interested him most and to pass that knowledge on to students in an atmosphere of respect and honor, prestige and generosity. He could see himself already within ivied walls, serene, his hair a little gray, passing learning on to those who regarded it most.

"What are you thinking?" Anna asked, seeing the dreamy expression on her husband's face. "What is going on in your mind?"

The words startled Edmund; he blinked and took another pull on his cigar. "Nothing much, my dear," he replied carelessly. "I was merely enjoying the feeling of relief, I imagine." He blew a long feather of cigar smoke into the air. "It's been a trying time for us all."

"For you especially. You've given us all such courage."

Edmund smiled. "You've shown great strength yourself, my dear," he said generously.

They gazed at each other across the little table and were contained. They loved each other comfortably, affectionately, without the demands of passion. Anna bent her head and smiled from beneath the wing of her hair; Edmund's eyes crinkled. They exchanged an act of mutual encouragement.

UPSTAIRS, in the room with Simon, Miss Harris stroked the child's hair, brushed it back from his less fevered forehead, whispered to him. Simon stretched his neck and buried his head a little deeper into the pillow; he seemed relaxed and easy. He seemed to be recovering.

"The miracle of it," Miss Harris whispered. "To think what a cold bath can do. I'd never have imagined."

She took a teddy bear which had been lying beside the bed

and placed it on the pillow by Simon's golden head; she patted it into place, making both of them as comfortable as she was able. She smiled and sat back, watching her charges. She dozed.

EDMUND Blackstone was on a green hillside tapping ancient mudstones when he first became aware that he was being called. In the pale gray rock he could see the shape of tiny trilobites. They were like none he knew. The piece he was tapping contained an almost perfect specimen. It was nearly his when he heard his name being shouted urgently, frighteningly, from a distance. For a moment he attempted to ignore the call but its insistence demanded. The trilobites dissolved and the greenness of the hillside turned into the darkness of night and he found himself awake, groping to turn up the heavy brass paraffin lamp which stood beside the bed.

Its flame jumped as Anna awakened, and the voice which had been calling Edmund's name came closer, seemed to rise in pitch, then break. Suddenly Edmund realized who it belonged to and what words were being shouted, screamed now, down the long hotel passageway.

The voice belonged to Miss Edith Harris. "Mr. Blackstone ... oh God ... Mr. Blackstone," she was crying. "Come ... come quickly. He's dead ... dear God ... *Simon's dead.*"

Edmund stumbled, almost fell, from the bed. In his nightgown, he ran down the passageway toward the crying voice. Anna followed. Together they forced their way into Simon's bedroom to find Miss Harris standing, her hands over her face, screaming her words of futility and death loudly, endlessly, without hope. Quickly Edmund went to her, roughly he pulled her hands from her face and without hesitation slapped her harshly on both cheeks. Miss Harris stopped screaming. Her face went white and although her mouth remained open, framing the last of her despairing cries, she became silent; she stood numbed, looking down at the body of Simon Blackstone in the bed.

Anna was already at the bedside leaning over her son. Edmund joined her. Together they bent over the tiny, incredibly still body. Edmund took the child's wrist, felt for the pulse but found none; pulling aside Simon's nightgown he placed his head on the unmoving chest listening for a heartbeat but there was nothing to hear; he took a glass from beside the bed and held it beneath the child's nostrils hoping that condensation would indicate a remnant of something living; but there was none, no sign, nothing.

In the end he stood slowly and looked down at his son, bewilderment, disbelief, tragedy stamped cruelly on his face. Anna watched his every move and when he finally stood she read clearly his defeat.

"No," Anna cried loudly, despairingly. "No, it is not true. I don't believe it. No."

Edmund's expression did not alter.

"Oh, no," Anna repeated and buried her face in the child's body. "Oh, dear God, no."

By now there were other faces at the doorway of the bedroom, other voices were raised in curiosity and concern. A mixture of other guests, dressed and semi-dressed, frightened or disturbed, peered about the lintel of the door with their questions.

"Please go away," Edmund said, turning to them. "There is nothing you can do here. Please go."

But they remained, persistent, curious, intrusive.

"Go," said Edmund once more, his voice controlled. Then, when there was no response, his anger snapped and he stepped quickly to the door and shouted, "Go. Get out of here. Leave us alone," and with one swift action slammed the heavy wooden door shut in their inquisitive faces.

The crash of the door echoed down the long corridors of the hotel, it reverberated, it bounced and slowly it died. As it vanished its sound was replaced with a hollow, tragic sobbing which came from the dead child's room.

CHAPTER TWO

A LITTLE after seven the following morning the Bavarian doctor trudged up the icy road to the hotel for the second time since the child's death. It was still dark. The cold air stung. As he breathed, icicles formed in his nostrils, his eyes watered constantly, his bootheels rang like steel on the frozen roadway. Earlier in the night, when he had been called for the first time, after Edmund had failed to find any life in his son's body, his reception at the hotel had been hostile. Edmund had blamed the doctor and his brutal treatment for the child's death; he castigated the man for his inefficiency, his inability to diagnose Simon's condition, the shortcomings of his whole profession.

All this the little doctor withstood patiently, understanding the outrage and the grief. Listening calmly, he examined the corpse, placed his stethoscope on the pale chest, and pumped air in and out of the tiny lungs. But he, like Edmund, failed to find any trace of life in the body. Ultimately he pulled the sheet up over Simon's face and covered him from the world. Then, and only then, did he turn to the distraught parents and speak.

"I am truly sorry," he said with dignity. "But I assure you the treatment is not to blame."

Edmund had opened his mouth to reply, but Anna, who throughout the examination had remained silent, put her hand on her husband's arm to quiet him.

"Do not say more, Edmund," she said, her voice resigned, patient, weary. "It will not help. Nothing will bring Simon back to us."

At these words, Miss Harris burst into harsh, despairing sobs. Anna went to her and led her from the room. Edmund hesitated a moment longer, then he too began to leave. As he went the doctor called to him softly.

"I will give you some sedatives," he said, reaching into his bag. "I think you will all appreciate them this night."

Edmund's face sagged. Suddenly the tremendous truth of the situation struck him; the loss was profound. "Is there truly nothing we can do, Doctor?" he asked, regretting his earlier outburst, needing assurance now, and help.

The doctor shook his head. "I'm afraid not, Mr. Blackstone," he replied. He turned toward the body on the bed. "There was little we could do from the outset apart from being able to administer some temporary relief."

Edmund turned blindly away and left the room. Later he saw to it that Anna and Miss Harris took a sedative; then they retired to their beds. All slept fitfully, falling between phases of deeply sedated sleep and restless turning, waiting for the morning, wondering how something so precious could be taken from them with such finality.

Now, as the doctor returned to the hotel in the frozen dawn, he went immediately to the child's bedroom. A maid let him in and, without disturbing the Blackstones, he went quietly to where Simon lay. There was something about the death the doctor did not fully comprehend. He had not referred to it the night before as he did not himself understand the anomaly, and its mystery could only have made the parents' grief more piercing. But the fact was that although there was absolutely no sign of life in the child's body the immediate signs of death were not apparent either.

The doctor went into the bedroom and began a re-examination

of the corpse. What he had suspected was confirmed. There was no real rigor mortis. There was some stiffening of the child's frame but it was not the same. It was almost as if the body had become fixed, firmed, rather than clamped with the rigidity of death. There was no darkening of the skin, nor—and the doctor was more perplexed by this than by anything—did the temperature drop to that of the room. There was a slight falling away of body heat. The doctor's thermometer registered 64.3 degrees Fahrenheit, but nothing like he would have expected in the usual circumstances, nothing like he would have expected with a normal death.

When he had completed his examination, the doctor stood, cupping his chin, looking down at the remains of Simon Blackstone. He had no professional explanation as to why the usual signs of death were incomplete; there was nothing in his experience which shed any light on the anomaly. As far as he was able to determine the child was dead, yet the signals were unclear, the requirements unfulfilled. There was something about the death which more than puzzled the doctor. He was beginning to fear it.

There was one further test he could make. He took a pin from the lapel of his jacket and picked up the child's hand; he bent the thumb and quickly pierced it with the pin, then pressed the pinprick. If there was any life at all, blood would flow. The doctor continued to apply pressure—there was nothing. He made another small puncture and again pressed the wound, but again there was no sign of any fluid; nothing flowed from or within the body. It was clearly a corpse.

Behind him he heard the bedroom door open and stood guiltily, a little startled at having been caught in so primitive an act.

Edmund Blackstone came into the room, his face gray with sleeplessness and pain. When he saw the doctor bending over Simon he experienced a momentary and overwhelming sense of reprieve, as if the events of the night had been nothing more than a bad dream, a nightmare born out of worry and concern; something which would vanish with the return of rational day. When Edmund spoke there was hope in his voice.

"How is he ...?" Edmund began, but the words died on his tongue. The expression on the doctor's face told him everything he needed to know. The pale, still body on the bed bore more witness than he required. "I'm sorry," he said, his voice faltering. "It's been so damned ... awful."

"I came," the doctor said gently, "to make a further examination, to see if there was anything else to be found. As you know, the child's illness has been most puzzling, right from the beginning. But ..." He paused and shrugged slightly. "Now we must make the necessary further preparations."

"Further preparations?" Edmund asked, then understood. "Yes, of course. I imagine there is a funeral parlor in the village?"

"I have the address."

Edmund closed his eyes; his face was lined, exhausted, dusted with early-morning beard; the moment had come now, the moment of decision. Simon had to be finally interred, buried, placed in the earth and sealed away forever. Hope, love, affection, presence would all disappear into a black hole cut from frozen soil as the child's body was lowered from sight. The thought was unbearable. Edmund opened his eyes and stared; there was no avoiding the compelling truth: his son was dead, nothing would return him to life.

"Here," the doctor said, handing Edmund an undertaker's card. "You will find him most ... efficient."

"Thank you," said Edmund, taking the pasteboard. He paused, uncertain of how to phrase his further question. "How long ... I mean, how soon need it be done?"

"At this time of the year there is no hurry," the doctor said matter-of-factly. "Within a few days is plenty of time."

"I see."

The doctor came to Edmund's side. "May I suggest you

leave all arrangements to me." His accent was unusually thick. "I know how distressing this is. It might be better if you let me attend to the details."

For a moment Edmund hesitated. It would be an easy way out, it would relieve him of intimacies he would rather avoid, heartache he could be spared, but as he was about to affirm the doctor's suggestion something within him rebelled. It was too easy, it was escaping the reality of his son's death, it was burying pride and responsibility and something amounting to faith beside the little corpse. He could not hide to that extent, his scientific mind rejected it.

"No," he said firmly. "Thank you all the same, but I'll see to it myself." He tapped the card with a finger. "I shall visit the undertaker this morning. The sooner the better. There seems to be no good reason for not having the funeral as soon as possible. There is nothing to wait for here."

"Very well," said the doctor. "If there is anything I can do . . ."

"Thank you all the same," said Edmund flatly, without rancor or judgment. "But I feel you have done enough as it is."

Later, having shaved and dressed with extraordinary care, Edmund spoke to Anna about that which had to be done. Anna appeared as exhausted as he. Her eyes were red-rimmed, her face looked as if lines had been drawn on the flesh with charcoal, her hands trembled continuously; but she held herself as firmly as she could, and when Edmund spoke she lifted her chin bravely. "I agree," she said, her voice steady. "There is no point in delaying things. The sooner we leave this place the better."

Edmund put on a heavy coat, took his hat, stick and gloves, and walked down the icy road to the village. The cold was penetrating. It seemed to ooze through his clothing; when it reached his skin it spread in undulating layers over his body. He quickened his step and moved his arms briskly, yet it persisted, it ran over him like liquid, chilling him to the bone. About him the countryside was gray, occluded, sodden, barren of anything save the ubiquitous snow and ice.

When he reached the funeral parlor, a small shopfront between a baker's and a butcher's, Edmund was surprised to see a small branch of holly with its bright red berries hung over the doorway. Its freshness was startling in the gray, overcast day.

My God, he thought, it's Christmas Eve.

Edmund Blackstone rang the bell and the undertaker himself came to the door. He was a strange mixture of a man whose work-worn hands—those hands used to hew wood for coffins and to turn the earth—were incongruous with his dark suit, white shirt and frayed black tie. The interior of the establishment smelled warmly of wood shavings; there was a fire burning cheerfully in a small black stove with a mica front.

"Merry Christmas," said the undertaker. He had a mountain accent. "What is it I can do for you?"

Quickly Edmund explained the purpose of his visit, his needs, his concern that things be attended to as soon as possible, his desire to leave as rapidly as he was able.

"I understand." The undertaker nodded solemnly. "But at this time of the year . . ." He left the excuse incomplete. "And what is more, I do not have anything of that size."

"Then you will have to make something."

"Yes, of course, but . . ."

"How long will it take?"

"Who knows?" The undertaker shrugged his workman's shoulders. "At this time of the year . . ."

Edmund's face grew stiff with impatience. "Look here," he began, tiredness, distress, concern heavy in his voice. "I need a casket and I need it quickly. Now will you stop dithering and do something?"

The undertaker, responding to Edmund's determination, lifted a work-worn finger. "Ah," he said in an enlightened voice. "I think I have just what you are looking for." The finger beckoned. "This was not exactly, as you might say, built for the

purpose, but it is beautiful and rare and I think you will like it."
He sounded more cheerful. "It is also," he added, "of a size that
will fit."

Edmund followed the undertaker to a workroom behind the
shopfront. Here the walls were lined with raw timber; the smell
of shavings was stronger, intermingled with that of glue and
resin. Tools littered a workbench, there was sawdust on the
floor, and at one end, standing against a wall, was a new pine
coffin. The sight of it caused Edmund to close his eyes and turn
his head painfully away.

"Here," the undertaker said proudly, bending, pulling something from beneath the workbench. "Do you not think that is
beautiful?"

He held in his hands an elaborate wooden casket. It was
heavily built but the woodwork was delicately carved. Below the
lid and about the sides of the box was a rolling, entwined leaf
motif studded with the dull bloom of malachite. The design
trailed down all four sides, flowing subtly to the base. The lid
was a massive affair that rose to a mound in the center of which
a heavy-petaled rose was carved, its heart encrusted with dark
red rhinestones. The clasp was of thick unpolished silver.

"It is beautiful, you agree?" The undertaker watched Edmund's uncertain expression. "It would be most suitable, do
you not think?"

"It certainly is . . . unusual," Edmund remarked. "But I
don't think it is exactly what I had in mind."

"There is not another like it."

"That I can believe."

"Then you will accept it?"

Edmund hesitated.

"It would be a simple matter for me to . . . alter it," the undertaker pressed, sounding as if he was referring to a suit. "I would
be able to reline it, *in the time*," he added significantly. "By
tomorrow evening it would be ready."

"Where did it come from?" asked Edmund. He touched the solid wood. "You did not make it yourself?"

"No." The undertaker shook his head. "You do not see such workmanship these days."

"Then where did it come from? Not here?"

"You are observant," said the undertaker. "The truth is that it belonged to a Spaniard who, well, died here some years ago. The family, unfortunately, were unable to pay for my services at the time. So they asked me if I would accept this instead."

"I see," said Edmund dryly. "In effect, if I take this, I am paying for someone else's funeral?"

The undertaker shrugged. "The world is a circle," he said philosophically.

"Very well then," Edmund said abruptly; somehow the ornateness of the casket seemed appropriate. He glanced quickly at the raw pine coffin leaning against the wall. By comparison it was crude, rough, ugly; he could not think of placing Simon's body in anything so brutal. "I'll take it," he said. "Have it ready by tomorrow."

"Of course." The undertaker paused. "There is only one small matter more."

"Money?" Edmund suggested bitterly.

"That too," agreed the undertaker. "But also I will have to take measurements. For the lining, you understand."

"Is that all?"

"Now that you ask, there is a further detail." The undertaker's face showed new interest. "The casket possesses a secret lock. Not that you will have any need for it, sir," he added, watching Edmund's reaction. "But it is a curious aspect of the workmanship." The undertaker closed the lid and slipped the thick silver clasp into place, then put the palm of one hand on the center of the rose and pressed sharply. The center of the carving gave beneath his hand and he twisted the core of the flower to the right. From inside the casket came a muffled clicking. The undertaker's lips curved into a small, proud smile. "That is all that is necessary to lock the casket," he said. "But, of course, you will have no need for such a device."

"I scarcely think so," Edmund said coldly.

"I point it out only to show the superb craftsmanship of the piece," the undertaker consoled. "In those days they really did such fine and lasting work."

"Of course."

"I shall have it ready for you by tomorrow. In the afternoon at the latest." The undertaker's voice was humble. "You may rest assured."

"Thank you," Edmund replied and left the warmth, the woody smells, the tall dark figure of the undertaker and his cluttered premises.

WHEN Edmund told Anna about the casket she was dubious; it seemed vulgar, to make more of the event than she would have wished.

"It really is quite handsome," Edmund assured her. "I think you will find it acceptable."

"If you are satisfied, then so am I," Anna replied. She shuddered quietly. "Dear God, how commercial it all becomes."

"I know," said Edmond. "But, sad as it may seem, there are necessary transactions to be carried out."

"Very well," said Anna. "Let us have done with it as soon as possible."

"By Boxing Day it will all be over."

"Boxing Day?" questioned Anna. "How distasteful."

From that moment until the time the casket arrived was a period of numbness for them all. Somehow the Blackstones and Miss Harris managed to survive those hours which lay between them and the undertaker's delivery. They slept little, they ate, sat by the fire, gazed out of windows at the endless, snowbound landscape. For twenty-four hours time had no beginning and no end, it drifted as the snow drifted; it lay heavy and numbing. It was monochrome, like a black-and-white lithograph.

Once or twice they spoke or were spoken to. The landlord, his normally genial face heavy with condolence, talked to both Edmund and Anna, the muffled sentences of his sympathy falling on polite but closed ears. A number of the guests approached and extended their hands, their eyes half shut in sympathy, forgiving the disturbance in the night. But they were shapes only, unrelated to the pain within, sounds only, which had no place or function amidst the thin, demanding cries of grief which persisted in the Blackstones' hearts. It was a parade of manners, a form of self-indulgence.

Christmas Day with its color and its quiet German festivity passed in a long slow caravan of shapes and faces, sounds and singing, the going to and the coming back from churches, the gathering of families and the expressions of goodwill. From their rooms the Blackstones and Miss Harris heard the voices of children chanting, women chattering, men lifting glasses to toast the occasion, while they sat quietly and waited for the hands of all the clocks to turn and the period of hiatus to be over.

Finally, late on the darkening Christmas afternoon, the undertaker walked up the hill to the hotel with the casket on his shoulder. He mounted the stairs to the Blackstones' rooms and held it forward in his gravedigger's hands for them to see. He had lined it with purple velvet, he had polished its elaborately carved exterior, he had shined the malachite and the rhinestones. It was even more handsome now; on its fine gloss, ice crystals, which had formed as it had been carried through the frozen air, glistened and shone. The face of the undertaker was proud as he laid it on the settee in the Blackstones' suite.

"You see," he said, raising a finger. "I told you there was not another like it."

"I'll grant you that," replied Edmund. He turned to Anna. "What do you think of it?"

"It is very handsome," said Anna; she wished she were able to admire it in some other context. "Very . . . handsome."

Edmund turned to the undertaker. "Thank you for what you have done," he said. "What else is there?"

The undertaker explained. They, the Blackstones, would hardly be involved; assistants would arrive and lay out the child on the velvet lining, they would then remove the casket to the undertaker's parlor where it would remain overnight; in the morning a small procession would bear it to the graveyard on the other side of the village and there Simon Blackstone would be laid to rest. It would be an undemanding matter, the undertaker pointed out, all they need do was appear the following morning at eleven at his establishment in the village.

When the undertaker had finished, Edmund turned to Anna and raised his eyebrows, seeking her opinion.

"It sounds all right," Anna said hesitantly. "Except for one small aspect."

"What is that, my dear?"

"I hate to think of Simon spending his last night in something so . . . foreign." Anna closed her eyes and pressed an embroidered handkerchief to her lips. "I couldn't bear him to be shut away down there in the dark."

"My rooms are comfortable," the undertaker said consolingly. "They are clean."

"That is not the point," said Anna. "He'll just be so far away."

The undertaker shrugged, not understanding their concern; perhaps it was because they were English.

"Please, Edmund," Anna said. "Do not let them take him away so soon."

"Is there any reason why our son should not spend his last night here?" Edmund asked the undertaker.

"No, there is no reason, but there are other guests."

"To hell with the other guests," Edmund replied. "Send your people along to do what . . . they have to do, then leave things as they are until morning. You can come and collect everything at ten."

"Very well." The undertaker shrugged; he hoped he would not be upbraided by the landlord but there was nothing further he could do. "The assistants will be here within the hour," he added, as helpfully as he thought appropriate. "It might be better if you, well, left them to do their work alone."

Edmund nodded. "I understand." He took Anna's hand and after the undertaker had gone, he said, "Let us go for a walk outside, my dear. It will do us good to get some air." He placed Anna's coat over her shoulders, took his own and together they left.

They did not walk toward the village but took the higher road which ran above the hotel toward the line of pine trees some two hundred yards away. It was already almost dark. The last filtering fingers of light threw the landscape into a series of deepening shadows causing trees, rocks, houses to lose their definition so that everything seemed to merge into everything else; the landscape was without definition, almost kaleidoscopic.

It was ice-cold. The cold drifted clammily, it came up from the ground, clinging; it pervaded, it reduced, in the end it over-powered. Anna's fingers and toes became numb, her face felt as if it had been scraped raw, her breathing became more and more difficult; suddenly she knew she could not walk another step away from the warmth of the hotel.

Quite soon, before they even reached the lee of the pines, she said, "Let us go back, Edmund. I can take no more of this."

"Yes," agreed Edmund. "It is bitter."

"Perishing."

They turned in the cold, darkening, milky air and began to descend the winding path back to the hotel. Below, the lights of the village came up clear and twinkling and the bell on the pointed church tower began to ring. For a moment both felt, in the beauty of the compact scene, something of Christmas, something of hearth and fireside, warmth and companionability.

Then the cold embraced once more and they stumbled downward toward their destination.

They were less than fifty yards from the hotel and could almost feel its welcoming warmth, when Edmund saw the old woman who had spoken to Anna at the station the day they arrived in the village. The crone was sitting by a gatepost on a small side road absolutely still, wrapped in her unending rags; she was staring at them with her piercing, burning eyes.

Edmund stopped when he saw her; the intensity of her look arrested him. "My God," he whispered. "What on earth's that creature doing out here?"

When she saw the woman Anna's fingers tightened on Edmund's arm and she clamped a hand over her mouth. Immediately she again heard the old woman's words; immediately she knew again the fear, the panic of that moment in the station. Her fingers bit into Edmund's arm with such force that he turned to her.

"Who is she?" he asked. "Do you know?"

Instinctively Anna shook her head.

"She seems to know us."

"No," said Anna, her voice rising. "That's not possible."

As they watched, the crone lifted her head toward them, without moving her body her head appeared to come closer; the eyes burned fiercely and the face was startlingly white. Then the crone's hand came up and she placed a single finger over the thin line of her lips. That was all, nothing more than a simple, silencing gesture, yet its effect was immediate. Anna's knees gave way and she would have fallen had not Edmund caught her.

"Oh, my God," she whispered, clinging to him. "Take me away from here. Take me away from that dreadful . . . thing."

"It's only an old woman."

"No," cried Anna, suddenly, fiercely. She gripped Edmund's arm and began to pull on it, urging him away desperately. "She's more than that. I know, I tell you, she is evil."

"But she's old, helpless." Edmund glanced back at the rags,

the white face, the burning eyes. "She may need help out here in the cold."

"She is *evil*." Anna's words rose, shrill, defiant. "Get me away from her at once. Don't let her speak to me."

"Speak? What do you mean, speak?"

"Edmund . . . for God's sake." Anna began to tremble.

Edmund hesitated no longer. Anna's distress was too demanding. With a last look over his shoulder at the creature with its intense eyes, Edmund half carried, half led Anna up the steps and through the heavy, wooden doors of the hotel, and immediately they were in the warm, sane interior he seated her in a large leather armchair and beckoned a waiter.

"A cognac. No, two cognacs," he said. "Bring them quickly, please."

By the time the brandy arrived Anna had recovered sufficiently to be able to sit steadily in the chair, her face still pale and drawn and her eyes full of terror. She lifted the glass to her lips with both hands, sipped the warming liquor and stared at Edmund over the rim with her large frightened eyes.

"Oh, Edmund," she whispered. "That woman."

"I do not understand why she upset you so much," Edmund said carefully. "She looked in need of help herself, if you want my opinion."

Anna took a deep breath; now there was no avoiding her first contact with the old woman. Perhaps having seen her himself, Edmund might understand her fear. "I *have* seen her before," Anna began. "The day we arrived, at the station. And she spoke to me." Anna shuddered, took another sip of brandy.

"*Spoke to you?*"

"*She said something about Simon.*"

"What on earth did she say?"

"I don't remember clearly." Anna closed her eyes. "You and Simon were waiting for the porter and she said something about him. I . . . I do not recall her words but they . . . frightened me at the time."

"Why did you not tell me of this earlier?"

"I do not know, Edmund. I suppose I thought it would sound silly." Anna's hands began to tremble; as she put the glass to her lips it clinked against her teeth.

"Anna." Edmund put his hands about Anna's so that the small tulip-shaped brandy glass was enclosed within his hands and hers. "You must tell me everything. No matter how silly or unimportant it seems." Suddenly he seemed very close. "Everything," he continued, and Anna saw pain in his eyes. "After all, we've no one else but ourselves now."

Anna nodded, afraid to speak lest her voice collapse and the words turn to tears. "Very well, Edmund," she was able to say finally, "I will tell you everything, but there wasn't *anything* really. Nothing the woman said made sense on its own. It was the fact she spoke to me at all that made me so upset."

"You've not seen her since?"

Anna shook her head.

"Then I'd not think on it further," Edmund said softly. "It is obviously some sort of mistake, some sort of ghastly misunderstanding."

"But . . ." Anna's lips trembled. "Tonight, when I saw her by the gatepost, I think . . . I'm almost certain she was trying to tell me something more."

"What?"

"I am not sure, but I think she was telling me not to say anything . . . anything about her or our meeting."

"Now why should she do that?"

"I do not know, Edmund, I really don't, but that is the feeling I had."

"Anna," Edmund said firmly, realizing how near to collapse she was, how close to complete hysteria. "We, both of us, have had a terrible time, our nerves are in dreadful condition. Anything at all is likely to seem much more than it is." He caressed Anna's hands. "But we must go on, Anna," he said softly. "We have our lives to live. We must build from this . . . disaster."

Anna waited. Edmund's words encouraged, they filled. They did not replace the great ache of Simon's death, but for the moment they were enough. She closed her eyes and felt the hot tears run; crying for Simon, crying for herself, crying for the comfort Edmund was attempting to give.

"Anna. My poor, poor Anna."

Anna wept.

"My darling. Things will get better from now on, you'll see."

Anna breathed deeply; she knew that nothing would ever be the same again but she loved Edmund for trying to make her believe otherwise.

The Blackstones remained together in the lobby of the hotel, regaining composure, something of peace. From time to time the waiter approached and hovered but was ignored; once or twice a guest stopped to whisper a word of condolence or sympathy but did not seem to be heard; the manager came toward them to ask if the presence of the child's body in the hotel could be kept as discreet as possible, but when he saw how unapproach-able they were, he went away. They remained until dark had clotted the outside air and there were sounds of small festivities coming from the dining room, until the undertaker came down-stairs and told them his task was complete and that they could go up and see their son if they wished.

His clumsy intrusion broke the cocoon of their unity. "It is all done as far as we are concerned," the undertaker said. "Your son, if I might.say so, looks at peace." He moved his hands to emphasize the condition.

Anna sighed.

"If there is nothing further," the undertaker added, "I will return in the morning."

"Thank you," replied Edmund. "That will be all."

The undertaker ducked his head in a small bobbing bow and left. Presently Edmund and Anna went upstairs to Simon's room and uncertainly, hushed as if they were in a church, ap-proached the casket.

Simon lay serene amidst the purple velvet plush; his face was calm, faintly colored, almost rosy; his golden curls were like spun metal as they caught the light; his hands were folded over the velvet cover and he looked for all the world as if he were sleeping gently, dreaming, about to wake on the instant.

"Oh, Simon," said Anna when she saw him. "Oh, my little son."

Edmund swallowed. When he spoke it was softly, almost in awe. "I must say he does look peaceful. We can at least be thankful for that."

"Should he stay here, I wonder?" Anna asked. "Alone all night?" She turned to her husband. "Perhaps one of us might remain with him?"

Edmund hesitated. "Do you really think that's appropriate?" he questioned.

"Something should be done," Anna replied bravely. "Perhaps Edith would oblige."

When Miss Edith Harris was summoned to the casket, when she saw Simon laid out so angelically, she fell to her knees, placed her head against the elaborately carved woodwork and wept. Her heavy, round country face reddened with emotion, her voice became thick with tears. "Oh, ma'am," she blubbered. "He does look peaceful, doesn't he? He does look at rest."

"Yes, Edith, he does." Anna helped the governess to her feet. "After all his suffering, he does seem at peace."

"Oh, poor, poor Simon." Miss Harris' tears began to flow again. I just can't believe . . ."

Edmund coughed. "We wondered if you'd mind sitting with him for a while this evening, after dinner. It doesn't seem right, somehow, to leave him alone," he explained.

"Oh, you're right, Mr. Blackstone. You're right. I wouldn't want him left out alone on his last night on earth, really I wouldn't. I'd be happy to sit with him, nothing would give me greater pleasure."

"Thank you, Edith," Anna said. "You're very kind."

"I wouldn't have it any other way," Edith replied, pulling her shawl about her resolutely. "He shouldn't be alone at all." She peered into the casket and clasped her hands together. "Oh, doesn't he look lovely, lying there? Doesn't he look nice?"

"We'll leave you here then, Edith," Edmund said. "Have you had supper?"

"Yes, thank you, sir." Edith nodded. "Yes, I'll be all right here, never you mind. I'll be fine here with my little Simon."

The Blackstones left Miss Harris and went to their rooms; there they rang for supper. They ordered an omelet each and a compote of preserved peaches together with a bottle of the young, crisp Riesling. But when the meal arrived they picked at it dispiritedly and barely touched the wine. There was none of the contentment, the sense of well-being, the dreams of ivied walls which had accompanied their meal of two evenings earlier; this was a quiet, sad affair, and almost as soon as it was over they went to bed, each taking a double amount of the sedative the doctor had left them.

About them the hotel buzzed and hummed with conversation, the somewhat lethargic leftovers of Christmas: a small ritual supper here, a quiet drink there; from the Smoking Room came the steady click of billards. Soon, too, those sounds ceased, and the hotel fell silent.

Miss Edith Harris was dozing, seated in a heavy chair, a blanket about her shoulders to keep away the creeping cold, when she became aware of a strange light in Simon's bedroom. At first she was unable to determine where it came from; sleepily she moved her head and looked toward the window, but the curtain was drawn and nothing came from that direction. She leaned, peering, at the little night light which burned with a steady flame on the table by the bed, but there was no more effulgence from that source than she would have expected. She frowned and moved her lips, pondering.

The light seemed to come from nowhere, yet everywhere. It

glowed, it filled, it pervaded. It touched every corner of the room softly so that Miss Harris was able to distinguish shape and form and detail.

"That's strange," she said sleepily, her voice bewildered. "Simon . . . ?"

She stood and approached the casket. She bent over it, her eyes hooded with sleep, and stopped, astounded. One hand went to her throat while the other came forward to stop, to ward off, what she saw. The whole interior of the casket was glowing. It did not appear to shed light, it did not seem to be the source of light, nothing came from the casket itself, but the whole inside was lit, and through some process of diffusion, association, contact, everything else in the room was reflected in an eerie glow.

Wide-awake now, Miss Harris took a step backward, tried to say something, but her throat was dry, closed to sound. She looked wildly about the room as if help or explanation might lie there, as if somewhere in the dim, phosphorescent glow there might be an answer. There was nothing, the whole room was clear now, vivid, lit as if by an early dawn with neither shadow nor direction.

Miss Harris broke then and whimpered. A small, frightened crying sound rose dry and voiceless in her throat but died even before it reached her lips.

Oh, dear God, she thought. What is going on?

She forced herself to lean forward and peer into the depths of the casket once more, at the gentle face haloed by its golden hair, lying serene and peaceful on the purple velvet. Simon was still, bathed in light.

Then, as she gazed down on his still face, Simon opened his eyes and looked at her fully, clearly, absolutely.

The effect was terrifying. Miss Harris felt her legs give way, she sank to her knees. Her hands gripped the sides of the casket. Her head rested against its elaborate woodwork. The whimpering sound rose again in her throat and again it died.

She clung to the casket, frightened, bewildered, paralyzed by what she had seen. The face was no longer Simon's face, the eyes were no longer those which belonged to her darling. There was a stranger staring up at her from the purple velvet.

"Simon," she managed to whisper, her head pressed against the carved scrolls, the malachite. "Simon, my baby, what has happened to you? What have they done?"

She knew she must assist, must do something, must remove him, unlock him from whatever presence possessed his small body. Slowly she raised her head and, holding her fear as if it were glass, something fragile which any uneven move could shatter and release, she forced herself to look into the deep, spreading glow which came from the casket. She was illuminated by it now, it shone on her round country face like light from the mouth of a furnace. She blinked, held her fear, and steeled herself to gaze into the depths of it.

She saw that the little face she knew so well was lit and glowing, that the eyes, as familiar to her as her own, were open; they too glowed as they stared up at her with a fixed, relentless expression. It was like no look she had ever seen before, it was like nothing she had ever known from the child. It was totally alien.

"Simon?" she whispered. "Is it really you?"

The face below her own smiled. The lips parted on the glowing countenance, rolled back into a smile the like of which she had never witnessed. They curved into a shape which contained neither warmth nor familiarity; they bent into a travesty of everything Miss Harris had ever known. As the smile increased, the eyes burned. They grew round and large and compelling, they forced the full, unyielding attention of Miss Harris, even if she had wanted to she would not now have been able to break their hold, they were magnetic, demanding, total.

"Simon?" Miss Harris whispered the name in hope, in request for something she might recognize or comprehend, in a plea for sanity. "Simon . . . dear Simon?"

There was no answer in the child's face, no response; the smile grew larger, the fire in the eyes increased. The whole room seemed to be flooded now, filled with light which spread, diffused and formless, from the child's eyes.

"Oh, Simon," Miss Harris whispered in the little voice which was all she was capable of. "Please, what are you doing?" She begged for something she might understand. "Please, Simon, tell me. Tell Edith."

She reached to touch the face, perhaps to discover whether contact might confirm or contradict that which her eyes held real, but she stopped short, her fingers frozen, because at the moment of her movement the figure in the casket made one of its own.

A hand came up toward her.

Miss Harris stopped, chilled by the gesture, held by the coals which burned in the child's eyes; she watched spellbound and helpless as the hand came up and groped for her. Gently, effortlessly, as if it had all the time it would ever need, the hand lifted and took her by the throat. At first it was nothing more than a caress, a gentle stroking of the governess's neck, but slowly, surely, irreversibly, the grip became more firm, the fingers tightened and Miss Harris began to feel the pressure of the nails on her throat. Then, and only then, did she make an attempt to escape, to break the grip, to turn, run, flee from whatever it was which lay in the casket, whatever it was which Simon had become. But by then it was too late, the time for escape was over. The fingers held her throat, the grip was like iron, the fingernails bit into the flesh and life began to leave the poor, doomed, helpless, innocent figure of Miss Harris.

She fought for a moment or two, but not violently. Her fingers scrabbled at the hand which gripped her but there was no strength in them; she had neither the will nor the ability to resist; she had neither the will nor the ability to survive. What Simon had become drained her of life, whatever possessed her charge took all that was vital from her body. Like a bird she died, her heart thumping until it was stilled, her body twitching more and more softly until it was as stone, her eyes growing round until they were empty.

With the hand still gripping her throat she slumped over the casket, motionless, lifeless, destroyed. The hand remained about her throat for a time or two after life had left her body, then it was slowly, gently, effortlessly removed, going as if it had all the time in the world, returning to its place on the velvet. As it went, so the coals dimmed in the child's eyes and light began to go from the room; it died slowly, listlessly, allowing the dark to invade once more. On the face in the casket the smile reversed until the small, neat, haloed head was as it had been: still, at peace, looking as if it had never been otherwise.

Only one small aspect of Simon Blackstone's body remained permanently altered. The nails on the hand which had taken the governess's life had grown as they gripped the throat, had become long enough to pierce the white skin of Miss Harris's neck, leaving tiny drops of congealed blood on her flesh. Now they remained longer than they had been, gnarled, permanently changed by the metamorphosis which had overtaken Simon. Now they were distorted, more deadly, more prepared for the future than they had been. Known or unknown, an inevitable, irreversible alteration from one form to another had commenced.

CHAPTER THREE

Aɴɴᴀ Blackstone discovered the body of Miss Harris early the following morning. Anna had taken two of the little Bavarian doctor's sedatives and they, combined with her exhaustion, had caused her to sleep deeply. She had awakened early, while it was still dark, while cold fingers of night gripped the hotel; sleep clung to her like a blanket. Beside her Edmund lay on his back, his blond hair ruffled, his face relaxed. He looked remarkably like his son. The thought gave Anna both pleasure and pain. Quietly she left the bed, wrapped herself in a thick gown and walked silently along the passageway to Simon's room.

At the door she paused. "Edith?" she called softly. "Are you awake?"

When there was no reply Anna pushed the door. It opened and she entered. For a moment, in the gloom, she was unable to absorb any detail of the scene; there was insufficient glow from the night-light for her to distinguish what the room contained. She called again softly, and when there was no reply, assumed Miss Harris had fallen into a deep sleep.

"Poor girl," she whispered. "She must be exhausted."

She went quietly to the form slumped over the casket and shook it gently by the shoulder. As soon as she touched the body she was aware of something unusual, a stiffening of the frame, an unexpected heaviness. Gripping it more firmly, she lifted Miss Harris' body away from the casket. As it came toward her she felt the weight of it and began to understand that a profound change had overcome the governess. Miss Harris' body rolled from the casket, the momentum of the swing carried it; it fell across Anna's knees and tumbled from there to the floor where it lay motionless, the broken throat open, the dead eyes staring sightless.

The moment was so absolutely terrifying that Anna was unable to scream. She was paralyzed by fear, completely contained within its hold. She stood frozen, inept, disbelieving, staring down at the lumpy form of Miss Harris at her feet. Forcing herself to turn, she looked into the coffin containing her son and was stupidly, abruptly relieved to find Simon's body as she had left it, serene, untouched, complete. Then she slowly walked from the room. Her step was steady, her footfalls made no sound; she neither hurried nor delayed but returned to her bedroom at the same even pace at which she had left it. She opened the door and went in. Edmund lay on his back, sleeping.

Only then did a small cry escape her lips. "My God," she whispered. "What shall I do?"

Her immediate fear had faded, replaced by numbness; now she was faced with the awful responsibility of communicating what she had seen. She could not imagine how she was going to inform anyone of what her eyes had witnessed.

Numbly she sat at the side of the bed and waited; presently Edmund woke, turned lazily onto his side, opened his eyes and stared up at the chalk-white countenance of his wife. For a second he remained still, bound by the last touches of sleep, then came fully awake and lifted his head in alarm.

"What's wrong?" he asked; his voice dry, unused. "Anna? What has happened?"

Anna shook her head in silent disbelief.

Edmund took his wife by the shoulders. "Come now," he said firmly. "Tell me what has frightened you so?"

"Come and see for yourself," Anna said woodenly. "I do not know that I can find words to describe what I have seen."

The evenness of Anna's voice galvanized Edmund. Quickly he rose, put on a dressing gown and slippers. Anna led her husband along the corridor to Simon's room, walking stiffly, without pause. When they reached the room Anna stood to one side so that Edmund might go in alone. He entered as Anna had done, pausing, his eyes confused by the dim light, not seeing immediately the body on the floor. Then he became accustomed to the gloom and gasped at the sight of Miss Harris. Carefully he stepped toward the body. Anna followed slowly, waiting for her findings to be confirmed.

"My God," Edmund whispered. "She's dead."

"That is what I thought."

"You knew?"

"No," Anna replied, shaking her head. "I was not sure." She could not avoid the lie. "Not absolutely."

"What could have happened to her?" Edmund bent over the body. "She wasn't ill that I knew of."

The simplicity of Edmund's statement caused Anna to laugh; small, bright, hysteria formed on her lips and filled the room. "Ill?" The word bubbled in her throat, uncontrollable, frightening. "What do you mean, *ill?* She's dead, is that not ill enough?"

"Anna." Edmund's voice was sharp. "Control yourself."

"My God!" Anna cupped a hand about her mouth. "Do you realize what you've said?"

Edmund stared at his wife. "Anna," he commanded, taking her by the shoulders, knowing he must calm her immediately. "Stop this. Stop it at once."

Anna's laugh died, slowly it trickled away to stillness. Then tears began to form and hysteria would have risen again had not Edmund drawn her to him and held her as he might a child, whispering comfort.

"Anna, Anna, Anna," he said softly. "Calm yourself. I know

what a shock it must have been to find poor Edith like this, but you must stop this now. Come along. Pull yourself together. Be strong. You know you can. Be strong."

The simple, nursery phrases quieted Anna. Gradually she regained control of herself; tears died as laughter had died, leaving a dry, empty hollow inside.

"Oh, Edmund," she whispered pitifully. "What is happening?"

"I'm not sure," Edmund replied with more confidence than he felt. "Some sort of ghastly coincidence, it seems. We had better call the doctor at once." He glanced at Anna and saw a reflection of his own alarm. "I am sure he can explain everything," he added uncertainly.

Once more the little Bavarian doctor climbed the icy road to the hotel, bag in hand. He examined the body of Miss Harris slowly, scrupulously, taking note of the damage to the throat. There was no doubt that the governess had been murdered; he was almost relieved to be certain of the cause of death and to find that on this occasion the condition of the body was as it should be. Only once, for an instant, did something uneasy cross his mind, but quickly, actively closing his bag, he put it aside. The thought was monstrous.

After he had completed his examination the doctor took Edmund to one side and spoke to him quietly. "Have you any idea how this occurred?" he asked.

"None. My wife found the poor girl this morning."

"Did you hear anything . . . strange in the night?"

"Nothing. Why?"

The doctor raised his eyebrows. "Don't you realize that the woman has been murdered?" he asked, his accent suddenly thick.

Edmund's face stiffened, he took a step away from the doctor. "Would you mind repeating that?" he whispered.

The doctor did, adding, "There is no doubt about it. The marks on her throat are unmistakable."

"Could they not have been caused by a fall?"

"No. She has been strangled."

"But, but that is not possible. She was here all night. She said she would sit with . . . Simon."

"Was the door locked?"

"I do not believe so."

The doctor sighed. "Then anything could have happened," he said almost to himself.

Edmund shook his head in disbelief.

"The woman has been murdered," the doctor persisted. He looked away. "I have no alternative but to inform the police."

"No," Edmund protested stolidly, thickly, appealing to the doctor. "That can't be necessary?"

"It is the law."

"Oh, my God. This is appalling."

"I realize that," the doctor responded sympathetically. "After what you have suffered this is doubly difficult to bear. I am truly sorry but there really is no alternative, the police must be notified."

"If it is your duty, then do it," Edmund said stiffly. "But can we be circumspect about it? I mean, will everybody need to know?"

The doctor sighed. "I'm afraid so, Mr. Blackstone," he said gently. "Murder is almost impossible to keep quiet. The whole village will know by nightfall." He went to the body, took a sheet from the bed and covered it, his face heavy with pity, touched with a mysterious doubt.

The doctor telephoned the local police station and Sergeant Obelgamma, a bald, gray man in his fifties, came from the village. After the doctor informed him of Miss Harris' death, his immediate reaction was to believe the governess was part of a *ménage à trois* and that either Edmund or Anna was guilty of her death.

"You knew the woman well?" he later inquired of Edmund. "She had been long with you?"

"Three years," Edmund replied.

"You were fond of her?"

"We both were. She was Simon's nanny."

Sergeant Obelgamma nodded wisely and ran a hand over his bald pate. "You will please not leave the hotel," he ordered. "We will need to talk further."

"I have the funeral to attend."

"She will be buried so soon?" the sergeant asked, then realizing what Edmund referred to, nodded. "Of course you may go to that. But please do not leave the village."

Edmund sighed. "For how long?" he asked.

"It is hard to tell," Sergeant Obelgamma replied briskly. "There will be many more questions to answer." He went on with a determined stride to talk to others, to organize the removal of the body. It was an exciting time for him; seldom did anything so dramatic occur in the village. Seldom was he able to flourish. He hoped he might conclude his investigations without the need to consult Munich. That would be success indeed.

THE conversation between Edmund Blackstone and Sergeant Obelgamma took place in a corner of the dining room, where the emptiness of the oaken-beamed room and the spread of white-clothed tables added to the unreality of the death of the governess.

Miss Edith Harris had come to the Blackstones when they moved from Tonbridge to London and her presence among them had been constant. Perhaps the only time she had been absent was when she had taken a train to visit her parents outside York while the Blackstones had come to the mountain village two years before to walk among the summer hillsides. Thus, her death was a family affair.

Edmund Blackstone sighed, took a small silver container from his waistcoat and removed a wax vesta. Carefully he lit the match and ignited a candle which stood in a brass stand on a table before him. It was all he could think of to do. For a moment he watched the yellow flame grow tall in the still air, then, snapping the match carrier shut he returned it to his pocket and left the room, went into the drawing room and stood before the fire.

Edmund remained gazing into the flames, denying the images the doctor's words demanded, until the undertaker arrived with one of his assistants.

"It is ten o'clock," the undertaker announced as he approached. "The time has come to remove the coffin." He stood heavily, his hard hands hanging by his sides. Behind him the assistant waited with equal ungainliness.

"Of course," Edmund replied. "We will be at your establishment within the hour."

The undertaker and his assistant went into Simon's room and closed the lid of the casket; they clamped the silver clasp into place and, lifting the wooden box between them, took it away.

Edmund saw them go, then went to his own suite of rooms. Anna had preceded him. Edmund suggested that she rest until it was absolutely necessary for her to leave the hotel. Her condition worried him; the strain of the past fortnight had been intense and the death of Simon followed by that of Miss Harris had plunged her deeply into shock. Her hysteria of the early morning had been alarming, it was clear that he needed to take her peacefully back to London where she might quietly recover her equilibrium.

As he entered the rooms he was surprised to find Anna sitting at a dressing table applying rouge to her cheeks; she looked more controlled than he would have imagined. She appeared almost gay.

"I thought I'd put a little color on my face," she said as he entered. "Do you like it?"

"Of course," Edmund replied carefully. "It does suit you."

"You do not think it out of place?"

"Why, no . . ."

"You do. I can tell by your voice. I will remove it if you wish, but I thought I'd try to appear a little cheerful. When you think of it, Edmund, Simon was always so happy, so alive, it seems a shame, somehow, not to make an effort for him."

Edmund went to his wife and put a hand on her shoulder, suddenly realizing the determination it had taken to appear brighter. "You are right," he said. "If Simon had the choice this is how he would wish to see you." He patted her shoulder comfortingly, hoping she had recovered sufficiently to sustain what he next had to say. "There is something else, however," he began uneasily. "Something further you must know."

"What?" Anna's face turned quickly. "What else could there be?"

"The doctor says . . ." Edmund began carefully, feeling for his words. "Well, he thinks that poor Edith was murdered. In fact, he's already called the police."

Anna sat absolutely still; she had almost forgotten Miss Harris. In concentrating on Simon's funeral she had been able to put the death of the governess from her mind. Now it vividly returned, compounded, magnified, with additional elements of horror and disbelief. She shook her head suddenly, explosively, as if to eliminate her husband's words.

"I can't believe it, of course," Edmund went on. "But that is what the doctor thinks. And the police sergeant appears to be of a like mind."

"*Murdered?*" Anna asked.

"Yes."

"But that is absurd. Who would want to murder poor Edith? She hardly knew a soul in the whole place."

"I agree," replied Edmund. "But, as I say, there are others who think to the contrary." He coughed to lessen the effect of what he was about to add. "You see there were . . . well, marks on Edith's throat, which brought the doctor to the conclusion that she had been strangled."

"Strangled—no." Anna dismissed the thought abruptly. "Now you *are* being ridiculous, Edmund. I can no more imagine Edith being strangled than I can you doing it." She returned to the looking glass and examined her face in it, hiding from whatever the idea contained. She had absorbed all she was able. "I am quite sure the poor girl caught what Simon had and that was that. She just didn't suffer the way he did. Her release was much more merciful." She peered at a cheek and applied a little more color. "As for whatever marks she might have had on her neck I can only conclude she damaged herself when the final spasm came." She glanced at her husband. "That little doctor didn't know what was wrong with Simon. I am certain he is just as mistaken about poor Edith. Do you not agree?"

Edmund sighed deeply and nodded. There was no point in prolonging the matter. Anna needed whatever respite she could get. "You are probably right, my dear," he replied evenly. "I am sure it will all be cleared up in a day or two."

"A day or two? Surely it won't take that long?"

"We shall see," replied Edmund. "It depends on that officious little sergeant as much as anything."

THE first thing Sergeant Obelgamma did when he left Edmund was to seek out the landlord. Here was his opportunity to impress and the landlord listened intently. "But are you sure?" he queried when the sergeant had completed his explanation. "The English servant was actually strangled?"

"It has been confirmed by the doctor."

"Who would do such a thing?" The landlord raised his eyebrows; he had a sudden fear of rumor spreading like wildfire, guests departing in droves, reservations being canceled, the hotel suddenly empty. "There has never been anything like this before."

Sergeant Obelgamma ran a hand over his bald pate and stepped a little closer to the landlord. "It is my opinion that the English are to blame," he said in a low, conspiratorial voice.

"But why?" the landlord asked, hoping for more information. It would be most convenient if this were the case—no blame would rest with the hotel or the other guests. "To me, the English seemed ... well, a little strange, but then foreigners are much the same. However there was nothing violent I was able to detect."

Sergeant Obelgamma moved his lips shrewdly. "I suspect there was an emotional relationship between all three." His gray eyes were calculating. "Either the husband did away with the girl because she was becoming an embarrassment to him or the wife acted out of jealousy." He sounded satisfied.

The landlord's eyebrows went up even further. As much as he would have liked to believe the sergeant's theory, he could no more imagine the passage of anything sexual between the neat, blond Englishman and the lumpy governess than he could see Anna with her hands about Miss Harris' throat.

"I have more questions to ask, you understand," the sergeant continued. "It will be necessary to have the body examined thoroughly, but I think I will be able to confirm my theory in a day or so."

"Excellent," the landlord said, his voice humble. "But, there is one small matter you might be good enough to consider. It concerns, well, the body of the English governess. Do you think it could be removed?" He shrugged. "You appreciate, it is not pleasant for the other guests to know that ... there is ..." His voice trailed away significantly.

"Of course," Sergeant Obelgamma puffed with authority. "It will be taken away at once."

"That is so kind." The landlord rubbed his hands together. "Would you care for some schnapps, perhaps? A little something for the cold?"

"Thank you," replied the sergeant. "That would be most appreciated."

The landlord was sitting with Sergeant Obelgamma, a bottle of his best schnapps on the table, when Anna and Edmund Blackstone came downstairs to the hotel lobby on their way to the funeral. Immediately the landlord came to his feet and approached the couple, his face long, pale, sad, his voice heavy with compassion.

"I cannot say how sorry I am," he said. "Is there anything I can do?"

"You can arrange to have our bags packed," Edmund told him. "We will be leaving as soon after the funeral as we are able."

The landlord could not avoid a quick, oblique look at Sergeant Obelgamma. "When do you think that will be?" he asked.

"Tomorrow perhaps," Edmund answered. He moved past the solid figure in its ubiquitous Bavarian green. "Now, if you'll excuse us . . ."

"Of course." The landlord bowed slightly. "I will have your luggage attended to at once."

He returned with his information to Sergeant Obelgamma. "That was interesting," he said, picking up his glass.

Sergeant Obelgamma lifted his head questioningly.

"The English are leaving tomorrow. Were you aware of that?"

Sergeant Obelgamma smiled a knowing smile. "We will see," he said cryptically. "We will see where it is they go tomorrow. For all they know it may be to our cells. *Prosit*," he toasted.

OUTSIDE, the Blackstones walked slowly down the hill from the hotel. The road was as icy as it had been since their arrival and the air as cold, but the sky seemed to have lifted a little and the little gusting winds had died. The village spread below like a Christmas card: thin columns of smoke rose vertical in the steady air, the church spire was clear and solemn. The cluster of houses about the village square were patterned and picturesque. It seemed to the Blackstones that at any moment the sun might spill forth and the whole valley burst into sparkling life. There was electricity in the air, a note of change, as if one era had passed and another, new and different, was about to begin.

They turned a corner, walked beneath an overhanging pine,

its branches laden with gloves of snow, its bark sheathed in ice, and came to a smoother stretch of road where Anna suddenly halted, her whole body rigid. Her grip on her husband's arm became intense. She raised a hand and pointed to one side of the road where beneath a holly bush laden with snow sat the old woman they had seen the previous evening.

"It's her," Anna whispered unsteadily. "She is waiting for us."

"Don't be absurd, Anna." Edmund kept his voice reasonable. "This is merely a further coincidence."

"No." Anna was sure. "She wants to speak to us, Edmund. Of that I am certain."

"Why on earth . . . ?"

"I do not know." Anna was calmer, her voice steadier. The moment of shock had passed. "But I intend to find out. This is the third time she's approached me. Now I must discover what it is she wants."

Without uttering a further word Anna released her arm from Edmund's hold and approached the old woman—the bundle of rags, the burning eyes, the dead white face. The crone watched with neither sound nor movement. She sat still, her form shapeless, lost in her unending, ragged wrappings, her eyes the only live element in her whole unkempt being. She waited until Anna was but a few yards away, then raised a hand, palm outward, and spoke for the first time since her voice had been released at the station.

"Do not come any further," she said, her old words thin and silky. "I am not sure of you yet."

Anna paused. "What do you want?" she asked, a tremor in her voice.

"You will speak with me now?" the crone questioned with a hint of mischief. "You will deign to speak with me now?"

"I thought it was you who wished to speak to me?"

The crone put a dirty hand to her lips and laughed a small, silent laugh. "You are right," she spluttered. "I have much to tell." There was sudden life in her face, a curious animation.

"What is all this?" Edmund stepped forward. "What do you have to say?"

"You will see."

"What can you possibly want from us?"

"Nothing."

"Nothing?" queried Anna, recalling the first meeting. "You have used that word before."

"You did not wish to know me then."

"I did not know what you wanted."

"Do you now?" The crone's eyes flashed briefly—something new had been added to the conversation. "Now, missus? Do you know now?"

"Yes," Anna whispered, suddenly aware of the nearness of a great truth, accepting, if not knowledge, then the presence of something profound. "Yes," she repeated. "I think I do."

"What *is* this?" asked Edmund.

"Be quiet, Edmund," Anna said swiftly.

From her rags the old woman watched the Blackstones. She listened to their interchange and again the hint of mischief was in her eyes. "Come closer now," she said to them both. "I will say what I have to say." She lifted an arm, beckoning.

Uncertainly, hesitantly, the Blackstones moved a step closer; they stood almost touching the old woman. The pressed, tailored formality of their funeral attire contrasted weirdly with the gray raggedness of the crone. They stood uneasily, waiting for the old woman to utter what she had to say.

"You know it is about the child," the creature began abruptly. "You know that is why I am here?"

There was a tiny, absolute silence, then Anna nodded. "Yes," she whispered.

"Simon?" Edmund questioned.

"It has always been about Simon," Anna replied, her eyes fixed on the old woman.

Edmund began to speak again, but Anna put out a hand,

touched his arm and silenced him. The old woman nodded approvingly.

"You are wise," she said to Anna. "You understand."

"I have only just come to understand," Anna replied. She had no fear of the old woman now, no sense of revulsion, only a clear knowledge that what the crone had to say was vital and that she must know it. "It is only now," Anna added, "that understanding has come to me."

"Then listen," the old woman replied. "I am from these parts—" she began—"where many strange things occur, and what I have to tell you I have seen only once before, when I was a child in this village." She listed her head and the fire in her eyes caught the Blackstones. "What I have to say is not pleasant. It will not be easy to accept, but if you have courage and if you have sufficient love, you will do what has to be done."

"What in God's name is all this mystery about?" Edmund moved impatiently. "Get on with it, woman."

"You will be informed soon enough," the old woman replied. "And then you may wish you had not been told at all." She raised a hand. "I have contained this knowledge for two years," she continued. "I was aware of it first when I saw you that summer you came to walk in the mountains. But I could not speak then. The time was not appropriate and you would not have listened to me." She gazed at Anna. "Do *you* understand how important it is that you listen?" she asked.

Anna nodded. It was occurring now as it would occur later. She felt it draw. Her eyes were fixed on the crone.

"Are you prepared?"

Anna waited.

The crone half-closed her eyes and her voice was startlingly clear. "Your child is a Moonchild, missus," she said. "That is what I have to say. Your child is a child of the moon."

Anna shuddered. The icy air seemed as fire. With neither knowledge of its condition nor experience of its significance, she knew suddenly that a great truth had been told. She remained still as rock and waited for the old woman to continue. Edmund, too, was silent.

"He is, without doubt, a Moonchild," the crone went on ruthlessly. *"His soul is no longer his own."*

"No." Anna whimpered. Beside her Edmund gasped. Horror moved them. Anna felt the drawing of an ancient, unknown force. "No," she cried. "Please say that is not so."

"He is doomed." The crone's voice pierced them both; her devastating words took breath from their bodies. "He will go on forever, becoming more and more distorted until he is nothing but a gnarled creature hiding in the dark. *Unless you do as I say.*" She opened her eyes fully and her gaze singed. "You cannot change him," she said. "But if you do what I say, you may bring him peace."

In the cold, clear air the woman's words scorched, tore, pierced. Anna stumbled beneath their impact. Half-kneeling before the old woman, she whispered, "This cannot be my Simon?" Her words fell like leaves on snow, soundless, without impact.

"You know it is," the crone replied.

"I don't." Edmund stepped back harshly. "I do not believe a word of this . . . rubbish."

"You must," the old woman replied calmly. "If you do not, the child is lost forever."

"He is dead," Edmund said bitterly. "That, you old fool, is surely lost enough."

"No," the creature answered. "He is not yet dead. He is not yet at peace." She turned her face away. "I waited for you yesterday to try to make you understand. But it was as useless then as I can see it is now. You do not wish to accept the truth." She began to go from them then, to withdraw; the fire in her ancient eyes began to die. She drew her rags about her and climbed stiffly to her feet.

"Wait," Anna called. "I will listen."

The crone's eyes went to Edmund. "But he will not," she said bitterly. "And one is not enough." Then her voice softened a little. "It is neither your fault nor the child's," she said, tiring now, becoming feeble. The fire in her eyes was almost gone. "It is an accident of the moon. No one person is responsible. I do not know the reasons. My duty is only to tell you all I can."

"I must know more," Anna implored.

The old woman smiled. "The doctor here is not as foolish as he seems," she replied.

"How do you know of this?"

The old woman paused, half-turned. "The other, the only other Moonchild I have ever seen was my brother," she said in her disappearing voice. "He was exactly as your son . . . his appearance . . . his walk . . . his laughter." She faced away from them so that the windy voice floated. "I do not want to see that happen again. I do not wish to know that your son would walk forever seeking peace and never finding it." She sighed. "Take him home. Take your son home, to the place of his birth, and bury him there." She walked away, an old, gray, listless bundle of rags.

"Wait, please." Anna scrambled after her.

"The doctor . . ." The old voice faded.

She went then round the bend of the road and was gone. Edmund and Anna followed quickly, but when they turned the corner there was no sign of the old woman. She was neither on the road nor beside it. There were no footsteps in the snow to indicate where she had been. The windy, icy road was empty all the way down to the village.

"Good God," Edmund said. "How incredible."

"She has gone." Anna sighed deeply. "We will not see her again."

"You don't believe any of that nonsense by any chance?" Edmund spoke critically.

"I do not know," Anna replied. "We must speak with the doctor."

"And the funeral?"

"Let it wait."

Edmund Blackstone studied his wife. There was a change in her he did not comprehend. Her face had the same drawn look, there were lines of pain and anguish beneath the eyes. The mouth looked as if it had been carved from stone. All the strain of the past fortnight was clearly defined, but something new had been added in the past minutes, a strength had developed he had not been exposed to before. He stared at her in awe.

As if sensing her husband's thoughts, Anna spoke. "We have much to do, Edmund," she said. "We have much to discover and I suspect we have little time. Let us go now and postpone the funeral." She took his arm and began down the road to the village.

"But what she said was monstrous."

"We cannot hide from the truth," Anna replied. "Anyway—" she paused and glanced at her husband—"if there is any veracity in what we heard, there is hope as well."

"Hope?" Edmund frowned. "I don't understand."

"It is very clear," Anna said, her voice strong. "If Simon is what she says he is, then he is not really dead, is he? In some way our child is still alive."

"Anna." For a few disbelieving seconds Edmund was not certain he had heard correctly. He peered into Anna's face. It was solemn, determined, set in its vision. Edmund shivered. "Are you sure of what you're saying?"

"I am not sure of anything," his wife replied. "But I do have a sense of hope. For the first time since Simon's death I feel things might not be as bad as they seem."

Edmund could not take his eyes from Anna's face. He was dismayed by the serenity it contained, the calm beneath its pain-worn façade. Here was the beginning of insanity. The proposition growing in Anna's mind was as abhorrent as the idea which had bred it.

"I must point out to you, Anna," Edmund said formally, "that what you are suggesting is quite bizarre."

"That may be," Anna responded. "But somehow that—creature—had a quality which made me think *she* believed in what she said."

"But you yourself only yesterday considered her evil."

"I know," Anna replied evenly. "But it is our duty to be sure." With that she increased her pace and continued briskly down the empty road.

Edmund followed, his face torn with concern. He believed Anna's reaction was one of frantic grasping, the clinging to any straw which might release her from the awful, absolute, unavoidable truth that their son was dead, in his coffin, about to be buried, sealed away for all time—but its intensity and the thought of where it might end filled him with new horror.

He was fearful as they walked the remaining distance to the village lying painted and delicate in the thin, gray light. The church spire was clear in the cold, open air and the little houses were as neatly joined as if they had been placed together by a child's careful hand.

CHAPTER FOUR

Edmund and Anna Blackstone walked without speaking
through the twisting streets of the village until they came to the
undertaker's shopfront. They walked through cold, crisp air,
over frozen pavements from which snow had been swept into
piles by the roadside; they passed a snowman with a corncob
pipe and a broom in his hand; they weaved their way through
a group of laughing children throwing snowballs; they walked
steadily, stiffly, obstinately through the ragged ends of Christmas
and the joyful voices. Neither noticed the scene about them;
both were intent.

When they reached the undertaker's, Edmund was again
surprised by the holly above the doorway. The green leaves and
the bright red berries belonged to another time, another experience, they lacked the right to be there.

The Blackstones entered the parlor to the smell of wood shavings and the warmth from the fire in the small black stove. To
one side of the room, laid on a table covered with a white cloth,
was the casket; its woodwork shone sleekly, rhinestone and
malachite gleamed; the hinged lid was thrown back and the
purple plush visible, but neither Anna nor Edmund made any
move to look at the child who lay within.

When he heard them the undertaker approached pleasantly,

almost cheerfully, as if welcoming old friends. "Ah," he said, raising a heavy finger. "You are ready?"

Edmund shook his head. "There is something we must discuss," he said abruptly.

"Is that not why you are here?"

"Not exactly." Edmund glanced at Anna. "We would, actually, like to postpone arrangements for a short while."

The expression on the undertaker's face altered; his professional charm was replaced with a mountain shrewdness. "But it is all arranged," he said carefully. "We have been working since midnight, digging."

"We regret that," Anna said sharply. "But there is no alternative."

"But what of my assistants?" The undertaker raised his workworn hands. "At this time of the year?"

"They will be paid, whatever happens," Edmund said tersely. "In the meantime, please be patient."

"This is a patient business," the undertaker replied philosophically. "I am in no haste, it was your good self who wished the service to be conducted with speed."

"Things have changed somewhat," said Edmund. "I should prefer to wait a little longer."

"As you wish," the undertaker replied, touching his frayed tie. "Just advise me when you wish to proceed."

Anna spoke again. "I imagine it will be all right if everything remains as it is?" she asked, her eyes going to the casket.

"Absolutely," the undertaker replied, following her gaze. "The coffin can stay here."

"Thank you." Anna smiled politely, then added an afterthought. "Would you mind closing it, please?"

"Now? Before the funeral?"

"If you don't mind." Anna was unsure why she issued the request. She merely felt it appropriate, immediate, something that must be done. "And see that it remains closed," she added.

"Whatever you wish, madam." The undertaker turned quickly to conceal his baffled expression and closed the lid with a small, muffled thud. "Anything further?"

Anna shook her head, took Edmund's arm, and they left. Their footsteps echoed clearly on the plain wooden floor.

The undertaker watched them go; he scratched his head and spat. "I do not understand the English," he said. "They are cold and they have no manners." He went into the other room where his assistant stood picking his nose. "This is the first English I have had, and I hope it will be the last." He shrugged his heavy shoulders. "First they want the child buried yesterday and now they put it off until tomorrow."

"What has changed their minds?" the assistant asked, wiping his nose with the back of his hand. "Have they no money?"

"Who knows?" the undertaker replied. "But I would put the child away for nothing if only to get rid of them."

The assistant shrugged. "There's no living in that," he pointed out.

The undertaker smiled a long smile. "This is not what you'd call a living business," he replied.

Outside, in the chill and twisting village streets, Edmund and Anna Blackstone found their way to the doctor's quarters. It was a slow journey, retarded by wrong turnings. Finally they were directed to the doctor's by a man on a horse.

There was a curious alertness about them now. As they paused outside the wooden door which led up, over the apothecary's, to where the doctor kept his rooms, they felt the presence of mystery.

They knocked loudly and waited. Shortly the door was opened by an elderly woman wearing a long black dress and a small black bonnet. "Yes?" she inquired, swinging the door inward, peering into their faces.

"I . . . we would like to see the doctor," Edmund said. "The name is Blackstone."

"Do you have an appointment?"

Edmund shook his head. "No, but the matter is urgent," he explained.

The woman appeared doubtful but stepped aside and showed the Blackstones up the stairs to the floor above, where she asked them to remain in a small waiting room with engravings of mountains on the walls. They stood nervously, expectantly, looking at the mountains and not seeing a line in any of them.

Presently the woman in black returned, and they were ushered into a large, warm, carpeted room, the walls of which were lined with books. Behind a handsome walnut desk sat the doctor; he rose when he saw them and offered his hand. On his face was an expression of wariness.

"Good morning," he said. "This is something of a surprise." When they arrived, he had been completing a report on the death of Miss Harris. Whatever occurred, the report would not be altered.

Edmund and Anna sat and waited. The doctor watched, sensing the difference in their bearing, fearing its significance.

"Well?" he inquired. "What can I do for you?"

Edmund raised a hand to his lips. "This may sound rather strange . . ." he began nervously. "But . . ."

Anna interrupted. "It is about Simon," she said positively. "We have had some rather peculiar information about him."

"Simon? Your son?"

"That's right." Anna leaned forward in her chair intently. "There is an old woman in this village we have encountered once or twice. A rather dilapidated creature." Her eyes pierced suddenly. "Do you know her?"

The directness of the question shook the doctor. He licked his lips. "An old woman?" he asked to regain composure, to put his fear aside. "Is that what you said?"

"That is correct," Anna replied. "It was she who gave us what little information we have about Simon and suggested we come to you for more."

"What exactly did she say?"

"Something quite monstrous."

"I beg your pardon."

"All quite impossible to believe." Edmund moved his chair uneasily. "I doubt her sanity, to tell you the truth."

"What exactly did she say, Mr. Blackstone?" The doctor's tone was intense. "I need to know everything."

"Well, to come to the point," Edmund went on, "she did not seem to think Simon was actually dead at all."

"I see." The doctor sat very still; a small nervous twitch appeared below one eye. "I wonder—" he added, his accent so thick some of the words were indistinguishable—"I wonder if perhaps you could be more specific?"

"That, I should have thought, was fairly specific," Edmund remarked. "What else would you want?"

"I regret I am unable to assist you," the doctor replied, raising a hand to touch the tic beneath his eye. "That is, unless you supply me with something more factual."

There was a small, even moment when none of them spoke; then Anna lifted her head and issued the words which would release or condemn them all. "She said Simon was a Moonchild." Her voice was unusually loud. "She called him a *Moonchild*. Does that mean anything to you?"

The tic beneath the doctor's eye leaped; he felt its movement beneath his finger. For a moment the whole scene was still, blank, void. The books seemed to stretch endlessly, the couple seated before him were mummified. His mouth was dry and there were sounds in his ears he had not heard before.

"Well?" Edmund asked. "*Has* the name any significance?"

"I am not sure . . ." the doctor began but had to pause. He had a sudden image of his grandmother seated by an open fire in a cottage, her hair long and straggly, her clothing nothing more than a bundle of rags. There was a cooking pot hanging from a chain above the fire, and the old woman, cutting the tongue from a frog, was about to throw it into the pot where other objects he would rather not think about boiled and turned in a dark liquid. The doctor shook his head and tried to put the image aside, but the chalk-white face of his grandmother and her burning eyes remained. He knew, suddenly, he should never have denied his earlier suspicions—he was too close to his mountain ancestry, his roots too deep beneath the soil of the village. "I am not sure what the old woman meant," he lied, his face desperate. "Could you possibly tell me more?"

"Well . . ." Anna replied. "She did say something about returning Simon to the place of his birth. Something about not burying him here." She paused and stared. "Does that not help you at all?"

The doctor nodded reluctantly. There was no doubt about it now. They knew enough. He was now incapable of not telling them everything. He could not deny the climate of his birth. The mysteries were too ancient, their presence too deeply ingrained. He should have accepted the truth earlier when he found the signs of death incomplete: the temperature of the body, its flexibility. He should have admitted it when he examined the corpse of the governess.

The doctor sighed. "I have to confess that the matters you speak of are not unheard of in these mountains." The tic beneath his eye had ceased. "There are many mysteries here, things unknown in other parts of the world."

"Then Simon is not dead?" Anna's voice penetrated. "He is still, somehow, alive?"

The doctor spread his hands defensively. "I must warn you, Mrs. Blackstone," he said, keeping his voice even, recognizing hope and trying to lay it, "that what I am about to tell you verges on the Satanic. It is deep in the heart of those practices we hide from, that we condemn. It is, in short, evil." He watched Anna's face while he spoke and was distressed to see no change in it.

"Is he alive?" Anna persisted. "Answer me that."

"He is not alive," the doctor replied. "Nor will he ever be, as you knew him, again. But also, he is not yet laid to rest."

"Then there must be hope."

"There is no hope whatsoever. In fact, the contrary is true. You are faced with despair."

"But . . ." Anna began when Edmund interrupted. "I understand how difficult this must be for you, Doctor," he said simply. "But if I am correct, are you saying that Simon is under some sort of spell?"

"*He is possessed,*" the doctor replied and his words stilled the room. For what seemed a long time no one breathed. "Perhaps," the doctor said at last, "this might be easier for you to accept if I told you what a Moonchild is."

He went to a bookcase and searching to the highest shelf, took down an ancient, leather-bound volume heavy with dust. Blowing the dust from its pages he turned them with care until he found what he was seeking, then returned and laid the tome before the Blackstones.

"This has been in our family for generations," the doctor said. "It is one of the very few copies still in existence." He was easier now; his knowledge was openly confessed. "It is the only written reference I know of regarding Moonchildren, their acts and their salvation."

"Salvation?" Anna's voice shook.

The doctor nodded. "The old woman you met was, at least, specific about that. Sadly, there is no way to restore your son to the life he knew, but you can save him from eternal, damned wandering. He can be laid to rest," he said.

"I do not understand." Edmund spoke with marked irritation. "How can Simon possibly be alive and yet not alive? It makes no sense to me."

"Sense is a word you cannot apply." The doctor read as he spoke. "Part of what I am about to tell you is based on fact, inasmuch as the physical, the lunar, the mathematical processes are concerned. But what has occurred to your child is unrelated to sense as we know it. Its cause is a mystery." He lifted his head. "Have you heard of Callippus?" he asked.

"Callippus?" Edmund frowned.

"A Greek philosopher."

Edmund nodded. "He had something to do with a calendar, I believe."

"Correct," confirmed the doctor. "In the fourth century B.C. he altered what is known as Meton's Cycle. Meton discovered that at the end of every nineteen years new moons fell on the same day of the week in each month. In other words, a cycle was complete."

"I remember now," Edmund said. "Callippus found an error in the Metonic Cycle."

"Yes, he found an error." The doctor referred once more to the book. "He altered the Cycle of Meton. He felt his own calculations to be foolproof and that by using them one would be able to predict the coincidence of new and full moons with absolute accuracy, right down to the same hour."

"There are those who believe that still," said Edmund and paused, aware of a strange significance. "But . . ."

"Exactly," continued the doctor. "Yet there was also a flaw in Callippus' calculations. He, too, made an error, the result of which is that every five hundred and fifty-three years *a day is lost.* It is gone forever. According to his calendar it is totally irrecoverable." He looked levelly at them both. "And it is believed that those born on that day are also lost," he added.

"No." Anna's voice was muffled. "Simon cannot be lost."

"This surely is merely a matter of calculation," Edmund protested. "Something arbitrary. It can have nothing to do with life itself."

"Not according to the beliefs expressed here." The doctor tapped the leather-bound book, causing a little cloud of dust to rise. "The facts I have so far recounted are well known, you will find them in any work of reference; but what is concluded from them here is quite another matter." His voice gained power. "Here facts merge with mystery. Here calculations and the beliefs in children of the moon begin."

"What does it say?" Anna whispered. The old woman's words were suddenly clear. She saw the face of her son.

"Essentially, it says that if a child is born on that single lost day in the Callippic calendar, he, too, may be lost forever and his soul may be eternally damned."

" 'May be'?" questioned Anna. "Then there is some chance?"

"I'm afraid not," the doctor replied, his tone hopeless. "Your son has not passed into what they call the second stage."

"What does that mean?"

"It is not encouraging. Had he survived his seventh birthday, he would, more than likely, have gone on to live a normal life, but now..." The doctor looked up. "I take it the child is not yet seven?"

Anna looked away. "His seventh birthday will be on the seventh of January." Her voice was listless.

"In that case there is no hope." The doctor examined the faces before him. They were committed now. They were involved. "You see," he went on, keeping his voice even, "while the child is vulnerable, anything that takes him away from his birthplace to where the mystery is active..." the doctor swallowed... "where they accept such things, as they do here, then he is damned." He closed his eyes. "Don't ask how, there is no explanation. But here we have been under the influence of the moon as long as we can remember. There are things in this place that will never be explained."

"Do you mean now?" said Edmund. "Even today?"

"Yes." The doctor cleared his throat. "Even today." He held up a hand to prevent further interruption. "Let me complete what I have to tell you." He returned his gaze to the book. "It says here that should a Moonchild fall under the influences which exist here, he is not only doomed but dangerous. There is nothing that can be done to restore him to normality. All that is possible is to lay him to rest."

"What in God's name does that mean?"

"It means once he has fallen into the death state, once he

has killed, taken the first life, tasted blood, he will continue. He will take any life then, without discrimination, unless he is returned to the place, the very spot, where he was born, and buried there deep in the earth." The doctor laid a hand on the book. "That is what it says here. That is the only way your son can be given any lasting peace. That is the only way to save him. You must take him home immediately. And do what has to be done."

"If I understand you correctly," Edmund said coldly, visibly shocked, "you are saying that Simon killed poor Edith?"

"There is no doubt about it," the doctor replied wearily.

"No . . ." Anna whispered, pleaded. "That cannot be."

"Murder is part of the condition. If you believe any of this—" the doctor tapped the open page before him—"you must believe it all."

"I find *that* quite impossible to accept . . ." Edmund began, but the doctor interrupted him. "Do you also find your son's condition impossible to accept?" he asked, a harshness creeping into his voice. "Do you find the fact that your English maid is discovered dead by his side impossible to accept?"

"Now, just a minute . . ."

"I do not wish to sound unsympathetic," the doctor said. "But there seems to be no other way to impress you." He stared at Edmund. "What has happened to your son is horrific; what has occurred to your maid an abomination." His voice rose. "Don't you realize that unless you return your son to wherever he was born and bury him there as soon as you can he will kill again . . . and again . . . and again?"

Edmund blanched under the impact of the words. "I object to your tone," he said stiffly. "You seem to forget that both my wife and I have been considerably distressed by the death of our son and also by that of our governess. You seem to forget that we were advised to come to you by some half-crazed old woman to see if you could enlighten us further. Do you understand that? To enlighten us, sir, not to deliver us a lecture on parental responsibility."

The doctor stared at Edmund, not believing his words. "But it is critical that you take my advice," he said. "You must do as I say. It is essential." He felt the tic begin to move beneath his eye once more.

"Tell me." Anna's voice was hollow. "Why does he . . . why does a Moonchild take another's life?"

"No one is certain," the doctor replied, grateful for the acceptance implied in Anna's question. "This book suggests it has something to do with blind vengeance, a hatred of all living things, a seeking of some sort of replacement for that one lost day on which it was born." He touched the twitch below his eye. "There are others who believe that because the child was born on an empty day his soul was also empty, ready to be possessed. And whatever possesses slaughters in the way the demon world has always seemed to slaughter." He shook his head. "There is no real answer." He looked at Anna. "Your son had been here before, I understand?"

"Two years ago. We all came."

"Then . . ." The doctor moved his hands, indicating helplessness. "It could be that something began its possession then. There are those who believe such things." The doctor paused, wondering how much he could tell them, how much they could accommodate. "There was one who could have told you more. My grandmother. She was closer to these mysteries than most. But she is dead and all I have is this." He tapped the book.

"That is all very interesting," Edmund said. His manner remained stiff. "But where is the proof?" He put up a hand to prevent the doctor's interruption. "I know, Simon is dead, and it, well, it does seem unusual, to say the least. But as a scientist I find all this mystery, all this folklore, somewhat unconvincing." Edmund paused. "I mean," he went on, "if I were to make a presentation of this to the Royal Society I should need a great deal more evidence than we've seen here to make any impression at all."

"Edmund," Anna chastised, "if what the doctor says is true . . ."

"*If* what he says is true," Edmund interrupted.

"But . . ."

"There are no buts involved," Edmund continued determinedly. "We have been told that Simon is possessed by some sort of devil. That he murdered Edith, whom he loved dearly. That if we don't go through some sort of primitive ritual burial he will haunt us for the rest of our lives." He raised his eyebrows. "The whole idea is preposterous, based on nothing but the words of some deranged creature by the side of the road, on a book of clearly dubious origin, and the memory of someone's grandmother. None of it would hold up in any court of law. There is no evidence whatever."

"Evidence?" the doctor suddenly hissed. "Is that what you want? Then I shall supply you with all the evidence you need." He recalled an echo from the past, a sentence or two, an old woman's voice chanting. *Once the change has begun,* the old voice lilted, *once it has commenced there is no regression. Progress recapitulates ancestry. The hoof of the goat will remain.* The words were ancient, the voice dead. "I shall give you more evidence than you would wish to see." The doctor's hot eyes met Edmund's. "Whether you present it to a court of law, the Royal Society or your own troubled conscience."

Edmund stared, incapable of reply.

The doctor rose from his desk and took a dark coat with an astrakhan collar from a stand by the door. His movements were brisk and decisive. "Come with me," he said. "We will go to the body of your son."

In unison the unlikely procession left the warm, book-lined room and descended the stairs. They went past the woman in black who stood by the door and opened it as if some unknown voice had announced their descent. They left the rooms above the apothecary's and walked slowly, determinedly, through the little village toward the undertaker's shopfront with the holly above the door and the casket containing the body of the child inside.

They went silent, intent, together, past the children playing in the snow, walking through the laughing group as if it had no existence. As they passed, the children's voices were silenced. When they reached the undertaker's, the doctor opened the door and went in, greeted the undertaker briskly and walked toward the casket. Anna and Edmund Blackstone followed, their faces bleak, their coats held about them tightly.

The undertaker blinked and moved his feet. "Is it time for the funeral at last?" he asked, his tone hopeful. "Shall we proceed with the final preparations?"

"No." The doctor shook his head. "There will be no funeral, not immediately. In fact, I would be most grateful if you would leave us alone for a while."

"Alone?" The undertaker frowned suspiciously. "You are not thinking of disturbing my work, are you?"

"Of course not."

"What I'm saying is that, well, you have your area and I have mine." He drew his lips back in a smile, not wishing to offend so profitable a source of business. "I mean, once they leave you and come to me, that's permanent."

"I understand your concern," the doctor replied more amiably. "But this has been a most unusual case, quite unique in medical science. Consequently I must take a few more notes, check a few more details." He smiled. "I shall be preparing a paper on the disease and, of course, shall mention your cooperation."

The undertaker nodded. "That is very kind of you. If there is anything you want, please ask for it." He left the room. He would be relieved when the English finally decided what they wanted done with the body of their child. Their indecision was tedious.

When the undertaker had gone the doctor turned to the Blackstones. "You must listen carefully to what I have to tell you. And you must be ready to move with speed, because, if what I believe is true, we will not have much time," he said crisply.

"I'm afraid I do not understand," Edmund said.

"You will." The doctor's tone was firm. "I am convinced that what I am about to show you will prove beyond doubt that the mysteries of this village, those which have possessed your son, are real." His voice softened. "Also, I must warn you that what you are about to see may horrify you both." His eyes went to Anna's. "I wonder," he added, "if it might be better for you, Mrs. Blackstone, to avoid this altogether. Perhaps you should leave us."

"No." Anna's voice was determined, absolute. "I am prepared to see whatever has to be seen."

"It will not be pleasant."

"Nothing about this has been pleasant," Anna replied evenly.

"Very well," said the doctor and began to undo the heavy silver clasp which held the rhinestone-studded lid of the casket in place. "But what you see may not be at all what you expect."

As he began to raise the lid, Edmund put his hand on the doctor's, arresting the movement. "Just a moment," he said. "Do you not think it might be advisable to inform us exactly what we are about to witness? After all, this *is* the body of our child."

There was pity in the doctor's voice when he replied, "I wish I could help you, Mr. Blackstone, but I cannot."

"Then open it." Edmund lowered his hand. "Let us see the worst it contains."

Slowly, with infinite care, the doctor lifted the lid of the casket. Hesitantly they all peered into the coffin, and it was Anna who exclaimed with relief to see the fair and sweet golden-crowned face of Simon completely unaltered. It was as they had last seen it, seemingly asleep, looking as if it might awake on the instant.

"Simon," Anna said. "Oh, dear Simon." Turning to the doctor she demanded, "What do you mean? There is nothing changed about his dear face at all."

Without replying the doctor reached forward and took hold of the child's hands lying folded, one over the other, on the purple velvet. Calmly he separated them, lifting the upper one away. It moved easily, loosely, there was no stiffness in the flesh at all. The hand came up as if it were alive. Reaching for the other, the doctor took it and opened the curled fingers slowly. As they came into view, emotion moved him like a wave: the fingernails of the hand were coarsened, thickened, longer than those of the other, and beneath them were tiny crusts of congealed blood. Fear momentarily shook the doctor. His mouth dried. There was the voice of his grandmother and the odor of evil; there were sounds in the night and a cloying darkness; there was the sign of the hoof and the coughing of a goat. *The hand of Simon Blackstone was the hand of a Moonchild.* The gnarled fingers were proof of the change, the blood beneath them evidence of his first victim. With a feeling of complete doom the doctor stood to one side, Simon's hand in his own, and presented the truth to the parents.

"Tell me what you see," he whispered.

Anna peered. "The hand ... it's different." Her words trembled; her throat closed. "It is horrible."

"The fingers ..." Edmund stammered ... "Are ... changed."

"Of course," whispered the doctor. "They are monstrously changed."

"What does this mean?" Edward asked harshly.

"It is the evidence I was sure, yet afraid, was there," the doctor said softly. "It is said that once the change begins, once alteration is initiated, it never returns to normal. Something, some part of the Moonchild remains forever in the shape of the possessor. And it continues. Each time the Moonchild claims another life the alteration will advance a little further, become a little more pronounced. Each time he awakens he turns a little more into the demon which has entered his soul." The doctor's eyes were hooded as if trying to hide his discovery. "Finally nothing will remain of the original child. All that was your son will have turned into a creature distorted beyond recognition." He paused and his voice dropped even further. "Unless you do as you have been advised, unless you return him to his birth-place and lay him to rest, he will wander through eternal dark-ness, distorted, possessed, utterly evil."

"Oh, my God." Edmund's voice cracked. "It is . . . true."

Anna put her hands over her face. Her shoulders shook in silent, tearing sobs. "Cover it," she pleaded desperately. "Cover it quickly. I never want to see that . . . thing again."

"Wait," said the doctor. "First I must show you more."

"I will not look."

"You must. There is no avoiding it."

"No." Anna's voice broke. "Stop this . . . please. Stop it now."

"I'm sorry." The doctor's voice was compassionate. "But what I insist you see now is even more imperative."

"Nothing could be more imperative than that distortion."

"This is. Watch the eyes." Even as he spoke there was a slight movement of the child's eyelids. They quivered, trembled, be-gan with infinite slowness to open. "You must see this," the doctor continued, "in order to know absolutely what danger there is in a Moonchild."

"My God . . . they're moving."

All three stared as Simon's eyelids gradually, irrevocably opened and his large, burning, translucent eyes glared with neither love, recognition nor any quality which was human. As the eyes burned upward, the glow which had awakened Miss Harris in the night began to emerge. It was like the beginning of dawn: white light from the pitted surface of the moon, a huge, overpowering, desolate glow which illumined everything. All stared, their breath caught in their throats, their faces alive with horror, until, in one final movement, the doctor slammed shut the lid of the casket and clamped into place the heavy silver catch. He was gasping now, sweat stood out on his forehead. Once more he heard voices in the night and smelled the smell of death. What was to the Blackstones a fearful distortion of their son—that painful, hideous, crippling enough—was to him confirmation of all he had ever denied. He would never be the same again, his mind would not survive this instant.

"By all that is holy," the doctor whispered for himself alone, "forgive me."

Anna Blackstone shouted, "My God, my God, what have you done?" Her words hurled themselves at the doctor in hatred and fear. The sound of her voice brought the undertaker running. "You fiend," she cried as he came into the room.

"Do you need me?" the undertaker asked.

"No," the doctor replied with amazing calmness. "There is nothing we need immediately. Please leave us alone a little longer."

"Are you sure?"

"I am certain."

"Very well." The undertaker lifted his hands uncertainly. "If there is anything, you will ask?"

"I shall."

The undertaker left the room once more, leaving it quieter, more subdued; his mundane entrance had calmed them all.

"I regret deeply what has happened," the doctor said finally; his hand was on the gemstone-studded lid of the closed casket; his eyes were on the Blackstones standing shaken, bearing the evidence of Anna's outburst. "I apologize for whatever distress this has caused, but it was necessary, and, believe me, my anguish is as deep as your own."

"That is not possible," Edmund replied bitterly. "You cannot imagine what you have done."

"I know it and I regret it. For myself also."

"What do you mean?"

"I have discovered aspects of myself I never knew existed."

"It is evil," Anna whispered. "You are a devil."

The doctor shook his head. "That is not so," he said with

great sadness. "I am no devil. I am merely his messenger." As he spoke his eyes asked for compassion, understanding, release.

"You . . ." Anna began but no further words came. Edmund stepped between her and the doctor. "What is your explanation of what we have just seen?" he asked.

"The eyes," began the doctor. "The whole creature must be kept in total darkness, otherwise . . . you saw what happened. Light, any light, whether it be from the sun or moon or stars, is deadly. It activates. It causes the Moonchild to kill. Light is the one element the body must be kept from at all times.

"After your . . . after a Moonchild has killed, there is a dormant period of some hours, days even, as if the beast were satisfied. That is why it did not reawaken after the death of the maid. It may not do so again for some time, but the more it kills the shorter that period becomes, diminishing until the monster is insatiable. Then . . . nothing will stop it. It will burst free of its own accord." The words were steady, the doctor's sincerity evident. "Please understand that at all times the lid of the casket must be kept firmly closed. *Never* allow it to open."

"And if it does?"

"I have told you. He will rise, walk, kill again as he has killed before. Don't you understand? You've seen the blood beneath the fingernails, there will be more if there is light. And the change will continue."

"Change?"

"From child to whatever has possessed his soul."

"Dear God," whispered Anna. "Why did we ever come to this hideous place?"

"That too was predetermined," the doctor said quickly. "Believe me, all you can do now is return him to his birthplace and bury him deep in the earth on the spot in which he was born. Then, and only then, will he remain in peace, in darkness. At rest with what remains of his soul."

"There is nothing else we can do?"

"Absolutely nothing."

"What if he is buried here?" Edmund asked. "If he were placed deeply enough here, might that not suffice?"

Laughter interrupted Edmund; the doctor emitted a thin, high, frenzied sound which cut the air like a razor. "Here?" he said. He put a hand to his mouth, holding his lips in place. "To bury him here would be to condemn us all. Nothing would contain him here, not all the locks in the world. This is where he wants to lie." He desperately tried to control himself.

"We accept your advice," Edmund said firmly. "Simon will be taken home to Tonbridge and buried there."

"Move with speed," the doctor said, visibly shaking. "There are some who believe it must be done before the seventh birthday."

"The seventh of January," Anna said, her voice dry. "We have less than two weeks."

"Leave everything here to me," the doctor went on; his laughter had died. "I will speak to the undertaker. I will arrange for the casket to be ready to travel tomorrow. A carriage will call for you early in the morning and the body will be in it." He held his voice steady; his instructions were lucid. "When the carriage comes you must leave at once, you understand. Without delay."

"That is kind of you," Edmund said simply. "We appreciate all you are doing for us."

"It is not only for you. This village needs to be saved, there will be sacrifices here as well."

"Then you are doubly kind," said Anna. She had seen the doctor's pain and her heart responded. "We will do as you say."

"I shall speak to the undertaker now. In the meantime return to the hotel and prepare." The doctor paused, thinking. "You would be well advised to tell as few people as possible about your departure," he added.

"The local sergeant has asked us not to leave the village," Edmund pointed out.

The doctor's look sharpened. "Do you know why?" he asked.

"I'm not sure, but I imagine he suspects we had something to do with poor Edith's death."

"Does he know anything about your son?"

"I should think his theories were simpler than that."

"Then do not mention a word of your departure to anyone," the doctor said, his tone brisk. "I shall arrange for the carriage to call for you at six tomorrow morning. You should be able to leave quietly enough at that hour."

"Wait," said Edmund, remembering the undertaker's actions when the casket had been purchased. "There is something further which we might be advised to put to use."

He stepped closer and placed one hand on the gemstone-studded rose which lay on the lid. Pressing firmly downward he felt it give beneath his hand and, twisting it, turned it slowly to the right. From the closed casket all heard the muffled sounds of the secret lock sliding into place.

"What is that?" asked Anna.

"It is a lock, built to be secret for some reason," her husband replied. "The undertaker showed it to me when I first saw the casket." He shrugged. "He felt we would have no need for it but I fear he was wrong."

"I am glad you have secured it," the doctor said. "You must be as careful as you can with . . . this at all times. Do not relax your vigilance."

"We shall not."

"If you fail," said the doctor, "the consequences will be deadly." He shook his shoulders as if to relieve himself of the dread. "Return now to the hotel. A carriage with this aboard will come for you in the morning."

The Blackstones left the undertaker's and climbed upward in the midmorning light to the hotel. Neither spoke, accepting without words what had to be done. It was no longer a matter of fact or fantasy, belief or disbelief; Simon must be taken back to Tonbridge, that pretty, castled market town in Kent where he had been born, and buried there. The problems which lay ahead, the difficulties to be overcome, the possibility that the exact spot on which Simon had been born might be impossible to locate, did not enter their minds. There would be solutions somewhere, there would be aid available. All that concerned them as they climbed the hill, leaving the tiny, patterned village behind, as that in the darkness of the following dawn they must leave, taking with them the casketed body of their child, leaving behind not only the village and its mystery but the remains of Miss Harris as well.

Once Anna lifted her head and asked, "What of her, what of poor Edith? Should she not also come with us?" But her voice carried no conviction.

"Impossible," Edmund replied in the same tone. "We can only hope that the good doctor will look after her."

"I do hope so."

"I am sure of it," said Edmund, quickening his step. "What is more, we will write to her parents on our return."

Above them, heavy snow-filled clouds drifted and the leaden skies remained.

CHAPTER FIVE

THE following morning was even colder. Snow, which had frozen overnight, clung to railings and fenceposts, branches and the roofs of houses. Windowpanes were crystallized. The chilling, gusting wind had begun again. At five in the morning Edmund climbed from his bed and woke Anna. Both had taken a sleeping tablet the night before and were only half awake as they fumbled about the freezing bedroom for their clothes.

THEY had dined the previous evening in their rooms, avoiding the stares of the other hotel guests, the whispered conversations in corners, the oblique gaze of the waiters.

Earlier in the evening the landlord had approached them. "I have had your luggage prepared," he said, his breath heavy with the odor of schnapps. "Have you any idea when you will be leaving?"

"Not exactly," Edmund replied. "As you probably know, the sergeant from the village may want to see us again."

The landlord placed a hand over his mouth and coughed. "Is it true," he asked, his voice curious, "that the funeral of your unfortunate son has been canceled?"

"Postponed," corrected Edmund. "The doctor wished to take a few additional notes. Apparently the disease is most uncommon."

"You do not mind this . . . interference with your son's body?"

"Nothing untoward will be done," Edmund replied stiffly. "Under the circumstances, it was of no matter to postpone arrangements for twenty-four hours or so."

The landlord nodded. "Shall I have your bags unpacked in the meantime?" he asked.

Edmund paused before he replied. "That would be kind of you," he agreed. "But it can wait until morning. We shall take an early supper in our rooms and will not want to be disturbed."

"As you wish," said the landlord and belched discreetly behind a hand. "I will send a waiter for your order."

"Thank you." Edmund moved his neat head. "I regret our visit has been so short."

The landlord's face assumed an expression of sadness. He bowed slightly as if to say he understood, that no words could express his sorrow. As Edmund left, he stood watching the neat Englishman ascend the stairs, then shrugged and went in search of another schnapps.

Now, as the Blackstones dressed in the cold, half-lit bedroom, fearing to turn up more light in case they attracted attention, their breath smoked in the freezing air.

When dressed, Edmund went downstairs and found the night porter, a rumpled old man who had been in a half-doze when the crisp, well-dressed Englishman wearing a tweed traveling cloak approached. He rubbed his eyes and stared at Edmund.

"We are obliged to leave immediately," Edmund spoke briskly. "I wonder if you would be good enough to assist with our baggage."

The night porter blinked and scratched his neck. "Of course, sir," he said uncertainly. "But could it not wait until the manager is called?"

"I fear not. There will be a coach for us in about ten minutes."

"I see." The night porter swallowed; responsibility overpowered him. "Is there a matter of settlement, sir?" he asked.

"Of course," Edmund assured him. "If you would be good enough to present the bill."

"I, ah . . . yes." The night porter searched through several ledgers until he found the figures he was looking for. He wrote them slowly on a piece of hotel stationery then handed the amount to Edmund. "I think you will find this correct, sir," he said.

Edmund glanced at the sum and took out his pocketbook, placed several bills before the night porter, whose lips moved each time one was laid on the desk, then added several others. "I wonder if you would also settle the doctor's account and that of the undertaker," Edmund said softly. "Any change I would like you to keep for yourself." He smiled at the rumpled man and added a further bill to the pile.

"Certainly, sir." The old man's hand closed about the money. "Shall I bring your bags down now?"

"Thank you," Edmund replied. "In fact, as there is no one else about, I shall give you a hand."

"I could find a bootboy, sir."

"There's no need," Edmund assured him briskly. "Come along now, we do not have much time."

Together they went upstairs and examined the leather cases, the brass-bound trunks spread out on the floor.

"I doubt if we will need all this," Edmund said on sudden reflection. "Perhaps we should selected only those cases needed for the journey. The remainder can be sent for later."

"As you wish, sir," the old man replied, grateful for the lightening of his load. "Which will they be?"

Quickly Anna and Edmund chose the few pieces they needed and together Edmund and the old man carried them down to the hotel lobby. As they placed the last by the large, wooden doors, the shape of a carriage drawn by two horses came up in the darkness. The driver, a formless man covered by a blanket, sat huddled in the driving seat. The horses stamped and snorted, their hides rippling with cold despite heavy woollen covers.

Stiffly the driver descended; he approached Edmund. "Are you Herr Blackstone?" he asked in a thick mountain accent. Standing, he was tall in spite of a bent back, and his left eye was blind. "If so, I have come for you. The doctor sent me."

"Thank you." Edmund turned his eyes from the ravaged face. "Would you help put the luggage aboard?"

"The first case is already here."

"The first case?" Edmund queried, missing the reference. "Which is that?"

"The one with the jewels."

"Of course," Edmund answered hastily, recognizing the casket and watching the night porter react to the description. "Now please get these others on board. The old man will help you. We shall leave as soon as it's done."

As the night porter assisted the one-eyed coachman, he observed what he could of the elaborate casket, its stones, its malachite. He knew now why the Blackstones were leaving with such dispatch. He wondered if he should call the manager before they departed but was afraid of the danger such an action might precipitate. He would wait, he decided, until questioned and then would describe what he had seen and heard. All would be done at the right time to the right person. He confirmed his decision with a nod and helped place the final case in the coach, then stood respectfully to one side as Edmund and Anna prepared to ascend.

"You have been most helpful," Edmund addressed him. "Please offer our regrets to the landlord and explain the reasons for our early departure."

"I will, sir," the night porter replied and watched the one-eyed coachman climb into the driver's seat. "I shall also inform him that you will send for the remainder of the luggage. Is that correct?"

"Perfectly," replied Edmund and followed Anna into the darkness of the coach. "Farewell."

"Farewell, sir," answered the night porter. The driver clicked the reins and the horses started; the old man watched them go, heard the splinter of their hooves on the icy roadway. His years of service made him bow as the coach moved off. "Safe journey to you both," he added.

The coach traveled slowly in the bleak early-morning air, the horses walking stiff-legged down the winding road to the black and frigid hollow where the village lay. Everywhere about was dark, only along the horizon did a little pale light filter, only the tops of the closest line of pines were shaped by the gathering dawn.

The coach reached the village and passed through the square, past the corner where the laughing children had played, past the frozen snowman standing guard with his broom in the dark. The Blackstones peered through curtains as the coach proceeded, not certain what they might or might not see and seeing nothing in the black and bandaged town, silent and umoving as the grave.

Only when the village was several miles behind and the light from the morning stronger did Edmund lift his head to call through the trap, "Where is it we are bound, my good man?" His cry echoed unnaturally above the steady clomping of the horses.

The crouched, curved figure of the coachman turned; his one eye gleamed in the filling light. "Kempten," he called in his mountain voice.

"The small town near Lake Constance, is that correct?"

"Yes, Herr Blackstone. From there you will obtain a train to Basel." He bent closer, a mountain of a man in the freezing dark. "That is what the doctor said to tell you. From Basel is a rail train to a Channel port."

"Thank you." Edmund told Anna what the driver had said.

"We owe that doctor a lot, you know. I'm afraid I have given little thought to our travel but imagine there will be a boat we can take from the coast to either Portsmouth or Southampton."

"I believe to Southampton there is such a service."

"Excellent, that means we will be in Tonbridge by the third or fourth of January," Edmund said. "We should have plenty of time for what we have to do."

Anna nodded. "I do hope there will be no trouble with passage," she said. "It can be quite difficult at times during the holiday period."

The mundane conversation continued, enabling them to avoid contemplating their real horror, to hide from that transformation in the ornate casket of what had been their son and this miserable journey through the freezing air. Its very triteness expressed their sanity in the early-morning flight.

THE manager of the hotel descended early, his face bright from the razor; from him came the smell of cologne. He walked with a springy step to the hotel door and peered out, sniffing the early air. He felt brisk this morning, efficient, and it was in this mood that he approached the rumpled old figure of the night porter bent nervously over the desk.

"Good morning, Hector," the landlord said cheerfully. "No trouble in the night, I trust?"

"No, sir."

"Fine, fine. Nothing to report then?"

The night porter shifted his shoulders. "Not really, sir," he said with some hesitation. "The English have left, but that is all." He kept his eyes lowered, hoping to pass off the news as casually as possible.

"The English have *left?*" The landlord's mood changed visibly. "What is that you say?"

"This morning, early." The night porter tried to sound unconcerned, as if the departure had been expected, as if the carriage in the early dawn usual. "There was a coach that came, from the village."

"I don't care if a dirigible came," the landlord said, his face dark with anger. "Why didn't you call me?"

"I did not think there was any need, sir." He scratched his cheek with a shaking hand. "They paid what they owed."

"Of course they would." The landlord glared. "Don't you know they are wanted by the police? Don't you understand that Sergeant Obelgamma had forbidden them to leave the village?"

The rumpled night porter blinked. "No, sir," he replied unevenly.

"You are an old fool, Hector," the landlord said bitterly. "We will need to find a younger man for your job." He thumped a hand on the desk in frustration. "Call Sergeant Obelgamma from the village. Tell him immediately what an idiot you have been."

The night porter stood as still as his fear would allow. Now was the moment to present his information; it was all he possessed to save himself. "Shall I also tell him about the jewels, sir?" he asked in a pale tone, his hope hanging clearly on every word.

"Jewels? What jewels?"

"The ones that were in the chest, sir. The ones that the coachman brought with him."

"I do not know what you are talking about, Hector." The landlord began to wonder if the old man had lost his reason.

Fumbling for words, trying to control his nervousness, the night porter repeated the conversation he had overheard. He told how Edmund had reacted, what the jeweled casket looked like. He told the landlord how his first inclination had been to call him from his bed but the calm, efficient Englishman and the tall, blanketed, one-eyed coachman had frightened him.

The landlord listened carefully, recognizing the casket for what it was, but deciding not to contradict the old man. He wondered how the information could be used to advantage.

Finally he reached out and put a paternal hand on the night porter's shoulder. "I wish you had told me this earlier, Hector," he said in a kinder tone of voice. "It makes all the difference." He chewed his lip thoughtfully.

The night porter sighed with relief. "Thank you, sir," he said gratefully.

"Not at all, you have been most observant." The landlord patted the old man absently. "Now, run along and telephone the sergeant. I am sure he will be interested in what you have to say."

The morning was bright again as far as the landlord was concerned. He had no doubt that the night porter's ramblings would add fuel to the police sergeant's theories, all of which suited him nicely. Whoever was responsible for murdering the English governess now was unimportant; what was certain was that the English couple would be blamed. No mystery would surround the hotel, none of the other guests would have any cause for alarm, there should be no cancellations. In fact, the landlord mused, as he watched the night porter grapple awkwardly with the heavy, enameled upright telephone, the whole event might give the hotel a certain picturesque charm, turn it into an interesting topic of conversation, create business. Only one small nagging doubt lingered in his mind; he hoped if by any chance the English were not responsible for the death of their governess, that whoever was would have committed all the mayhem necessary for the time being and that no further bodies would be found. He smiled happily, went off to find a glass of cold white wine and wait for Sergeant Obelgamma to arrive.

Sergeant Obelgamma had been shaving when he received news of the Blackstones' departure, and in his urgency to leave nicked his jaw. Placing a small piece of toilet paper over the wound, he hurried up the icy hill to the hotel, which seemed to loom menacingly in the early mists.

"This is criminal," he said to the landlord as soon as he arrived, the small piece of paper moving with every word. "How did it happen? Who is responsible?"

"That is difficult to say." The landlord spoke mildly. "Did you not yourself give them permission to leave the hotel?"

"Yes, yes, but not the village. I told them specifically not to leave the village."

"Unfortunately our night porter was not informed of that fact." The landlord's tone made it quite clear the hotel was in no way responsible. "However, you may thank his observation for, well, any additional information he is able to supply."

"Of course, of course." Sergeant Obelgamma spoke rapidly and the tissue on his jaw flicked up and down. "It is my opinion that the English have accomplices."

"Accomplices?"

Someone sent the coach. Someone must have supplied the jewel casket."

"Have you any idea who that might be?"

"At the moment, no." Sergeant Obelgamma raised a finger. "But I intend to find out."

The landlord nodded thoughtfully and stepped a little closer. "I might just be able to assist." He was close enough for his winy breath to cause Sergeant Obelgamma to blink. "It is possible I can help."

"Is that so?" the sergeant asked. "How?"

"The undertaker might just know something about the casket." The landlord raised his innocent hands. "Not that I am suggesting he is in any way involved, you understand. But he might, just might, know something of the casket."

"In that case I will question him." The police sergeant closed his lips and sighed, and a certain resignation came over his face. "I am afraid I will need to inform the outside authorities," he admitted reluctantly. "Now that the English have left the village, this case has become a national matter."

"That is unfortunate," the landlord muttered. "We here in

the village, all of us, you understand, would not wish for any unfortunate publicity."

"That is true," the sergeant admitted. "But there is no alternative."

"You will be discreet? After all, we know who the criminals are."

"Of course, of course." The sergeant spoke quickly. "I will contact Inspector Fuchs of Police Headquarters in Munich. He is a clever and sympathetic man who deals with foreign crime."

The sergeant nodded briskly enough to cause the small piece of toilet paper to float to the floor.

IT was some time before Sergeant Obelgamma contacted Inspector Fuchs. First he listened to the night porter's story, further elaborated, slightly more dramatized. The sergeant realized he would not be disgraced by the flight of the English— the very fact that they had chosen to leave in the darkness of early dawn served to indicate how clever, even accomplished, they were. Their single error, so far, had been to indicate that someone in the town was in league with them.

As he listened, Sergeant Obelgamma's theory about the Blackstones altered. It was obvious now why the governess had been murdered: she had not been involved in a triangle of passion, but had in fact discovered her master's secret. The Blackstones were, without doubt, international jewel thieves who moved from hotel to hotel taking what they could and, had it not been for the illness and subsequent death of their son, would clearly have removed every piece of jewelry from this hotel and vanished without trace.

"You have shown excellent observation," he congratulated the night porter. "I will mention your assistance to Munich."

"You are very kind," murmured the old man humbly. "I was merely doing my duty."

"You will be rewarded," the sergeant assured him and left the hotel. He returned to the village and made for the under-

taker's. Entering the establishment beneath the sprig of holly
nailed above the doorway, he found the undertaker seated
before the little black stove, his heavy hands held toward the
warmth. "Ah," began Sergeant Obelgamma without any cere-
mony. "I have a few questions to ask."

"I will do my best to answer them," replied the undertaker
unenthusiastically.

"It is about the English," the sergeant said, pulling up a
stool. "The couple with the dead son. What do you know
about them?"

"Too much." The undertaker shook his head sadly. "I know
more of them than any man would wish to know. They come
to me for a burial. First it has to be yesterday, then it is put
off until tomorrow." His tone was monotonously grieved; he
stared at the fire, past the shape of his outspread hands, and
lamented. "You would think that the one reliable thing in
this unreliable world was death, would you not? You would
imagine that once a body was in your hands for burial that
would be the last of it, eh?" His head moved solemnly from
side to side in deep regret. "No, not with the English. Not
only do they postpone their arrangements but they take the
body away as well." His melancholy eyes came round and fixed
themselves on those of the sergeant. "What do you make of
that? God knows what they intend to do with it. There is no
competition they could take it to, I am the only man in my
profession for miles." He sighed. "The English are beyond my
understanding."

"That is true," agreed the sergeant and waited a few seconds
before asking his next question, hoping to surprise an answer.
"Tell me," he said loudly, "what do you know of the other
English death?"

The undertaker closed his eyes. "That is the worst news I
have heard all week," he replied truthfully. "And it has not
been, what you would call, a good week for notices."

"You have no idea who was responsible?"

"I swear it."

"On your mother's grave?"

"On my mother's grave." The undertaker smiled a long, slow smile. "And what more could you ask of a man in my position?"

Sergeant Obelgamma stared at the heavy figure of the undertaker, his hands extended toward the mica of the stove for warmth. The man's replies rang of honesty, no one could affect such melancholy merely to elaborate a lie. The depth of his professional soul was clearly bewildered by their comings and goings, their bringing in and taking away of bodies. The sergeant shook his head thoughtfully.

"Very well," he said at last. "Tell me what you know of the jewel casket."

The undertaker's puzzled face came round slowly. "The what?" he asked mildly. Nothing would surprise him now.

"The jewel casket," Sergeant Obelgamma persisted, knowing he had lost a suspect. "The one the English had with them."

The undertaker nodded sagely.

"I see you recognize it." Sergeant Obelgamma's hope was a little revived. "Tell me about it. Immediately. Everything you know."

"I know they have not paid me for it," the undertaker said sadly.

"Explain the jewels to me, then." Sergeant Obelgamma leaned forward but knew in his heart he was to be disappointed. "I want the truth, understand."

"You shall have it," the unhappy man replied and proceeded to tell exactly how the Blackstones came into possession of the ornate casket with its rhinestone-studded lid and the dull bloom of malachite on its carved sides. "Then," the undertaker sighed, "just when you would expect your difficulties to be over, the Englishman came back and took it all away. Everything: the casket, the body of his son, even the velvet lining I had so carefully installed."

"When was this?"

"Yesterday morning, not ten minutes before the funeral was due."

"He took it with him then?"

"Not exactly," the undertaker replied, recalling the events.

"When?" Sergeant Obelgamma's nose twitched; he felt close to something. "When was the casket removed?"

"Later," the undertaker told him. "When they returned with the doctor."

"So the doctor is involved?"

"You could say so," replied the undertaker thoughtfully. "In fact, you could say he was a large part of it."

Sergeant Obelgamma took out his notebook, found a pencil and carefully licked the end. Holding the pencil over the notebook he said, "Tell me everything you know about the doctor. He could be the very man I am looking for." There was a gleam in the sergeant's gray eyes.

Once more the undertaker's monotonous tones with their mountain accent filled the room as he told of the Blackstones' second visit of the morning of the day before. "My own establishment," he said. "And I am banished."

"Do you know why?"

"If I did I would tell you."

"What happened then?"

"What happened then?" The undertaker's voice rose. "You might well ask, but I was not there to see it. I was next door, waiting to be allowed to return to my offices." He rubbed his hands together. "It is considerably colder out there, you understand."

Sergeant Obelgamma wrote rapidly in his notebook.

The undertaker shrugged. "Finally I was permitted to return," he said, then paused, recalling Anna's voice raised in horror. "No, I lie," he added. "First the Englishwoman screamed, I had almost forgotten it. She screamed and I rushed in to see what I could do to help. When I arrived the husband was holding her and she was calling the doctor something, some name. I forget what it was."

"Try to remember."

The undertaker closed his eyes and concentrated. Sergeant Obelgamma ran a hand over his bald pate nervously. Finally the undertaker opened his eyes and shook his head. "I cannot recall what it was," he said. "But she was furious with the doctor, that I remember clearly."

"What happened then?"

"I was sent away again. Later, when I was allowed to return, the doctor himself came to fetch me. The English were gone, the casket was shut and the doctor asked me to deliver it to his rooms." The undertaker spread his gravedigger's hands, emphasizing his loss. "I ask you, what else could I do?" His eyes were on Sergeant Obelgamma. "After all, the doctor is my main source of business. I could not afford to offend him."

Sergeant Obelgamma's gray eyes became shrewd. "Then why are you telling me all this?" he asked cleverly.

"It is a choice of evils, that I will admit," the undertaker confessed. "I cannot afford to fall out with the police either."

Sergeant Obelgamma nodded. "What else?" he asked.

"Is that not enough?"

"Perhaps so." Sergeant Obelgamma felt as if opportunity had turned in his favor; a prime suspect was suddenly his. "You have done well to tell me all this," he said, tapping his notebook. "I will see that you are amply rewarded.

"I have only done what I must," the undertaker said gloomily, then raised a quizzical eyebrow. "What reward did you have in mind?"

"We shall see." Sergeant Obelgamma stood, looked important. "It is a matter I intend to discuss with Munich. I will now go to the post office to make a telephone call to Inspector Fuchs."

The undertaker returned his gaze to the fire. It was not his day; he sat sullen and silent while the sergeant took his leave, he neither moved nor spoke as the sergeant said farewell but remained gloomily despondent as the bald man went out into the street. Only the little gust of freezing wind that entered his establishment as Sergeant Obelgamma opened the door caused the undertaker to move at all; he shivered and edged a little closer to the small black stove.

When Obelgamma's long-distance call to Inspector Fuchs in Munich finally came through it was not as satisfying as the little sergeant hoped it would be.

At the other end of the line Inspector Fuchs stood upright, the funnel-shaped handpiece clamped to his ear, and listened to everything Obelgamma had to say. Every now and then he asked a further question and, his face expressionless, absorbed the answer. Inspector Leopold Fuchs was a large, heavily built man with a handlebar moustache and thinning hair which he brushed straight across his forehead; he had long been with the Munich Municipal Police, and through a series of successful arrests and his own interest in travel had developed a reputation for solving those crimes which involved foreigners. He spoke English and French fluently, and in all three languages knew what questions to ask and what to extract from the answers. He was a careful man, and the replies he received from Sergeant Obelgamma disturbed him.

"Have you talked to the doctor yet?" Inspector Fuchs asked after an extended reply from the sergeant. "Has he been questioned?"

"I am about to proceed with that now."

"Don't."

"I beg your pardon, Inspector."

"The word was: *Don't,* Sergeant. Not until I get there."

"You wish to question him also?"

"Not exactly," Inspector Fuchs replied. "I wish to question him first."

"Is that necessary, sir?"

"Essential, in my opinion."

"I see."

"I will also wish to question the others: the undertaker, the landlord, the night porter. All of them."

"Very well. If that is the case, I shall organize it for you."

"Please do not," the large inspector requested. "You have done enough as it is."

Sergeant Obelgamma placed the flat of his hand over his bald pate sadly. "You seem displeased with what has occurred," he said as discreetly as possible.

Fuchs sighed. "Not exactly," he said. "But these international matters can be very delicate. Especially when the English are involved." He altered his voice so that it sounded less condemning. "This type of work requires years of experience, it needs a special nose, Sergeant. All in all, it would be much better if we went over the ground again together." He raised his eyes to the ceiling. "I am sure what you have done will be most valuable, most valuable indeed."

"Thank you, sir." Seregant Obelgamma raised his voice. "When can we expect you?"

Inspector Fuchs took a silver half hunter from his waistcoat pocket and looked down at it. "I will organize a special coach," he said. "The journey will take about ten hours through those mountains. Are the passes open, do you know?"

"I feel confident they are, sir. There has been no fresh snow although it is very cold."

"In that case I should be with you before midnight tonight. Please reserve a room for me in the hotel. As Herr Fuchs, not Inspector. Tomorrow morning I shall visit you at the station-house."

"At what time, sir?"

"After breakfast." Inspector Fuchs took the telephone from his ear and replaced it on its hook. "Imbecile," he muttered and stared out the window. "Dunderhead."

Something was missing from the facts the village sergeant

had supplied. Something vital, central, convincing was absent from the simple theory heard thinly over the long-distance telephone. Inspector Leopold Fuchs grunted with dissatisfaction as he prepared himself for the journey up into the cold mountains. He wondered how he might further reduce the little sergeant's activities, but nothing short of murder came to mind.

PART II

THE JOURNEY

CHAPTER SIX

THE valley air was cold, damp, penetrating, the sky overladen
with heavy cloud. The coach bearing Anna and Edmund
Blackstone and their deadly casket descended the mountainside;
about them snow became less and more greenery was seen.
Once a bird flashed beside the trotting horses and both Anna
and Edmund fixed their eyes on its shunting life. Only the
coachman remained unmoving. His blanketed figure was rock-
like, crouched over the heaving backs of the horses, his one eye
fixed firmly on the icy road ahead. Around him the chill air
clung to his ribs, and moisture in his nostrils crusted.

As the coachman drove, only part of his mind was on his
mission, that which he had been hired for. Another part, more
primitive, more basic, shifted in wonder, dwelling on the ornate
casket the English carried, turning over possibilities of what it
might contain. Their possession of the splendid case, coupled
with the extreme earliness of the departure, caused him to
wonder exactly why they were in such a hurry to reach Kempten, the rail town.

He had been told little enough by the doctor, merely that the
English were to be collected at a certain time in a certain place;
he had been given the casket as part of their luggage; but what
he had seen was sufficient to set his mind alight. Now, as the
coach proceeded, his conjectures flourished and grew. If he had

the opportunity, he thought, if the chance came, it would do no harm to look inside the elaborate box. It was his right to know what his coach carried, it was his duty to be informed. He clucked his tongue at the horses and came to a decision: all he needed was an opportunity, and that could be provided easily enough; there must be halts along the way, pauses for refreshments, a meal at an inn. Once the English were out of sight he would examine the contents of the casket they so carefully carried. The coachman smiled in anticipation: it could prove profitable. And after all, if one is called from one's bed at five in the morning to sit all day in the freezing air, one deserved a little more than one had been offered; if there was gain in the casket he had earned the right to it, that much was clear.

The one-eyed coachman shifted the reins in his hands and the horses moved more rapidly; they would be in Kempten by nightfall, and if he was lucky, he would arrive a richer man.

WITH this thought in mind the coachman paused once, later in the day, by a small wayside inn and leaned toward the Blackstones hopefully, asking if they would care to refresh themselves, to take a little *Glühwein* perhaps. But Edmund waved him on; he was hungry, as he knew Anna must be, but he was aware of the danger of any delay so close to the village. He had glanced at Anna who nodded in confirmation.

"It is best," Edmund argued, "to keep going."

"I agree," Anna replied. "There is no point in delaying."

"We have had a good journey so far."

"We have been lucky, apart from the cold."

Thus the coach proceeded steadily, past the turning of the day, until it took a final corner on the icy road before it reached a stream. It was here that the accident occurred. At this point the road doubled, curving back as it came to the stream leaping and glistening in the valley bottom. The water ran swiftly; the rocks it bounced over gleamed with a patina of ice; the sound it made as it fled the valley was quick, rushing, and it came up suddenly as the road entered its course. The sudden roaring caused the already unsettled driver's attention to lapse. He failed to rein the horses as the coach turned the bend. Velocity spun the vehicle on the icy roadway and it crashed into a stand of willows growing on the bank.

Everything happened very quickly.

One moment the coach was traveling steadily toward the unseen stream, the next it had swung wide and the iron-rimmed wheels were sliding on the treacherous roadway, driving sideways in the direction of the stream bed, spraying powder ice as they cut into the surface. The horses, feeling the weight behind them shift, lost their gait and scrambled sideways, taken by the body of the coach. Their legs tangled. Their heads were raised in fear and pain. Above them, the one-eyed coachman gripped the reins; he stood on the footboard and dragged backward to stay the horses, attempting to straighten the drive of the coach. But it was too late, nothing would halt the sideways motion of the coach now save the willows growing by the riverbank. With a huge and overpowering crash the coach plunged into the stand of trees, heeling toward them as it went, skidding violently into their bulk with a sound of splintering wood.

The driver was flung clean. He fell past the willows onto the edge of the riverbank where he lay dazed and unmoving, his boots dangling in the freezing water. The horses reared and plunged, tearing at their harnesses, tugging at the coach bulked against the trees, but they failed to move it. Their actions broke more of the bodywork, added to the sound of splintering, but did not free the vehicle. After a short while they quieted and stood in their tangle of leather waiting to be led.

INSIDE the coach, the crash had taken both Anna and Edmund with equal surprise. As the slide began, Anna clutched her husband. Edmund grasped her tightly as they were enveloped by sound and furious movement. They heard the cries of the horses and the grating of iron on ice. The thrust of sideways motion tumbled their cases around them. They were dimly aware of the standing figure of the one-eyed coachman hauling on the reins, shouting at the horses, and the shifting of the ornate casket, bearing the body of the child as it slid from beneath the seat where it had been wedged. As Edmund held Anna, in those few seconds that remained between his instinctive, protective action and the crashing of the coach into the trees, he saw the casket move, and he thrust a foot against it, clamping it as best he could in its place of safety, realizing that in spite of the lock and the clasp it might fly open on any violent impact.

"Good God," Edmund gasped, grasping Anna, attempting to secure the casket. "We must hold . . . this."

But even as the last word escaped his lips the coach crashed into the willows; the sounds of shattering wood and the agony of the horses cut him short. Both he and Anna had one clear second of thunder before their heads cracked together and they were knocked senseless. Unconscious, they lay in the corner of the coach, which was stuck, tilted into the stand of willows. One wheel, lifted from the highway, spun crazily. They lay amidst fallen cases, some open, some split, while against the door, hurled into it, its condition masked by swirling dust, was the casket containing the body of Simon Blackstone, the Moonchild.

For a few moments after the horses calmed there was peace. The spinning wheel slowly came to a halt; the sound of cracking wood, the tearing of metal on ice had ceased. Only the rushing of the stream through its bed surrounded the remains of the coach and its contents.

Of the three, the first to recover was the driver. The freezing water washing over his boots revived him and he sat, a hand to his head, and turned slowly to look at the wreckage behind him. Then, realizing he had no bones broken and that there was no sound from the others inside the coach, he climbed to his feet and walked stiffly toward the horses. They whinnied when they saw him and rolled their frightened eyes; but he clucked his tongue and spoke in a voice they recognized, and they were still once more.

Then the coachman approached the body of the vehicle. He walked round to the side farthest from the willows and reached for the door handle, but it was beyond his grasp, so he circled to the other door and took hold of the handle there. The coach itself was jammed between the trunks of two willows, leaving the door on that side unobstructed. Crouching beneath the body of the tilted vehicle, the coachman turned the handle and felt the door loosen; he pulled and it opened a few inches, then stuck. He struggled a minute or two longer, then, with a heave, flung it wide. It swung open and through the dust the coachman caught a glimpse of Anna and Edmund Blackstone, unconscious, huddled against the side of the vehicle. He was about to reach for Edmund, to pull him forward in search of signs of life, but he stopped as he saw the heavily carved casket. Its rhinestone-studded lid glinted, the malachite glowed about the sides. It was within touch, it lay at the feet of the Blackstones against the door the coachman had just opened. He reached for the casket instead.

This is luck, he thought, as he ran his hands over the carved surface. This is a sign, surely.

As he touched the casket it slipped on the tilted floor and edged toward him as if in agreement. Swiftly he caught it and, surprised and delighted by the weight of the valuables he believed it to contain, lowered it slowly to the ground and began to examine it carefully. His lips pursed as his eyes took in the detail of the carving and the inset jewels; these alone, he knew, would be worth his while. He moved his hands over the casket, touching it gently, with awe, until he came to the heavy, ornate lid. It was open, sprung by the force of the crash. The secret lock had been released and the silver clasp was free. It hung broad and loose beneath the coachman's fingers. In the casket's dim interior he could just make out the rich purple of the velvet and something which looked like spun gold. Glancing over his shoulder to determine that neither Edmund nor Anna had moved, the coachman turned quickly to the casket and swiftly opened the coffin wide.

The sight within shocked him. He had expected jewelry, furs, gold, valuable garments, and to discover the unmoving, cherubic, golden-crowned body of a child lying on the purple velvet, the hands evenly folded over the chest, took the coachman's breath away. The body had survived the battering in the tilted coach with neither mark nor movement. The child lay still, seemingly rested; the hair was unruffled and the hands untouched. The sight in its simple beauty caused the purblind coachman to stare at it silently for a second or two and then emit a small, deeply felt sob of pity.

"Poor little one," he said, understanding why the Blackstones had left in the cold and early dark, why they were intent on keeping the strictest timetable for their journey. They were taking their beloved child home for burial, they could not bear to leave this sweet innocent behind, buried in some corner of a foreign field that was not part of England. "Oh, what a pity," the coachman whispered and reached forward to touch the child's porcelain brow.

As he did, he froze, became rock-still, his hand poised halfway toward the cherubic face, his one eye wide, blank, fixed in horror: because in the instant he began his movement the Moonchild embarked on a similar gesture, a mirror of the coachman's own. The child's eyes opened and blazed with their intense, magnetic, paralyzing twin beams of white light. At the same time the hands unfolded, and the underhand, the Moonchild hand, with its growing nails and gnarled knuckles, began to lift with time-arresting slowness toward the coachman's throat.

The coachman's mouth opened but no words came; voiceless he remained crouched, as he had remained crouched most of his working life, stunned, motionless, incapable of either flight or defense, his one eye glued to the Moonchild as the hand came up and clamped itself about his throat. Only then did the man try to scream, but now the hand about his windpipe prevented his crying from emerging. The last thing the coachman ever saw, as the fingers bit into his neck and blood spilled down his shirtfront, was the immensity of the white light which surrounded him. It came from everywhere; it grew inside the casket and it sprang from the child's eyes, it enveloped them both, filled the little hollow where they were locked together by the immovable arm; it spilled outward, alarming the horses so that they reared and cried and rolled their eyes in a new, an inexperienced, fear. While the life was torn from the coachman's throat the face of the child smiled its deadly smile.

The smile altered Simon's visage completely, twisting it into an epitome of evil, malevolence, corruption even more vile than the smile which had bid farewell to the poor, helpless life of Miss Harris. It was more developed, advanced, increased in mischief and madness; it distorted the face completely, it shattered the angelic image. It burned, as the eyes burned, into the dying coachman, it scorched the clouding sight of his single eye, it seared the final seconds of life. As it writhed over the child's face the iron-hard fingers ripped the beleaguered man and dashed his soul to darkness.

Then, its dreadful task accomplished, the hand returned to the coffin and the smile began to fade. For what seemed like seconds the coachman's body remained frozen after the hand had left it, hung lifeless on its heels, until with one final, convulsive movement it pitched onto its back and lay dead; the lifeless eye turned upward to the leaden sky, the torn throat open for all the world to see.

Only then was the devilish smile erased completely from the face of Simon Blackstone and the innocence of the features re-formed. The burning eyes closed and the moonlight died; all was as it had been except for the hand which had taken the coachman's life. The nails were longer now, the hand more twisted, distorted, misshapen; now the knuckles were rough and scarred. The demonic hand mismatched the arm which carried it. It was larger, unfitted to the slender child's stalk from which it grew; it was an old hand now, ancient, immeasurable in time and deed. The crooked nails, the swollen knuckles, the heavy veins which threaded it belonged to something dark and distant, evil and timeless, of odors and climates which the child's nostrils had never known, had not yet been experienced by the rest of the body.

The change was enveloping; what had been the innocent hand of a child was now a Moonchild's dreadful weapon. From the hand to the arm to the body and finally to the sweet face distortion would creep until, as the old woman had predicted and the doctor confirmed, nothing would remain of the original, every aspect would be reduced to a ragged, distorted figure, altered beyond description—haunted, haunting, destroyed forever—unless the remains were returned to Tonbridge and buried there in depth and darkness before the seventh birthday.

Now the Moonchild lay back on the velvet plush, the face calm, innocent; the hands refolded one above the other on the slight chest: only now the underhand was so hugely distorted that the one above no longer disguised the change. This perhaps more than anything else horrified Edmund when he recovered consciousness and staggered onto the scene. It was the dreadful incongruity of the hands that caused him to cry aloud with grief, slam shut the casket lid and refasten the clasp and the lock before Anna recovered and moved to join him.

Edmund turned his head away; he could not bear the distorted sight of what had been his son; the pain in his chest was greater than anything he had ever known; the cry which leaped from his throat spilled grief. The sound of it caused the horses to rear once more and splintering cracked from the coachwork. The panic of the horses calmed his own. Quickly Edmund approached them and, speaking softly, quieted their fear, his control born from the sudden, clear understanding that unless he acted, no other would. With the same measured pace he took the blanket which the coachman had worn and covered the man and the great, still-bleeding wound in his throat. As he did, Edmund heard movement behind him and turned to see Anna, one dazed hand over her eyes, the other holding the coach door for support, standing unsteadily.

"Wait," he called.

"Edmund?" Anna's voice was frail. "What happened?"

"We had an accident, my dear." Edmund thought quickly. "The coachman, I am afraid, is dead."

"Poor man. Is there nothing we can do?"

"Nothing."

"And Simon?" Anna's voice grew stronger. "What of him?"

"The casket is secure," Edmund replied. "And you, is there anything broken?"

"No." Anna separated herself from the coach and took her husband's arm. "I think you cushioned me." Her eyes went to the damaged vehicle. "Oh, dear, is there anything to be done with this?"

"We will need to get it upright once more," Edmund said. There was a strength in him now he had not known before. Until this moment he had remained in the hands of others, as he had remained in the hands of others all his life: it had been the doctor who made every decision regarding the condition of his son; it had been the police sergeant, the landlord, the undertaker who had instructed or acted or offered aid; it had been the coachman who had come for them and borne them away, choosing route and understanding timetable. Nothing had been Edmund's own, the few simple decisions he had made had affected them not at all. Now there was no other to aid or advise; the journey before them was his own responsibility; the problem of the splintered coach his to solve. He looked at Anna, dazed and uncertain and said, "It will be all right, my dear. I shall harness the horses to the side of the vehicle. They should be able to pull it away from the trees."

"Will it still travel?"

"I should think so," Edmund replied, examining the wheels. "Nothing else seems broken. The axles are sound and the wheels intact. Only the upper section has suffered."

Anna looked at her husband curiously, seeing the strength, recognizing the new authority. "I wasn't aware you could handle horses," she said, probing delicately.

"Every gentleman can ride," Edmund said, moving round the coach. "Would you mind, my dear, rearranging the cases while I attend to this?"

"Of course not," replied Anna. "I feel quite strong again." She began to sort the scrambled luggage. "Is there any other way I can be of assistance?"

"Not at the moment," her husband replied. "This should not take too long."

Edmund unharnessed the horses and, with the same strappings, linked them to the side of the coach away from the willows; he worked quickly, dexterously, thinking clearly. The activity put all else out of mind, it became its own objective, and, in spite of the freezing air, Edmund began to perspire as he shouldered the horses into place, climbed onto the heeling coach body, lashed the harnesses. When he returned to the icy roadway, Anna was beside the horses holding their heads.

"I have attended to the luggage," she said. Activity had calmed her. "Although I am afraid some of the cases from the roof are ruined."

"We must patch them as best we can."

"Perhaps we can purchase new ones in Basel."

Edmund nodded. "We will have to see," he said.

Then, taking the reins from Anna, he began urging the horses forward. He stood by their heads, the reins in one hand, the coachman's whip in the other, and softly, almost tenderly, coaxed them into action. At first they were reluctant to move; they stood stiff-legged, their eyes white in their heads, their ears uneasy, but gradually they grew accustomed to the Englishman's soft voice and his unyielding pressure. Once or twice Edmund cracked the whip over their backs and slowly they began to respond. The muscles in their shoulders straining, the harness creaking with effort, they pulled against the wedged coach. The coach was firmly stuck; it moved an inch or two, the sound of woodwork shattering was heard once more, the body of the vehicle shuddered, but for the moment it remained entangled in the willows. Unrelentingly Edmund persisted, his mind devoted to the strength of the horses. He permitted his mind to dwell on nothing more than each step as it was paced, each problem as it was solved, each inch as it was covered. He worked the horses, edging them, coaxing, breathing power into their widespread nostrils. They pulled and the coach tilted, they forced and the broken woodwork tore, they heaved and with a sudden shout and a crack of the whip Edmund carried their heads. With a thunderous splitting and a cloud of dust the coach heaved from the willows and came to rest free, scarred, crippled but serviceable on its four iron-rimmed wheels.

"Thank God," Edmund heard himself say. His breath came in gasps, sweat stung his eyes. "Come, Anna," he said. The coach was free and the journey lay before them. "Let us get aboard and away from this unfortunate place."

"At once," said Anna, a quiet pride burning within her. She would never have imagined Edmund to contain such strength.

Swiftly Edmund unharnessed the horses from the side of the coach and replaced them between the shafts of the vehicle. They seemed to understand the importance of their effort and were quiet in Edmund's hands, returned to their places with neither fear nor resistance. Then Edmund and Anna climbed into the coachman's seat and sat in the freezing air. With a crack of the whip Edmund set the horses in motion, and the journey to Kempten was resumed. Together the unlikely English pair braved the cold about them, the roughness of their movement. They continued, and that was all that was of importance in their minds.

Once Anna turned to her husband and placed a hand on his sleeve. "That man behind, there was nothing we could do?" She was forced to shout above the sound of the horses' hooves.

"Nothing," Edmund called back, wondering if there would be more to leave before they reached their destination. "He was gone when I found him."

"Poor man."

Edmund nodded. Anna's remark raised new concern. The fact that the secret lock had failed left open the danger the casket contained. Edmund considered trying to obtain something more secure but immediately realized how difficult that would be to apply without either admitting to Anna the real cause of the coachman's death or denying to the world the disguise in which the Moonchild traveled. The casket could scarcely be borne to Tonbridge bound with heavy chain or obviously padlocked— that was no manner in which to convey the loved body of a recently deceased son.

Edmund Blackstone shifted the reins in his hands. It was clear that not only was the secret lock to be used at all times but the casket itself must be retained behind locked doors whenever they were unable to guard it personally. He sighed and pushed the horses forward. The journey to Tonbridge would be long, dangerous, difficult.

CHAPTER SEVEN

As he had predicted, Inspector Fuchs arrived in the little mountain village before midnight on the day on which the Blackstones fled. He was tired, cold, irritable. All the way from Munich his mind had turned and re-turned the few facts Sergeant Obelgamma had supplied, and the more Fuchs sifted them the more his contempt for the sergeant's theory increased. It was too simple. It did not satisfy. Once again Fuchs sensed there was something missing, some fact the sergeant had not begun to suspect.

Inspector Fuchs moved his bulk angrily. Sergeant Obelgamma would be faced with several harsh questions, not the least of which was why he failed to inform Munich earlier. Anyone with any experience should know that the moment foreigners were involved Munich was to be called.

"The fool," Fuchs said aloud. "Playing his own command."

He grunted and peered upward through the coach windows seeking a glimpse of village light, but there was nothing save the freezing mist which enveloped the valley and the cold, damp smell of earth. He pulled the traveling rug more firmly about him and rubbed his hands beneath its cover, scowling.

Fuchs was certain the Blackstones were no jewel thieves. He had never heard of them, and even if that were not their real name, he would have been aware of such a couple's presence in Europe. The whole business did not taste right, some delicate fulcrum on which everything should balance was absent. Inspector Fuchs pulled the rug closer and sighed; there was much to be done and there seemed little time in which to do it.

"God in Heaven." Fuchs shivered. "Why could the English not commit their murders in the summer? Trust them to select the coldest winter in fifteen years."

He settled back uncomfortably, feeling the cold as fat men do, deeply, constantly, all over. He waited as patiently as he could as the horses clattered up to the village where there would be warmth and something to drink, if not immediate satisfaction.

FUCHS was dozing when the coach pulled up outside the hotel and his eyes were heavy with sleep as he heard the voice of the driver say, "We are here, sir. I have called the porter." Fuchs nodded and yawned and moved his bulk from the vehicle. Outside the air was even colder.

As the driver carried the single bag into the hotel, Inspector Fuchs was approached by the rumpled night porter, who glanced at the single unit of luggage and the large, heavily built man with the tall hat, the black cloak and the handlebar moustache who accompanied it.

"My name is Fuchs," the inspector said, rubbing warmth into his hands. "I understand a room has been reserved for me. And I would like an Asbach."

"Of course." The night porter remembered the booking. "You are from Munich, no?"

"I am from the outside, which is freezing," Fuchs replied curtly. "Now get me the brandy immediately."

Nodding, the rumpled night porter fetched a bottle of Asbach and a glass; he placed them before Inspector Fuchs. The driver had left the two men alone in the lobby of the hotel, Fuchs seated in a heavy leather armchair, the night porter standing beside. No one else was to be seen. There was the sound of soft singing from somewhere in the building, but the rest of the guests appeared to be asleep. Fuchs poured himself a large brandy and drank it without pause, then looked up at the rumpled old man who had received him. This must be the porter who had seen the English off that morning, the last person to speak to them in the village.

"What hours do you work, my man?" Fuchs asked.

"From midnight until eight," the night porter replied. "I have only just come on."

"Not a very cheerful stretch."

"It suits me, sir. I read a little."

"Or sleep?"

The old man shrugged. "At times one is not very busy," he said in agreement.

Inspector Fuchs smiled an expansive smile; he loosened his cloak and unwound the silk scarf from about his neck. "Here," he said, pushing the brandy in the direction of the night porter. "I am sure you also feel the cold." He watched the old man's face respond.

"I shouldn't, sir," the night porter replied. "Not on duty."

"No one will disturb you now, surely?"

"No, sir. You are the only guest expected tonight."

"In that case, be *my* guest."

"I would be glad to, sir." The night porter reached behind his desk and found a glass. "It is bitter, as you say."

They toasted each other and sipped their drinks, then Inspector Fuchs asked a question casually, as if it had only just occurred to him. "Anyway, you would not have many late comings and goings in a place like this," he said indifferently. "People like myself who disturb your *reading?*"

"That is usually the case," the night porter admitted. "Yet I was disturbed this morning early enough. Well before six." His head moved as he remembered the excitement.

"Really?" Fuchs commented, pushing the bottle toward the old man, who refilled his glass.

"This was actually quite an event." The porter edged closer. "The people who disturbed me were English. They were leaving and it is said they were involved in some crime."

"Interesting," Fuchs remarked and took more brandy, again pushing the bottle toward the old man, who accepted it readily. "I would not have thought crime was something that occurred in as peaceful a village as this."

"Let me tell you it does, sir," the night porter began, and slowly, between sips of his drink, related all that had occurred in the early dawn. He had told the story several times in the course of the day, and by now the Blackstones were a recognizably criminal pair: their bearing, their muttered conversations, the heavily bejeweled casket had all been extended to a major degree. "I was terrified, sir," he said. "I don't mind telling you. The day I saw them I knew they were not to be trusted."

"Interesting story," commented Fuchs. "Perhaps you should tell it to the police." He paused, then added, "Or have they been notified by now?"

"They have, sir. In fact Sergeant Obelgamma had been keeping a pretty close eye on them."

"Not close enough, it seems."

"He's a good man, the sergeant, in his way."

"And what way is that?"

"Oh, he's very keen, sir. Too keen, some say."

"Well, well . . ." Inspector Fuchs yawned loudly. "I really must get some sleep," he said. "It's been a long cold journey and the warmth has made me realize I am tired." He smiled broadly. "Thank you for your company," he added, shaking his head. "Who would have thought such things occurred?"

The night porter returned the smile. "I will show you to your room," he said with quiet pride.

"Thank you." Inspector Fuchs stood, took the brandy bottle by the neck and followed the night porter to his room. He tipped the man, wished him goodnight, climbed into bed and was almost immediately asleep but not before he had muttered to himself, " 'Too keen, some say'? We shall see about that."

As Inspector Fuchs drifted into sleep the Blackstones were about to do the same. They had arrived in the small railway town of Kempten well after dark. They were cold, so frozen their hands and feet were numb. When they breathed, the air was like fire in their lungs. Several times Edmund had urged Anna to take shelter in the coach, but each time she had refused. There was a bond between them now, a new welding born out of isolation and the fact that destiny was in their own hands. So they remained together in the freezing dark and together they arrived in Kempten.

In many ways Edmund was grateful for the cover of darkness. It hid the damaged coachwork and reduced their chances of being recognized. Edmund was aware that Sergeant Obelgamma might have telegraphed along the route requesting their detention, he was conscious of a need to be seen as little as possible. Even the slight glow their faces caught in the gas lighting of the streets was enough to cause him to turn up his collar and pull the brim of his hat down over his eyes. He saw to it that Anna did the same.

"We must rid ourselves of this coach," he said. "We have no further use for it."

"How can that best be done?"

"If we take it to a stable, that should do," Edmund replied thoughtfully. "We shall need to tell them some story about collecting it in a day or two."

Anna nodded. "There may be many such falsehoods ahead of us," she admitted reluctantly. "But that cannot be avoided."

"There is only one goal ahead," Edmund replied. "And that is to get Simon to Tonbridge as soon as is absolutely possible."

They drove about Kempten through side roads, often doubling away from the main street as they searched for a stable; once Edmund thought he saw a coaching sign at the end of a narrow lane but there were two constables standing beneath it so he continued past the lane's entrance, seeking further. Finally, in an area a little too brightly lit for Edmund's liking, they came across a stable opposite a restaurant above which was a pension.

"This will have to do," Edmund remarked as he drew the horses to a halt. "I think," he added as an afterthought. "It might be better if you were to ride inside for the last few yards."

Anna agreed, and a few moments later Edmund went to speak to the stable owner, a thin, wiry, pockmarked man who stood amid the dull gleam of leather and the stench of horse droppings.

"Good evening," the man greeted as Edmund approached. "You have horses, I see."

"I should like to leave them here for a night or two," Edmund said casually. The stable owner nodded and Edmund saw his eyes go to the wrecked bodywork. "We've had rather a bad journey," Edmund continued, speaking easily. "In fact, we had to leave the driver at an inn on the way. He broke a leg and it will be some time before he recovers."

The stable owner scratched a pitted cheek, suspiciously. "You were unable to find another coachman, I take it, sir." His voice combined a mixture of servility and disbelief.

"Impossible, I'm afraid," Edmund admitted. "I've had to drive the wretched thing myself." His tone became more businesslike. "Tell me, is there a decent hotel close by?"

The stable owner hesitated. "It depends on what you want, sir, but the Pension Arnoldi opposite is very good. Frau Krantz, who runs it, is very reliable, very clean, and an excellent cook." He sounded as if he would benefit from the transaction.

Edmund smiled. "After such a recommendation who could resist?" he said amiably, but glancing at the man's face saw doubt wrinkled on the pitted brow. "As we shall be here for a day or so," he added, "do you think you might take care of the coach?" The expression on the stable owner's face altered subtly as he heard the request, a new interest was born, a degree of profit was represented.

"I should think so, sir," he said. "How long will you be in Kempten?"

"We are in no hurry. It seems a pretty little place."

"It is, sir. You could spend a pleasant day or two here seeing the town." He moved closer to the coach. "Can I assist with your baggage?"

"That's most kind of you," Edmund replied. "Please have it taken across the road. In the meantime I shall speak with your highly recommended Frau Krantz."

Edmund helped Anna descend from the coach. "We shall stay here overnight," he said, seeing the weariness deeply etched in her face. "The stableman tells me the pension across the road is comfortable. It will suit us nicely for the night." As he spoke Anna sighed with relief at the suggestion.

"It would be nice to get out of this perishing cold," she said gratefully. "But should we not take a train as soon as possible?"

"There will be one in the morning, I am sure," Edmund said, taking her arm. "I will make inquiries later." He turned to the stable owner who, with a lad, was removing the luggage from the coach. "Do pay attention to the casket there," he said. "It's rather valuable and fortunately came out of the accident unscathed."

The man touched his pitted forehead. "Leave it to me, sir. I'll see it all gets to Frau Krantz immediately."

"Well done," said Edmund. "And you can proceed with the repairs as soon as you like. The sooner the better, in fact."

"Of course, sir," the stable owner replied, then added as if the thought had only occurred to him, "There is just one small matter, though. The repair work might be a little expensive, particularly as you'll be wanting it in a hurry, so to speak."

"I understand," Edmund replied, leading Anna away. "But, shall we say that the cost of repairing the coach is the least of my worries at the moment? Please go right ahead."

Frau Krantz's Pension Arnoldi was, as the stable owner described, neat, clean, warm, and rich with the odor of good cooking. A little, plump woman with her hair tied in a bun, Frau Krantz drew the English couple beside a fire as soon as she saw their cold, pinched faces and their mud-spattered traveling capes. She readily gave them coffee and small glasses of spirits and fussed endlessly, and both Edmund and Anna welcomed the mothering. They drank the warm and warming liquids and held their hands to the fire while Frau Krantz assumed total responsibility for their peace and comfort.

"I've had everything put in your rooms," she said. "And the jewel box, the special one, so they've told me, because it's valuable, isn't it? it's on the table. Like you asked, I've locked the door and I'm sure it will be all right in there. I must say, it is a handsome piece." She smiled and brushed a loose hair from her forehead. "I'd keep my furs in it, if it was mine, that's if I had any furs."

Anna sipped her coffee and did not reply.

"Well, then," continued Frau Krantz, "I've ordered you a schnitzel and fresh vegetables. Cook's gone, you see, and it is rather late. But I'm sure you'll enjoy it and there's beer if you'd like it or wine. Tell me what you'd wish and I'll see to it."

"You are very generous," Anna said gently; her face was smoother and the lines of tiredness had eased. "I think my husband might like beer. And I should enjoy a little wine."

"Very good, madam." Frau Krantz folded her hands before her.

Later the Blackstones ate and later still went to their rooms. Both had been surprised by their appetite. They ate hugely, and for the first time in days knew a sense of well-being, strength, purpose.

Before they retired there was one further task Edmund had to perform. Alone, he visited the station and inquired about trains to Basel and from there to whatever Channel port was most convenient. Anna remained in the pension with the casket, dealing as best she could with the damaged traveling cases; she reduced their number to three, leaving the most broken ones in the bottom of the wardrobe together with clothing she knew they would be able to do without on the journey.

While she was thus occupied, Edmund slipped quietly out the back entrance of the pension and walked to the Kempten rail station, which was no more than half a kilometer away. There, beneath the yellow glow of gaslight, he found a single clerk in the booking office. After consulting several train guides and peering for a long time at a timetable pasted on a green wall, the booking clerk was able to tell Edmund everything he needed to know.

There would be a train from Kempten at nine forty-five the following morning which would connect with another at Basel. They could expect a slight delay at Basel, but no more than an hour, and from Basel it was a direct run to Le Havre via Paris. No further changes would be needed, and, in fact, the Basel train should connect with a ferry from Le Havre to Southampton. It was all very simple, the clerk assured Edmund. He was certain the trains would be on time, he was sure there was no possibility of missing the ferry, and he could supply tickets for the entire journey, reservations complete. His face gleamed with pleasure as he organized the timetable and costed the tickets. He was positive nothing could go wrong.

His transactions complete, Edmund returned rapidly to the Pension Arnoldi and, as he entered, saw a young man wearing a striped apron whom he assumed to be either a barman or a waiter.

"Excuse me," Edmund addressed him. "I wonder if you could fix me with a nightcap."

"Certainly, sir," the young man replied. "What would you like?"

"Pour me a draught of your excellent beer," Edmund requested, taking off his coat and standing by the fire. "Is it a local brew?"

"It is," said the young man cheerfully. "We're very proud of it."

"You have every right to be," Edmund assured him. As he sipped the bright, clear liquid, he studied the young man. This was the sort of assistant Edmund might need the following morning. It might be difficult to leave quietly—particularly as the livery stables were opposite and there seemed to be a direct relationship between the suspicious owner and the motherly Frau Krantz. "Tell me," Edmund asked, "what is your function here? Barman, are you?"

The young man smiled. "I'm a bit of everything," he said. "Barman, waiter, whatever's needed at the time."

"And at the moment a barman is needed?"

"At the moment, yes," the young man replied cheerfully. "In the mornings I usually clean up. While Frau Krantz goes off to market I, well, I suppose I'm in charge really. Cook doesn't arrive until about eleven, in time to begin the lunches."

Edmund took another pull of his beer. "Sounds interesting," he said, wiping froth from his upper lip. "And responsible—if Frau Krantz goes off every morning leaving you alone."

"Every morning she's off, sir. She enjoys the market. Says most of her friends are there."

"A popular woman. I shouldn't be surprised, the way she looks after people." Edmund smiled knowingly, a signal between understanding men. "Even that rather strange chap across the way thought very highly of her. In fact, it was he who recommended the pension."

"Herr Issell," informed the young man. "Yes, he and Frau Krantz have an understanding, if you know what I mean."

"I believe I do." Edmund finished his beer. "Excellent," he remarked putting down the stein. "Well, good night, and doubtless I shall see you in the morning."

"I should think so, sir," the young man replied. "I come on about nine."

Edmund went upstairs to find Anna asleep; her face, flushed

after the cold, looked handsome, oddly young. He bent and kissed her softly.

"Sleep well, my dear," he said gently.

WHEN Inspector Leopold Fuchs woke the following morning it was snowing in the tiny mountain village; flakes the size of rose petals floated gently, relentlessly down outside the hotel window. The air was drenched with snow, he could not see more than ten or fifteen yards through the cottony mist. The sight pleased Inspector Fuchs; he stood by the window and stretched his large body.

"Good. This is good," he said. "Now it will be warmer."

He shaved carefully, delicately moving a cutthroat about the shape of his moustache; he dressed with slow determination, then descended to breakfast and there ate an expansive meal of cold meats, cheeses, rye bread and coffee. He sat for a long time at the breakfast table watching other guests come and go, beckoning to the waitress frequently for more coffee or bread or meat or cheese. Breakfast was Inspector Fuch's most enjoyable meal, his appetite was keenest in early morning. He felt, then, a greater need to be refueled.

As he pushed his chair a little farther back from the table and dumped his linen napkin on a plate, the landlord ap-approached and stood genially beside the inspector's chair.

"And how did you sleep?" the landlord asked, after the initial greetings. "You were quite late arriving, I am told."

"I slept as I always do," Fuchs replied. "Extremely well."

"A fortunate talent," suggested the landlord.

"A determined training," corrected Fuchs. He waved an arm at a chair. "Please be seated, I have one or two questions I would like to ask."

"What sort of questions?" replied the landlord, unaccustomed to anything but a casual and undemanding stroll about the breakfast room, welcoming new guests, comforting the old.

"Ones with honest answers, preferably."

"I'm afraid . . ." began the landlord, backing away a step or two. "This is not the place for . . ."

"Don't be afraid," Fuchs interrupted smoothly. "And let me assure you, there is no better place. You can have coffee while we talk." He took a wallet from a breast pocket and produced a document. "I am an inspector of police from Munich," he continued in the same friendly tone. "And I have come to make a few inquiries, as they say, about the English couple and their dead governess. Foreigners involved in crime, whether they be on the giving or receiving end, are my specialty. So, you understand, there are questions I must ask."

Very slowly the landlord sat down; he raised a finger and, when the waitress came, ordered a glass of wine. "It was not made clear you were an inspector," he said warily. "There was no mention of it when the reservation was made."

"Would it have made any difference?"

"No, but . . ."

"In that case let us proceed." Inspector Fuchs smiled, took a sip of coffee, wiped his handlebar moustache and leaned forward. "Now," he said in a firm voice, "tell me about the English."

When Fuchs had finished questioning the landlord there was a fine line of perspiration along the hotelkeeper's hairline; his hands were unsteady, and, in spite of three glasses of wine, he felt quite without confidence.

In his easy, unrelenting, penetrating way Inspector Fuchs discovered when the landlord had recognized the ornate casket for what it was, and why he had allowed the night porter's fears and distortions to be passed on to Sergeant Obelgamma. Also Fuchs learned that the Blackstones and their son had been to the village during the summer two years earlier; ostensibly, their reason for returning was to experience a winter in the place where they had been happy. By pressing further Inspector Fuchs uncovered the information, after the landlord's second glass of wine, that Simon Blackstone's funeral had been postponed.

Where the body of the child was now the landlord was unable to disclose.

"That is all I know, believe me, Herr Inspector," he said, taking a silk handkerchief from his jacket pocket and touching his brow. "I have not withheld information, you realize. It is just that I have not been asked these questions before." He raised his hands, palms upward, displaying his innocence. "Why should I not help the police all I am able?"

"That is a question I won't ask."

"The English did have permisson to leave the hotel. Sergeant Obelgamma gave it to them himself."

"Did our very keen Sergeant Obelgamma know that the funeral had been postponed?"

"I am not sure."

"Do you know why your night porter lied?" Fuchs asked, but was aware of the reason himself. He had seen the old man's moment of glory, had heard the elaborate tale direct. "Have you any idea why he should make so much out of so little?"

"I think he was afraid."

"Of you?"

The landlord spread his hands.

Fuchs nodded and drained the cold dregs of his coffee. "Very well," he said. "What else can you tell me that will send me away?" He smiled a large, confident smile. "That is what you want, no?"

The landlord did not reply; he cupped his hands about his glass and shrugged his unhappy shoulders.

"There is one thing more," Fuchs said, watching the landlord's eyes. "Who sent the coachman?"

"I do not know."

"Think hard who it might have been."

"My God." The landlord's hands began to shake. "All I want from life is to run a good hotel."

"Don't you?"

"Yes, but when something like this occurs, there could be years of hard work, careful planning, excellent service all gone, overnight." He lifted his haggard face. "Don't you understand what it could mean if people believed that if you came to stay here you could be murdered?"

Inspector Fuchs laughed a robust laugh. "God in Heaven," he said. "How many guests *have* you lost?"

"It is not that," the landlord said miserably.

"What is it then?" Fuchs asked, enjoying the landlord's discomfort. "Who did the English know, meet, have contact with in this village?"

"No one special," the landlord replied. "Apart from the doctor, the undertaker. I know of no one else."

"He who failed to cure and he who perhaps did not bury."

"I beg your pardon?"

"It is not important." Inspector Fuchs stood, held out a massive hand, grasped the landlord's and shook it briskly. "Thank you very much," he said. "You have been more helpful than you know." He smiled genially. "There is only one thing more."

"What is that?" The landlord's tone was haunted.

"Please do not divulge my identity to anyone," Fuchs said. "There is a distinct advantage in remaining an anonymous policeman." With that he walked from the breakfast room, leaving the dismayed landlord wiping his forehead and lifting an unsteady finger at the waitress in order to obtain a further glass of wine.

Feeling quite cheerful, comfortably aware of his excellent breakfast, Inspector Fuchs walked briskly down the road to the village. Snow lay on the inspector's tall black hat like a crown, it hung on his shoulders as along a branch, small, delicate flakes settled on the spread of his moustache and these he blew away from time to time with a robust, huffing gesture. He walked confidently, enjoying the snow. It *was* warmer, as he knew it would be. It was crisp and fresh and he thought of the coming conversation with Sergeant Obelgamma with an additional degree of relish.

Inspector Fuchs considered himself a kindly person. He was fond of children, owned two cats, and hardly ever argued with his wife, but he did obtain a special pleasure in parting the fabric of men's lies and eying critically, in the hard light of truth, what lay below. He was an iconoclast, a destroyer of false idols. He believed there was enough truth in the world to appreciate, enough beauty to be enjoyed with a clear eye; there was no need for fabrication. That, of course, Fuchs always added with a smile, depended on which side of the law you stood. So he strode with light heart and clear mind down to the village, a tall, heavily built, snowbound figure, and approached the police station briskly.

In the small stone slate-gabled police station, the body of Miss Harris lying semifrozen in the cellar, Sergeant Obelgamma awaited the coming of Inspector Fuchs with trepidation. Ever since their telephone conversation Sergeant Obelgamma had felt deflated, restricted, suspended in activity: he was not aware of chastisement so much as of the fact that the game had been taken away from him. The case would remain dormant until Inspector Fuchs actually stepped through the police-station door and reactivated it.

When Inspector Fuchs did enter the station, the sergeant was standing by a heavy, oaken desk in the center of the room talking to a constable who sat behind it. Simultaneously they heard the door open, felt the gust of chilling wind and turned to see the large, snowcapped figure of the inspector approaching.

"Good morning, gentlemen," Fuchs said, removing his hat and depositing snow on the floor. "The weather has turned warmer, I see."

"Ah, Inspector Fuchs?" questioned the sergeant uncertainly.

"The one and only," confirmed Fuchs.

"I am Sergeant Obelgamma and this is Constable Kramer." Inspector Fuchs shook hands with them both, removed his cloak, deposited more snow on the floor, took the chair behind the desk Constable Kramer vacated, and ordered coffee. While Kramer carried out the order, Fuchs interrogated Sergeant Obelgamma in his direct, genial and deadly manner.

In spite of his concerns, Sergeant Obelgamma stood up well to Fuchs's questioning.

He agreed that perhaps he had jumped to conclusions, not once, but twice, but that surely was understandable. After all, the facts themselves were well-enough reported even if his reading was capable of being construed in other ways. He apologized profusely for not having notified Fuchs earlier, but, as he went to some pains to point out, the delay was at most twenty-four hours.

He admitted he had failed to detect the Blackstones' visit to the village two years earlier, but in his opinion that was a small detail. Yes, he had given them permission to leave the hotel, but who would have refused a request to attend the funeral of their only son? No, he did not know the funeral had been postponed, not until he questioned the undertaker; and as a result of that conversation, the undertaker certainly appeared to be innocent.

Inspector Fuchs sipped hot, bitter black coffee and listened. It was as the night porter had commented: Obelgamma was a good man, even if a little overzealous. Fuchs put aside his thoughts of castigation. The little sergeant had handled the undertaker well; there would be no need to question that man further. What was more, Obelgamma had uncovered a great deal regarding the doctor's activities. Fuchs hoped the doctor would disclose more than all the others put together.

"Why was the body of the English governess removed from the hotel with such haste?" Fuchs asked suddenly.

"The, ah, the landlord wished it taken away," Obelgamma replied, remembering the innkeeper's schnapps. "He felt it might cause panic among the other guests."

"Was it in full view of the public?"

"Of course not. The truth is," Obelgamma confessed, "the landlord was worried."

"Not as worried as he is now, I'll warrant."

Sergeant Obelgamma raised his eyebrows questioningly, but when the inspector offered nothing more, continued, "He felt there might be, well, unpleasant connotations if the corpse remained on the premises." Obelgamma swallowed. "I understood his concern, and as I had made a thorough examination of the room where the body was found and had a sketch of its position, I, well, I had it removed."

"Let us go and look at it," Fuchs said abruptly.

"The body?"

"What else? I have already seen the landlord and have some experience of his rooms."

Downstairs in the cold cellar, Inspector Fuchs examined the remains of Miss Harris with great care; he looked at the marks on her throat for a particularly long time and spent minutes studying her clothing, looking for rents, missing buttons, threads, any signs of struggle. Finally he replaced the sheet which covered the body and led Sergeant Obelgamma upstairs. The sergeant followed eagerly, knowing he had survived the interrogation better than expected. Also he began to realize he was in the presence of a great man, someone who knew exactly what he was doing.

"Well, sir?" he asked, on their return to the office. "What do you think?"

"I think we should go and talk to the doctor," replied the inspector crisply. "You have his address?"

"Yes, but so far I have not approached him."

"Very wise," said Fuchs and ushered the sergeant out into the snow. They walked through the village square, snow capping their boot tips. Sergeant Obelgamma had left the police station with such speed that he had neglected to wear a hat, and the heavy flakes settling on his bald pate melted and ran in tiny streams about his head, but regardless of discomfort the little gray-eyed sergeant took the tall, heavily built inspector to the door which led up to the doctor's rooms. "This is it," he said, pointing. "Up there."

"Then up we go," commanded the inspector.

Loudly, authoritatively, Sergeant Obelgamma rapped on the doctor's door, after which he stood stiffly, his hands behind his back, awaiting results. There seemed to be an unusually long time before the door was slowly opened by the woman in black—the woman who had admitted the Blackstones. Her dress was the same, the black bonnet did not appear to have been removed, but the face was different, haunted, destroyed. Beneath the eyes were heavy, dark rings, and the skin of the cheeks had shrunk. She trembled constantly as if in fever; she did not seem to have slept.

"Yes?" she inquired, her voice wooden, her words faint. "What do you want?"

"Is the doctor in?" Sergeant Obelgamma asked.

At mention of the doctor the woman's tremors increased and she clung to the door with both hands, steadying herself. "What did you say?" she whispered.

"We are police," Sergeant Obelgamma said briskly. "You know that. Now please let us pass."

"No." The single word was fearful.

"What do you mean, no? We have every right..." The sergeant's voice was forceful but Inspector Fuchs stepped forward and interrupted. "We are sorry to disturb you, madam," he said courteously. "Is there something the matter?"

"No," the woman said. "Yes."

"What is it?"

"The doctor." The woman shook again and her face twisted with distress. "I don't know. I don't know what it is. I've never seen him like this before. Ever since the night before last, ever since he, I just don't know. It's nothing like anything I have ever witnessed." Once they began, the words tumbled, fell from her shaking lips, jumbled, confused, senseless. She lifted her face to Fuchs as if in a confessional. "He's ... he's not himself, sir. I don't know what it is. I don't know what could have happened. I've never been through such a time."

Inspector Fuchs took the woman's arm gently, felt it tremble beneath his fingers. "Perhaps it would be better if I went up and talked to him," he said sympathetically.

"He won't see anyone."

"Let me try, all the same."

Holding the frightened woman's arm, Inspector Fuchs ascended the stairs to the rooms above. Sergeant Obelgamma followed closely. When they reached the small waiting room with the engravings of the mountains about the walls, the woman's trembling increased.

"He's in there." She pointed to the room beyond. "But he won't see a soul. He's been locked in there for hours. Ever since sometime last night, and he won't let anyone in. Not me. Not anyone."

"Do you have a key?" Fuchs asked.

"Yes. But he's threatened me if I use it. He's told me ..." The woman stopped, unable to repeat the threat. "He's told me to go ... away." There was none of the quiet authority she had shown when reluctantly permitting the Blackstones to enter the premises, none of the calculated efficiency with which she had seen them out in the company of the doctor. Her words were broken and her eyes tortured. She looked as if she were about to collapse. "He's said some terrible things," she added. "I think he's gone mad or something."

"Give me the key," Fuchs said.

"He'll kill me."

"I doubt it," Fuchs said, holding out his hand, waiting patiently while the woman searched through the bunch of keys she carried about her waist and unfastened one for the room next door. "The man sounds as if he needs all the help he can get."

Taking the key, Fuchs approached the door; behind him the

woman stood trembling. Obelgamma's face was alert. There was one moment of clear, distilled, perfect silence; then, before Fuchs could insert the key, a great, hollow, tormented cry came from the other side of the door.

"Take your hoof and your brew," the strangled voice shouted. There was the crash of something breaking. "Bury them. Leave me. Get out, get out, get out ..." The voice died in a whimper.

Inspector Fuchs stood very still, listening as the sound of a child's pitiful crying began in the room next door.

"There," whispered the woman in black. "That's what he's been like. Shouting or crying. Sometimes I don't even understand what he says. They're not words, sir." Her face was stained with dried tears. "Just sounds he makes. Like an animal." She put a hand to her face. "Don't go in there," she implored. "You don't know what he's like."

"I must go in."

"No ..."

"Immediately. While he's quiet."

"I'll come with you." Sergeant Obelgamma stepped forward. "He might be violent."

"Stay with her." Fuchs nodded to the woman. "She needs you more than I."

With that Fuchs turned the key quickly and went into the room, closing the door behind him. The sight which Inspector Fuchs encountered in the once-tidy book-lined study dismayed even his hardened eyes. The doctor sat on the floor in a corner crying like a child; tears ran down his raddled cheeks; his eyes were small, slitted, creased with weeping; his hair a tangled mess. He sat in a child's position, his knees under his chin, his arms clasped about them. He looked lost and desolate, lonely and bereft, as if his soul had been taken away. His feet were bare, and every now and then one hand would creep down and pick at the toenails, some of which were bleeding as a result of his self-destruction. The floor was littered with torn pages, broken book covers, scattered papers; and every picture in the room had been smashed, hurled from the wall, cracked, battered, destroyed with a force which expressed hatred, fear, despair. Within the room was a deep, overpowering smell, as if someone or something had lived there too long.

The doctor seemed unaware of the inspector's entrance; he sat curled in the corner, picking his bleeding feet, tears flooding, emitting a thin, lost wail. For a few moments Fuchs remained as he had entered, standing tall and still by the door; then he walked slowly toward the doctor, both hands held out as if to a child. When he spoke, his voice was soothing, cajoling, comforting.

"It's all right now," he said gently. "It's all over now, you'll see."

The doctor's eyes came up slowly, filled with tears, filled with hate; he glared at the inspector but did not speak.

"I'm going to get you something which will make you all better," the inspector continued, his voice addressing a child. "Now, I wonder where the doctor keeps his medicines? I wonder where he puts them?"

At the words the doctor's eyes slid sideways to a glass-fronted oak chest on one side of the room. Inspector Fuchs was surprised to see that its glasswork had remained unbroken. It had not been touched. It was a small island of sanity in a sea of destruction. The doctor glanced at it hastily, then his eyes went away again, back to his toes, which he began to pick once more. He started to whimper.

"Perhaps I'll just have a look in here," Fuchs said, talking aloud, keeping the man within the child informed. "Perhaps there's the very thing we're looking for right here."

The doctor picked at his toenails with increased fury while Fuchs searched the glass-fronted case for something to sedate the man. Fuchs picked up bottles and read their labels, looking for a name, a formula which might sound familiar, something he might recognize. Behind him the child's wail rose. It now contained a note of menace Fuchs had not heard before; he realized that quite soon the doctor's emotions would explode again, that something new would be torn, broken, smashed in the violent room. He knew also that in that frame of mind the doctor would be useless. Finally Fuchs found what he was looking for: a small, brown bottle of a liquid marked "Sulphonal." Somewhere Fuchs had read of the drug's use in cases of epilepsy and hoped it would be effective in calming the doctor. Quickly the inspector read the dosage, looked about and saw a small enamel washbasin in which three glasses had been smashed. Their shards littered the bowl, but a fourth had remained intact. With one eye on the restless doctor, Fuchs measured the dose, added a few drops more, splashed a little water into the glass and walked back to the figure crouched on the floor.

The doctor's slitted eyes never left the inspector. He ceased picking his bloodied toes and stared at the tall man with the handlebar moustache as if he had feared him all his life.

"Here we are," Inspector Fuchs said coaxingly. "Here's some nice medicine. It will make you feel well again."

The doctor's eyes began to weep anew.

"Now then, don't cry." Fuchs bent. "Just be a good boy and drink it all up."

"Don't want it," the doctor said in a voice that was not his own; it rang of childhood, punishment for petty misdeeds, standing in a corner, being deprived of supper. "Won't take it."

"Yes you will," Fuchs said firmly. "Open your mouth."

"No." The mouth closed sharply and the words were forced from between closed lips. "Not going to."

"I shall spank you if you don't."

The doctor did not speak, but more tears flowed, rolling down his unshaven, hopeless cheeks; he sniffed and moisture dribbled from his nose.

"There's a good boy." Fuchs reached and touched the doctor

under the chin, lifting it so the mouth opened a little. He brought the draught closer. "Drink it all up now."

The doctor tried to twist his head but Fuchs's grip was firm; the doctor thrashed weakly as a child might, beating feeble hands against Fuchs's arm, but the strength of the man was untouched by that of the child. Firmly, surely, relentlessly Fuchs brought the liquid forward and, unspilled, poured it down the doctor's throat. The doctor coughed, his stomach retched, his throat gagged as he tried to reject the Sulphonal, but Fuchs maintained his grip and the doctor had no alternative but to swallow. He did so, his face thick with reluctance, his eyes vivid with hate. Even after he had consumed it, Fuchs continued to hold the doctor, remained squatted beside the childish figure. It was only when the liquid began to work, which slowly and surely it did, that Fuchs released his grip. He sighed with relief and moved away.

It took a little more than ten minutes for the first effects of the Sulphonal to become apparent. The doctor's eyelids became heavy, drooped. His body relaxed, stopped twitching, and his fingers, which had plucked at his feet with such destruction, lay limp and placid in his lap. He eased further into the corner, folded into it more comfortably; he looked spent.

Fuchs stood slowly and placed the empty glass on the desk. "There," he said in his comforting voice. "That's a lot better, isn't it? Now we can have a nice little talk." He picked up an oaken chair with a maroon leather seat which had been knocked on its side and drew it up before the becalmed man.

The doctor sighed; when he spoke his voice was almost normal. "Who are you?" he asked weakly. "Where did you come from?" He sounded tired, drained, devoid of spirit.

"I've come to talk about our English friends," Fuchs replied casually.

"What English friends?"

"Those whose son unfortunately died." Fuchs shook his head

sadly. "They need help. God in Heaven, they need help. We must see what can be done for them."

The doctor looked upward sleepily, his hooded eyes on the inspector, then he turned his head to one side and said listlessly, "There's nothing we can do for them now." The tired voice was final.

"There must be," Fuchs persisted. "We can't just leave them like that."

"There is nothing more to be done, I tell you." The doctor closed his eyes. "All that could be done has been done. God speed their journey."

"I hope so," said Fuchs fervently.

"I tell you, they need such fortune," the doctor confirmed. "They have to take him home to Tonbridge, England. That is all anyone can do."

"There must be more, surely."

"No." The doctor's eyes came back; his tired voice held a note of frenzy. "Once the hoof is there, once the mark is made, once the claws have begun, there is nothing. *Nothing*, you understand? Except a proper burial in the proper place as soon as it can be achieved."

Fuchs sat thoughtfully, eyeing the drugged doctor, balancing the obscure sentences. "So they've returned to England?" he said at last, as if there was no alternative. "And they've taken the child?" His tone was casual; he spoke as if the thought was for himself alone.

"That's where he was born."

"Of course. It was fortunate you were able to advise them."

The doctor sighed—a pained, heavy, lost sound. "There was nothing else I could do," he said. "They did not know the condition. It is the only solution that is known." He closed his eyes and pressed his exhausted hands against their lids. "She is to blame," he whispered. "She told them first. It is in constant revenge for her brother." He sighed and rubbed his sleepy eyes.

Fuchs was even more confused. "Frau Blackstone, you mean?" he put forward.

"Don't be stupid." The doctor's voice was hostile. "She who has been here forever."

Fuchs thought. A pattern was forming. The elements missing from Sergeant Obelgamma's report were slowly becoming distinguishable, shaping something not only mysterious but cursed, unlike anything Fuchs had ever encountered. The crime committed in this village was not in any ordinance. Its image floated, ungraspable. In the coils of Fuchs's imagination, along the frontiers of his mind it swirled, surrounded by mists of myth and mysticism, fable and folklore.

Fuchs stared at the closed figure of the doctor on the floor—the man's mind was gone, destroyed, taken by whatever it was that lay central to the mystery in the mountain village. An ambulance would have to be called to take the man to Munich, more than likely in a straitjacket; there he would be confined to some institution until he either recovered his sanity or died—Fuchs suspected the latter. He regretted the doctor's condition but there was nothing else to be done; his only hope was that before the Sulphonal wore off or the doctor was violently attacked again by whatever possessed him, he, Fuchs, would be able to discover what route the English couple had taken.

Perhaps he might overtake, even circumvent, the Blackstones. One way or another it was clearly his duty to locate and if necessary hold them to determine what had turned them from normal English tourists into fugitives.

"Tell me," Fuchs urged, "that governess who was with them. What unfortunate luck that was. How really tragic when you come to think about it." He hoped the vague statement would evoke response.

"There is no reason," the doctor replied. "There is no selection. In the first case it was the mother. In theirs, the governess. The claw does not discriminate."

"I see," Fuchs replied, as if he understood completely. "She was not *selected*?"

"She will be followed." The doctor's eyes opened wide; he fixed his gaze on Fuchs's moustache. "There will be more. They will be numberless unless the instructions are carried out to the letter."

Fuchs turned away; the meaning escaped him. He lifted a hand and wiped his moustache. "They will need to be as swift as possible," he said as if musing the problem aloud.

"The shortest route is not always the fastest," the doctor said evasively. His eyes had closed again and his voice was fading; the Sulphonal was taking him to sleep. "One must do what one can with what is available."

"True," Fuchs agreed. "They must have proceeded well, for I did not pass them on my way from Munich."

"It was the coachman who suggested Kempten," the doctor said drowsily. "I believe he had a woman there."

"Of course. From Berne there is the Continental Express."

"Basel is closer," said the doctor, his voice receding. "Or Zurich, which is a lovely town." He moved, restoring a little wakefulness. "In the spring, Zurich," he said and shuddered. "I went there with my grandmother once. That is where part of it began." His eyes widened. "In that case, Basel, not Zurich."

Fuchs moved his head in agreement. If the English did not catch the Continental Express and he took the next from Munich, there was a chance he would arrive in Tonbridge either at the same time or slightly before them. It was just possible, if he moved with speed. In the meantime he would ask Obelgamma to telegraph ahead to some stationmaster or other, requesting confirmation which train the Blackstones had taken.

Fuchs neither knew exactly why he must follow the Blackstones himself nor his reasons for not obtaining police intervention farther down the line; he was only aware that the doctor's madness contained a simple message: the English urgently, desperately required help.

Fuchs was never sure how the pieces came together in his mind; how he became certain during that short, dislocated conversation with the doomed doctor that the English were not criminals in the common sense. It was clear that they carried the body of their son with them, which they believed must be returned to Tonbridge. They would travel to one or other of the Channel ports, and he, Fuchs, must follow to effect what aid he could, what intervention was necessary. That much Fuchs sensed only, but it was enough to precipitate him on the most fateful journey of his life.

The doctor began to fall into a heavy sleep; the lines eased a little as his face relaxed; the tearing hands were innocent in his lap; the tears dried on the raddled, unshaven cheeks.

"You can do nothing." The doctor's voice suddenly interrupted Fuchs's train of thought. "Not now."

"I can try," Fuchs answered quickly.

The doctor's eyes opened once again. "I did not tell them ..." he began. His mouth was rubber. "I was not able to warn them." He pushed a hand over his lips. "They had gone before I discovered ..."

"What?" Fuchs bent. "What more must they know?"

"Who it is." The doctor's eyes closed. "Who will be ..." His voice trailed away to nothing.

"Who is what?" Fuchs shook the man. "Tell me."

"The guardian ..." The doctor's voice was faint. "He who ... keeps it there ..."

"Doctor—" Fuchs slapped the exhausted face; the loose head rolled. "*Tell me what that means.*"

But the inspector's efforts were useless. Sulphonal had the doctor in its grip. Nothing more would come from his rubbery lips. Slowly Fuchs released him; he stood, looking down at the lost shape, then he turned, opened the door and peered out at the startled expectant faces of Sergeant Obelgamma and the woman in black.

Briefly he told Sergeant Obelgamma what had to be done:

that an ambulance was to be ordered from Munich for the doctor immediately and, in the meantime, to obtain a strait-jacket to preclude any further self-destruction. Fuchs glanced at the face of the woman and saw pain and sadness there.

"It is all we can do, madam," he said comfortingly. "I am afraid your doctor needs the best medical attention available. Meanwhile, he must be protetced from himself."

The woman's face tore. "What has caused this . . . madness?" she asked in a shocked voice.

"If I knew the answer to that," Fuchs replied, "I believe I should know the answer to everything."

He returned his attention to Obelgamma. "The English are on their way home," he said. "I was unable to discover the route, although I suspect they will have gone via Basel and Paris. If I return to Munich now it is just possible I can be there before them. Going through Brussels to Ostend." He wiped his moustache with the back of his hand thoughtfully. "There are several telegrams I would like you to send, Sergeant," he added and watched the excited expression on the bald man's face.

"Of course, sir." Sergeant Obelgamma took out his notebook and licked the end of his pencil in readiness. "I shall go to the post office immediately."

The first telegram Fuchs requested was to Munich Police Headquarters, in which he asked that a careful study of time-tables be made to determine which route would get him to En-gland fastest. He would leave the village immediately and should be back in Munich by ten that evening.

"Very good, sir," Obelgamma said, writing fast. "Is there more?"

Fuchs nodded. "Do you know anyone, a stationmaster, a reliable porter, someone you can trust on the Basel-Paris route?" he asked.

Obelgamma thought. "I have an old school friend who is stationmaster at Troyes. I believe that is on the way," he said helpfully.

"Are you sure the train does not go through Dijon?"

"I do not think so. Not from Basel."

"Very well. Telegraph him and ask him to keep watch for the Blackstones. Describe them and their luggage and ask him to telegraph me at the boat station in Ostend, letting me know if they pass through Troyes and when they should arrive in England. Is that clear?"

"Perfectly, sir." Obelgamma's pencil flew. "Anything else?"

Fuchs paused, then finally said, "There's an old acquaintance of mine, an Inspector Kearsley at Scotland Yard. Telegraph him and ask if he knows anything about the Blackstones. I doubt if he does, but a telegram is worthwhile. Kearsley can also contact me in Ostend or Dover." He looked into the excited gray eyes of the sergeant. "I hope you have all that clear, Seargeant. I am relying on you. I will not have time to check these communications myself." His voice was faintly critical.

"I have it all written down, sir. Don't worry."

"Sometimes that makes no difference." Fuchs turned to the woman in black. "Worry as little as *you* can," he said. "The doctor is sedated and should sleep for some time. Whatever you do, do not unlock the door until Sergeant Obelgamma arrives with a straitjacket. The ambulance from Munich should be here by evening. They will know what to do for him."

"Thank you, sir." The woman pressed a handkerchief to her face. "Thank you for all you have done."

"I have done little enough," replied Fuchs and began to depart, Sergeant Obelgamma at his heels. "Come along, Sergeant," he called over his shoulder. "I shall need a fast coach and my case from the hotel. I have no time at all between now and Munich."

The tall figure of Inspector Fuchs strode out of the doctor's rooms and into the street. It had stopped snowing, and, glancing at the fresh fall, Fuchs noted there was not more than ten centimeters, not enough to delay his coach in the passes. If everything went as planned he would be in England the day after tomorrow, the thirty-first of December. It seemed a fitting way to see the old year out. Fuchs walked silently, the semifrozen snow sticking to his boots, the short, bald figure of Obelgamma by his side.

After a while Obelgamma coughed and lifted his voice in what he already knew to be a hopeless request. "Do you think, sir—" he began—"I mean, is there any chance of my accompanying you?" His eyes were eager for recognition.

Fuchs stopped in the snow and looked down at the shorter man. "I am truly sorry, Sergeant," he said. "Your company would be most welcome. But there are things to be done here that only you can do." He made the rejection as graceful as possible.

"You are sure, sir?"

"Who will send the telegrams, Sergeant? Who will attend to the doctor? Who will receive the ambulance? Who else will see to it that the English governess is buried in a proper place?" His moustache moved in a smile. "But thank you for wanting to see this through with me. It does you great and good credit."

Obelgamma's chest puffed and he nodded wisely. "I understand, sir. It has been a privilege working with you." He nodded his shiny head several times to confirm the sentiment.

"On the contrary, it has been a pleasure working with you," Fuchs rejoindered.

Sergeant Obelgamma held out a hand, which the inspector shook stiffly. Then Obelgamma took a step backward and snapped his hand into a salute; he would have clicked his heels has it not been for the snow. He turned and walked importantly away, his brisk body determined, his head a small, bright hollow with envy of his association with the great Inspector Fuchs, heard them hang on every word he uttered as he re-signal in the gray day. Already he saw men's eyes in the taverns counted the strange events of the Blackstone case. As he walked away, his step was light in the snow.

Fuchs watched him go with an odd sense of loss; there was something about the little sergeant which would survive forever. Fuchs coughed and turned on his heel. "You're becoming sentimental in your old age," he told himself roughly and set up the hill to the hotel amid the pines.

CHAPTER EIGHT

By the time Inspector Leopold Fuchs had obtained a coach and was on his return trip to Munich, Edmund and Anna Blackstone were aboard the train from Kempten heading toward Basel.

They had slept well in Kempten after their long day in the cold, and they awoke early, slightly stiff as a result of their crash, but little more; Edmund had a small bruise on his forehead and Anna a swelling behind one ear, but both were alert and eager to be away.

They awoke to the rich smell of coffee and fresh bread baking. The air was warmer in Kempten than it had been in the mountains and a little pale sunlight filtered through the cloud, enough to make them feel something had turned in their favor.

While they dressed, Anna rang for breakfast, which Frau Krantz brought up herself, her eyes bright with early morning, her arms bearing a tray laden with coffee and warm bread; there were little pots of honey and strawberry jam, boiled eggs in woollen covers to keep them warm.

"Here you are," she said cheerfully as she placed the tray on a table. "Just what you need on a morning like this. Something to keep you going. I expect you'll be seeing the sights of Kempten, and it's not warm outside. Warmer than where you've

: 154 :

come from, I'll warrant, but not all that warm. And we get it damp down here as well. So eat it all up and if you want any more just ring and ask."

"Thank you," Anna said gratefully. "It looks delicious."

"Well, I'll just leave you to it," said Frau Krantz, making no move to go. "The eggs are fresh, they came in from the farm yesterday. And the bread's just baked. It was warm when I put it on the tray."

"Thank you," Anna repeated. She sat by the tray and began to pour coffee. "I believe I have quite an appetite."

"Glad to hear it," said Frau Krantz. "I made the jam myself and the honey comes from hereabouts as well. From the same farm, in fact, as the eggs. Everything's wholesome, I can assure you."

Edmund approached from the dressing room and, after greeting Frau Krantz, sat at the table and began to spoon his egg. It was clear Frau Krantz would go in her own good time, so he might as well ask the questions uppermost in his mind. "That's a friendly young barman you have down there," he said, breaking fresh bread and dipping in into the yolk of his egg. "He fixed me with a splendid nightcap last evening. We had a most enjoyable conversation." He popped the egg-laden bread into his mouth.

"Herbert?" confirmed Frau Krantz. "He's a lovely boy. Nothing is too much trouble for him."

"Told me you left him in charge of the place each morning," Edmund said. "While you're off to market. That right?

"That's right," Frau Krantz replied. "He's in charge while I'm out. I do all the shopping myself, of course. Everything. I like to see it all before I buy. I like to know its quality. And all my friends are there, at the market. It's a treat each morning." Frau Krantz smiled happily. "You'd be surprised at the news you pick up. They know everything that goes on, they do. Nothing passes them by."

"I bet," said Edmund, wondering if news of the dead coachman had reached the town. "A regular grapevine, I shouldn't be surprised."

"You're right, sir." Frau Krantz began edging toward the door. "They say, down there, that they know things sometimes before they even happen." She laughed, lifting her hands to touch the sides of her bun. "They miss nothing down in the markets. Not a thing." She smiled. "Well, I must be going. I have a day's gossip to catch up on."

As Frau Krantz bustled out of the room Anna turned to Edmund. "They will surely have heard of the crash," she said, her tone worried. "Possibly of the fact that the coachman is dead also."

"I was thinking the same thing," said Edmund. "We will have to leave as soon as she is gone."

"At what time is the train?"

"Just before ten." Edmund glanced at his pocket watch. "We have slightly less than an hour."

"Is the station close by?"

"No more than a few hundred yards." Edmund took another egg. "I shall go and talk to young Herbert shortly," he said. "We shall need his help with our baggage."

HERBERT was more than willing to assist. When Edmund informed him they had made up their minds to take the next train to Basel and required help with the luggage, the fresh-faced young man responded eagerly, enjoying the authority it gave. With a proprietorial flourish he presented Edmund with the bill for the night's lodgings and then saw to it that the cases were brought downstairs.

"Give me a moment, sir," he said, "and I shall fetch a carriage."

"That would be convenient."

"It is no trouble, sir. I assure you."

Edmund and Anna stood by the luggage, the casket and three

cases, waiting for Herbert to return. This he did a few minutes later but with a significant change in his bearing. The bright fresh-faced helpfulness had been replaced with something subtler, quieter, almost furtive.

"Did you have any trouble?" Edmund asked.

"No, sir," Herbert replied, not looking at the Englishman. "The carriage is by the back entrance as you requested."

"Then place the luggage aboard as quickly as you can."

"Yes, sir. I shall fetch help from the kitchen."

"There is no need," Edmund replied. "The only piece you'll require aid with is the casket. I'll take one end of that."

"Yes, sir." Herbert picked up two cases and went outside with them. Edmund frowned and turned to Anna. "Something has happened to that young man," he said. "His mood is strangely altered."

"I wonder what has upset him."

"More than likely us," Edmund replied. "I suspect word has arrived about the coachman."

"Dear God," said Anna. "I pray that nothing delays us now."

Edmund bit his lip nervously.

Once the coachman's body with its hideous throat was discovered, their departure from Kempten would not only be delayed but possibly prevented. Almost certainly the local police would become involved. Frowning, Edmund waited for Herbert to return for the third suitcase and the casket. When the young man did, his eyes avoiding Edmund's, they carried the body of Simon and the last case out into the street. There Edmund saw the answer to his concern standing beside the carriage: Herr Issell, his wiry body taut, his pockmarked face alive with suspicion, was pointedly blocking their path. And he did not seem about to move.

"Herr Blackstone," Issell called, his voice rough, confident, containing none of the servility of the previous evening. "You are going, I see."

"Correct," replied Edmund. "Kindly step aside."

"You are going without paying me for the repairs to your own coach?"

"You will be paid," Edmund responded stiffly. "But not until I return to England."

Herr Issell's face twisted with disbelief. "I do not find that easy to accept," he said. "If I had not seen Herbert with the carriage, and if I did not have a cautious mind, you would have gone and that would have been the last I would ever have heard of you or your money."

"I assure you, the money would have been sent." Edmund's voice was tight with anger. "Now, get out of my way."

"I will not move," Issell said, "until you pay me."

"Are you calling me a liar?"

"Until I get my money, yes."

Edmund turned quite calmly to Herbert. "Can you manage this the last few paces on your own?" he asked, referring to the casket.

"Yes, sir." Herbert's face was a mixture of confusion, guilt, curiosity. He dropped the suitcase and took both handles of the casket, releasing Edmund's grasp. "I can manage it alone."

"Very good," said Edmund and returned his attention to Herr Issell. "Now, I must settle with you," he said and hit the pockmarked stable owner squarely on the jaw with a crisp right-hand cross. Surprise had hardly time to register on Issell's face before he fell flat on his back and lay motionless on the roadway. "Right," said Edmund, adjusting his cuffs. "Let us be off."

The incident happened so quickly for several seconds no one else moved. Herbert stood, the elaborate casket held in front of him, his fresh face blank, his mouth agape. The coachman looked down from his seat at the flat form of Issell below, then turned his eyes away and shook his head slowly as if the incident were none of his business and he regretted having witnessed it. Anna put a hand to her lips and looked at Edmund, her eyes round with surprise.

"It could not have happened to a more pleasant fellow," Edmund said; he felt enormously elated with the success of his blow. "Doubting my word indeed."

"Edmund?" Anna's voice was breathy. "I do believe you have knocked him out."

"I am sure of it," Edmund replied. "What's more, I'm delighted at having done so." He glanced at Herbert. "Put the casket in the carriage, lad," he said. "And when that ruffian comes to, tell him he will be paid in full. Which is a great deal more than he deserves."

"Yes, sir." Herbert grinned boyishly and placed the coffin inside the carriage. "I regret telling him you were leaving, but I did not know he would behave like that." His grin widened. "I must say, sir, you do box extremely well."

"I was taught by one of the finest gymnasts in Berlin," Edmund replied, taking Anna's arm and helping her aboard. "Goodbye, young man," he added. "Tell Frau Krantz we enjoyed her pension immensely and we are truly sorry to be departing with such haste, but . . ." He shrugged briefly. "The explanation is long and complicated and it is highly unlikely she would believe it. Just tell her we were called away suddenly."

Herbert nodded. "She may get a different tale from Herr Issell," he remarked.

"So be it," replied Edmund and mounted the carriage. "To the station, driver," he called and waved briefly at the young man standing beside the prostrate figure of Herr Issell in the dust.

The remainder of the Blackstones' journey to the Kempten rail station was without incident. The coachman spoke no more than was necessary; porters carried their luggage through the barriers into the first-class compartment Edmund had reserved. The casket was placed on the floor by the window so no sudden movement of the train would dislodge it. Anna and Edmund settled in their seats to watch the little town with its Gothic spires disappear into the distance, feeling for the first time since they had left the village a degree of security.

Edmund, watching smoke from the engine coil past as the train climbed above the town, said, "I do believe we are at last on our journey proper."

"Its beginning was not without excitement," Anna said with a small smile.

"I must apologize for such a public display," said Edmund, rubbing his knuckles. "But the matter had to be settled as quickly as possible."

"Do not apologize. I thought you were magnificent."

"Really?" Edmund looked pleased. "I hope I shan't be forced to such extremes again."

THE train spun through splendid country, past farmhouse and village, spire and snow-clad barn. It traveled the rush-lined borders of Lake Constance until it came to the city of Basel. At Basel there was an hour's delay before the night express left for Le Havre via Paris. The Blackstones moved slowly from one train to the other, accompanying their luggage discreetly. Their passage through customs proved a simple matter. The little Bavarian doctor in the village, left far behind now, had provided them with a certificate declaring the death of their son and describing the elaborate coffin in which the body traveled. The sober appearance of the Blackstones, together with their documentation, ensured smooth and sympathetic transit through the uniformed channels.

Once aboard the night express, again in a private compartment, the casket once more secure on the floor, the Blackstones waited for the train to carry them through the night, across the final section of the Continent, toward the ferry which should be waiting for them some four hundred miles to the north.

"All that passed smoothly enough," Edmund remarked as the train pulled out of the cavernous Basel station. "The English customs will be as simple, I suspect."

"I trust so," said Anna. "How can we ever thank that little doctor enough?"

Edmund shook his head. "One can only hope he finds his own reward," he replied.

It was dark and the train from Basel was some two hours from Troyes when Stationmaster Punt received a telegram from his old childhood friend Sergeant Obelgamma. Punt and Obelgamma had been together at school in the border town of Singen, and, although they had since gone their separate ways —Punt to the railways, subsequently to be transferred to the SNCF, Obelgamma to the police—over the years they had maintained a steady contact with each other, so it was no surprise to Stationmaster Punt to receive a telegram from Sergeant Obelgamma.

The telegram read: SUSPECT ENGLISH COUPLE TRAVELING UNDER NAME BLACKSTONE ON BASEL PARIS EXPRESS IN POSSESSION OF JEWELED CASKET PLEASE CONFIRM LOVE TO CHARLOTTE OBEL-GAMMA.

Stationmaster Punt read the message several times by the light of an oil lamp with a keen air. His nose twitched. Punt differed from his old school friend Obelgamma in many ways; where Obelgamma was thin and wiry, Punt was short and fat. He waddled when he walked, his cheeks hung in heavy folds, his little eyes were almost lost in rolls of lard; years of French cuisine had altered the ambitious boy from Singen; but, like Obelgamma, he retained an enthusiasm for mystery. He held the telegram up to the light in a pudgy hand and stared at it for a long time. This was the first occasion he could recall when Obelgamma had consulted him in a professional capacity, and he could only conclude that it was significant.

"Jacques," he called to a guard in his heavily accented French, "when is the express from Basel due?"

"In one hour and forty-two minutes, sir."

"I see." Punt folded the telegram and placed it in a breast pocket for safety. "I wish to be notified when it is ten minutes from the station." His little eyes became shrewd. "I shall need to examine the train myself. Please be sure that you are able to organize a delay of at least fifteen minutes.

"But, sir—" the guard looked dismayed—"that could mean the train missing the morning ferry. You know what the steamship company is like."

"That cannot be helped." Punt tapped his breast pocket containing the telegram. "This is official business."

"May I inquire what we are looking for, sir?"

"Police business," Punt replied enigmatically.

"I see." Jacques removed his guard's cap and peered into it as if it might supply an answer. "Perhaps one of the wheels could be cracked, sir."

"I beg your pardon?"

"For the delay."

"Good thinking, Jacques," Punt complimented the guard. "Now, don't forget, be sure to inform me ten minutes before arrival. You'll get the signal."

"It will be done, sir."

Stationmaster Punt was fortifying himself with sweet milky coffee and a plate of pastries when Jacques arrived with the news that the night express was due in a little less than eight minutes. Immediately Punt got to his feet, wiped his mouth briskly and waddled onto the platform. Jacques followed dutifully, a little mystified.

"We must work this out," Punt said. "I shall casually stroll through the first-class section of the train, keeping my eyes open. You will see to it that the wheels are checked, several times if necessary. Don't concern yourself with the engineer or the guard. I shall explain exactly what this is all about." He found a crumb on the mound of his stomach and ate it thoughtfully. "Now, if this takes longer than I think, if I am not off in, say, fifteen minutes, please do not hesitate to send the train on its way."

"With you on board, sir?"

"With me on board, Jacques. Even if that means I have to travel as far as Romilly."

"Isn't that very inconvenient, sir? Could I not delay the train longer?"

Solemnly Stationmaster Punt shook his head, causing rolls of fat about his neck to wobble. "Police business," he said, tapping his breast pocket cautiously. "We can't afford to arouse suspicions." He breathed deeply, placed his feet squarely on the platform and looked out into the darkness in the direction from which the train would come.

Jacques nodded in uncertain agreement and took his place beside his master. The train was due in five minutes.

WHEN the train pulled into Troyes station with a cloud of steam and a shower of sparks, Edmund and Anna Blackstone were in the dining car. It had taken them a significantly long time to decide to leave the casket and depart their compartment. They watched the darkening landscape pass, seeing each mile take them closer to England and the end of their fearful journey, and when they first became aware of hunger Anna suggested they call a steward and eat without leaving the coach. But Edmund thought otherwise.

"We are able to lock this door and turn the gaslight down, my dear," he said persuasively. "There's no earthly reason why anyone should come in. Even if they did, our circumstances are well known. Everything is quite safe."

"If you say so, Edmund," said Anna doubtfully. "But the thought of leaving . . . well, it worries me."

"We've had nothing since breakfast."

"Are you sure it would not be better to have something sent along?"

"In my experience," Edmund persisted, "anything sent along is vastly inferior to what the dining car supplies. And for my part, I have quite an appetite."

So it came about that the Blackstones began a late dinner some twenty minutes before the train pulled into the station at Troyes. When it did, Edmund gazed out of the dining-car window and remarked on the prettiness of the lights of the town in the cold, sparkling air. Then he returned his attention to the onion soup, which was delicious, as was the rest of their meal, and they consumed it slowly and with enjoyment. It was only after the train had been stationary at Troyes for almost fifteen minutes that Anna looked about with a worried frown.

"Is there anything wrong, do you imagine?" she asked. "We seem to have been here for quite some time."

"A minor repair, I would guess," Edmund said reassuringly. "There have been a number of lanterns going by outside and I heard the wheel-tappers pass a short while ago."

"I've noticed, well, perhaps I am becoming oversuspicious but . . ." Anna smiled hesitantly. "But I thought I saw a rather fat railman looking at us most strangely."

Edmund laughed. "Really, Anna, you sound like something from a penny dreadful." His voice was amused.

"You may laugh," Anna replied. "But I assure you, a very fat railman passed through the dining car several times and on each occasion he peered at us most closely."

"And you imagine that is related to our stoppage?"

"I do not know what to think. But it does strike me as odd."

"Anna, my dear," Edmund said, a little more seriously, "we are no longer in Germany. We have even passed through Switzerland. Therefore it is quite unlikely anyone is looking for us in Troyes, of all places, and particularly not a fat French railway man. He was more than likely envying us our splendid dinner." He smiled. "Had you seen Sherlock Holmes, it might have been quite a different matter."

"You may joke about it, Edmund, but . . ." Anna's remark was interrupted by the sudden jerking of the window toward the platform, and she saw a guard standing under a yellow light staring at the departing train. He fell away into darkness. There was no unusual activity that she could see. "Well," she admitted, returning to her dinner, "perhaps you are right."

"Of course I am, my dear," replied Edmund confidently. "Would you care for a little more of the lamb?"

As the train resumed its journey, Stationmaster Punt was in the locked compartment reserved for the Blackstones, his eyes on the elaborate casket with its carvings, its rhinestones and its malachite. He looked upon it with envy, but with a feeling of success; his old school friend Sergeant Obelgamma would be amazed when Punt reported his achievements.

Punt had boarded the train as soon as it arrived at Troyes and had spoken to the guard and the engineer. To them both he had told slightly differing stories, neither of which contained any reference to the Blackstones, who were to be Punt's own personal triumph. The guard had been persuaded of the necessity of the delay on the basis that a thorough inspection of the braking system had been ordered by the SNCF due to a near disaster at Nevers the day before, the blame for which had been laid at the door of the stationmaster, who, it was said, had not been rigid enough in enforcing such inspections. The reason, Punt added, why the guard might not have heard of this was because security was tight on the matter. To the engineer Punt merely reported that he, together with the guard, were to carry out the inspection and that the engineer might as well take coffee while this was being done. Punt then examined the compartment lists, divided the train into two sections, took the half containing the Blackstones' coach and gave the other to the guard for examination.

With his master key Stationmaster Punt unlocked the door of the Blackstones' compartment and signaled to Jacques on the station platform, who had listened to everything which had been said with wide-eyed fascination, that all was well and to proceed after fifteen minutes.

Jacques nodded dutifully, turned his eyes to the station clock and watched critically until fifteen minutes had passed, then gave a signal to proceed, which the guard immediately questioned.

"I have found nothing," he said. "Is the inspection over?"

"It is over," Jacques replied. "The trackmen have indicated that everything is in order."

"Where is Stationmaster Punt?"

Jacques thought quickly. "He too found nothing, sir. He has gone to his office to make his report."

"I see." The guard frowned. "Does he wish to converse with me further? This seems to be a matter of some importance."

Jacques swallowed, his mind racing. "I doubt it, sir," he replied. "He has given the train a clean bill of health."

"Really?" The guard raised his eyebrows. "Tell me," he asked, "what exactly were we looking for? That was never made absolutely clear."

Tapping his breast pocket as he had seen Punt do, Jacques replied, "Official business." He spoke from the side of his mouth.

"Indeed?" The guard sounded impressed. "In that case I hope it turns out successfully."

"It will, sir," Jacques waved the train away. "I am confident of it."

As the train steamed out of Troyes, Stationmaster Punt, having made the last of his detailed notes regarding the Blackstones' luggage, placed his hands on the casket containing the Moonchild and pondered; his fat face was fixed with curiosity, his pudgy hands damp with excitement. This was obviously the piece Obelgamma had referred to, this was the jeweled casket mentioned in the telegram. Stationmaster Punt was consumed with such a sense of inquisitiveness, such a desire to know what the casket contained that his chins wobbled and his mouth ran with saliva. He moved his hands possessively over its surface and they left damp patches where they rested.

Punt felt the train start with a jerk, glanced out of the window to see Jacques' final conversation with the guard, and knew he would be closeted with the casket, alone and without fear of interruption, for a further twenty minutes at least. His ill-concealed inspection of the Blackstones at dinner indicated that they had reached only the main course, so at the very least there would be coffee and cheese to follow, possibly a desert as well. He realized there was plenty of time to examine the contraband (which he was sure it was), and the thought of it sent a shiver of delight along his fat spine.

"It is my duty," he said aloud. "Obelgamma would not want it any other way."

Punt waddled to the door of the compartment and checked that it was firmly locked. In spite of the dark outside he drew the curtains. He performed each action slowly, methodically. When he returned to the casket he stood before it a few seconds longer, savoring the delay. Then, very slowly, he bent, reached out his pudgy hands and, slipping the silver clasp, attempted to lift the lid.

Stationmaster Punt's disappointment at not being able to move the lid was profound. It closed on him like embarrassment, causing his cheeks to flush and fine beads of perspiration to form on his upper lip. All the anticipation he had known turned to guilt, and for a moment it almost defeated his purpose. He stood and gazed at the casket, staring down at the open clasp hanging loose, at the fine line where the lid joined the coffin. Then he breathed deeply, flexed his pudgy fingers and, moving forward, bent again.

This time he grasped the carved sides of the lid firmly and with a swift, determined jerk attempted to swing the top half of the casket back on its hinges. Again he was frustrated. Again the lid remained in place, although the force of Punt's action lifted the entire casket some inches from the floor of the carriage. Stationmaster Punt paused. Crouched on his fat knees before the tightly closed coffin, he pondered, the mystery urging him on, adding pace to his physical longing to open this elaborate box and know what it contained. His juices ran. A long, slow moan issued from his thick and greedy lips.

"There must be a hidden lock," he whispered. "No wonder Obelgamma asked me to intervene. These English must have a great deal to conceal."

With that, Stationmaster Punt stood again, easing the muscles in his legs. He put his head to one side and studied the casket, trying to imagine where the hidden clasp might lie, then bent once more, his aching legs protesting, several stitches in his uniform snapping beneath his bulk, and allowed his fat but sensitive hands to wander over the splendor of the box, to explore each detail of carving, each gemstone, in the hope something might trigger the concealed device.

For fully five minutes Punt remained before the casket seeking the lock he was sure was there, allowing his fingers to probe and roam until the strain in his knees would take it no longer —then, placing one solid hand on the center of the casket, on the heavy-petaled, gem-studded lid, he heaved himself to his feet.

All at once Stationmaster Punt felt the rose depress beneath the weight of his hand and knew he had discovered the casket's secret. Immediately, before allowing his strained knees relief, he returned to the box and, pressing downward with his hand, twisting the center of the rose this way and that, he heard the muffled clicking of the lock and felt the lid come loose beneath his fingers. Punt sighed deeply with relief, greed, success, then threw back the lid of the casket.

The sight he saw disappointed him greatly. He was not quite sure what he had expected, but the elaborateness of the exterior, the mystery of the English couple, the officialness of Obelgamma's telegram, suggested a great deal more than the body of what was quite obviously an embalmed child lying serenely on a bed of purple velvet. Punt shook his heavy head with bitter deprivation. There must be some mistake; surely Obelgamma could not possibly be interested in the body of a child—*unless*—Punt's mind raced like a machine—unless the child did not belong to the English couple, unless it had come illegally into their possession, unless they had kidnapped a corpse. Punt held his breath and peered more closely at the face. It appeared quite healthy, it looked as if it were merely asleep. Perhaps, Punt thought, it was only drugged, perhaps it was lying in a coma.

Carefully, Punt reached into the dimness of the interior and felt for the child's pulse, taking in his pudgy hand that of the child which lay uppermost on the chest. As he did so, as his fat fingers wrapped themselves about the slender wrist, *they brushed against the claw below.* For one long second Stationmaster Punt could not imagine what it was the back of his hand had encountered. It occurred to him it might have been the fabric on which the child lay or part of the infant's clothing; then, with a horror that turned his heavy stomach and a leaping fear that dried the saliva in his cavernous mouth, he realized it was not human. The hand below the one he held, which had been hidden by shadow, was grotesque. The nails were heavy, coarse, dense, shaped like those of an animal, the skin thickened and dark so that it resembled hide more than that which might cover a human body; the hair which grew from the monstrosity was dense, brutal, brushlike, and it scraped his hand like wire.

Immediately—Punt would have thought within the same second—as a hand involuntarily draws back from a flame, he released the child's pulse and began to retreat from the casket, but even within the perimeters of that speed the Moonchild hand moved faster. So quickly did it grasp Punt's own that he was not even aware of the movement, merely knew that instead of his hand holding the child's, a claw now grasped his own, firmly, fearsomely, like iron.

Punt opened his mouth to scream but terror incapacitated him; there were no words to issue, no cry to dispatch. His legs failed and he lurched, fell toward the casket, managing only to grab with his free hand the edge of the seat by which the casket stood. As he hung, heavy and terrified, his mouth open, his hand caught, in that filtered second when the horror became a reality and some long-lost nightmare enveloped him, the Moonchild opened its eyes, gazed up at Punt's heavy, shocked face and began its fiendish smile.

For a moment everything went black before Punt's eyes. It was not so much that he fainted but that his mind completely rejected what his eyes perceived. His senses refused to acknowledge the message they delivered. Everything was wiped clean for an instant. And in that black, blind instant, the Moonchild struck. In a flash the hairy paw released the stationmaster's hand and reached for the throat, gripping the heavy rolls of fat about the neck, plunging the deadly nails into the flesh.

Punt opened his eyes and gazed upon the last sight he would ever see: a slow, devilish smile distorting the dead child's face. Twin beams of white light emerged from the once-closed eyes. Punt gagged at the vision; his body heaved, his stomach thrashed, his eyes bulged. But in spite of his torment the claw at his throat did not move. Even as Punt died, as his great body lunged and twisted in its last seconds of life, nothing distracted the clawlike arm—its nails dug and its muscles bulged. As Punt pushed against the edge of the seat, as his massive legs tried to straighten and lift him away, there was no releasing the Moonchild arm, there was no dislodging the demon at the throat. Blood gushed suddenly as the nails bit. Punt fell and rolled. The arm held for seconds longer as if it wanted to be certain no dreg of life remained in the bulky body. As the claw impaled and the smile distorted, white sourceless light filled the compartment with such chill that every single item seemed to glow with formless illumination.

Slowly the body of Stationmaster Punt was released, the Moonchild's smile died, the arm withdrew, the light faded. It was as if a moving picture had been reversed, showing the action from end to beginning, as if all the forces contained in the

Moonchild withdrew to rest once more, leaving the bland and innocent face of Simon Blackstone serene on the velvet plush, leaving part of him as it had been, childlike and docile; but now the fingers, the hand, the whole arm of the demon on one side was manifest. From the shoulder downward the arm was distorted; from the neck itself the monstrosity grew, bulging with muscle, clothed in dark and hideous flesh, covered with coarse animal hair; and the pressure of it, its presence, forced the rest of the body to one side of the coffin, edged it away so that there was no disguising the change now, there was no covering of it by the other hand, which had returned to its original place and lay upon the travesty of itself like a flower amidst offal. The change was overwhelming.

The compartment was still once more, illumined only by the fishtail burners Punt had turned up. The train steamed steadily onward through dark and wintry French landscape, past the shapes of farmhouse windows rich with light.

In the dining car, unaware of what awaited them in the compartment, Anna and Edmund Blackstone completed their dinner in a leisurely manner, relaxed now that the train was in motion once again. They sat, lingering over coffee, talking almost idly while the express passed through Romilly and the entire personnel changed as the night shift came aboard and the new guards, carriage by carriage, began to examine the passengers' tickets.

Ultimately a guard approached the Blackstones' table and asked politely for their documents; Edmund searched, but not finding them, remembered leaving them in his black traveling coat which hung in the compartment. This he told the guard, adding, "If you care to wait a moment I shall fetch them."

"We can send a steward," the guard suggested.

"It is no trouble," replied Edmund, mindful of privacy. "The carriage is close enough."

"There is no hurry," the guard explained. "I am going in

the direction of your compartment. I can see the tickets there."

"Very well." Edmund turned to Anna. "Shall we return, my dear?"

"Of course," his wife replied. "The meal was delicious."

Walking within the rhythm of the train, the Blackstones made their way back to their compartment, listening to the clack of wheels, seeing darkness blur the outside windows. As they neared their compartment they passed a guard who asked them if they were returning, and when they confirmed that they were, offered to unlock the door; but Edmund, thinking again of their need for seclusion, refused.

When they reached their door Edmund stood beside it for a few seconds fumbling for his keys; then, seeing that the corridor was empty, he quickly turned the lock, not quite knowing why he was being furtive, merely becoming accustomed to the habit of caution.

As he opened the door he was aware of a change: someone was present, the curtains had been drawn, the lights were burning brightly and for one long moment he thought he was in the wrong compartment. He was about to back away, to tell Anna of his mistake, when he discovered the heavy, slumped figure of Stationmaster Punt on the floor beside the open casket. As soon as he registered what the raised lid signified and glimpsed the pale, golden-crowned face lying on the velvet, Edmund knew what had happened. His eyes went to the dead bulk on the floor, and a cold, devastating, blank fear filled him so completely for a time he could not move, but stood blocking the doorway hypnotized by the scene and all the horror it represented. It all came back: the corpse of Miss Harris, pale, wan, wide-eyed and lost; the dead coachman, his throat ripped, his one eye staring sightless at the leaden clouds; the distortion of that which had been his son corrupted almost beyond recognition. For some blind reason the peace of the past day, the simplicity of their journey from Kempten, the meal they had consumed, their closeness and their conversations had served to numb, to deaden. Edmund shuddered pitiably, incapable of moving forward or back.

Behind him he heard the voice of his wife. "What is it, Edmund?" Anna was saying. "Is something wrong?"

"Yes," he said, turning quickly. "Go away."

"What?" Anna asked, but even as the question was framed she knew. "Is it the child?"

"Do not come in."

Briskly Anna pushed past. "I will not be excluded," she said entering.

"Anna." Edmund felt weak. The sight of the dead station-master, the raised lid of the casket drained him of capability. "Oh, God, Anna," he said, "will this never end?"

"Come in quickly," Anna said with surprising calm. "Close and lock the door."

"But—"

"Do as I say. *Now.*" Anna was emphatic. "The guard will be here in a minute."

As Edmund moved numbly and locked the door, Anna gave her attention to the distortion in the coffin. The sight of what had been her son almost made her ill; she put a hand to her mouth and momentarily looked away. Bile rose in her throat. There was no hope in what she saw, no promise; the possibility that anything human might be salvaged from the monstrosity was absent. Anna knew, in that fraction of a second, that she must try to put from her mind all thought of resurrection. Simon was dead. All that remained was her duty to bury what was left of him, rid the world of it as soon as possible before all trace of her infant was destroyed.

Bravely, one hand still to her mouth, she reached and closed the lid of the shocking casket and replaced the silver clasp. Then, acting as she had seen Edmund do in the undertaker's rooms when they had first recognized the monster their son had become, she pressed downward on the rhinestone-studded center of the rose clasp and, twisting the core to the right, heard the secret lock click back into place. After that she stared at the body of Stationmaster Punt lying on the floor by her feet.

"We shall have to do something about this." Her voice was determined. "Edmund." She turned to her husband. "You will need to help me."

"Yes." Dazed, Edmund moved forward, his mind stilled, his action slow. "What shall we do?"

"Can we possibly get—it—out of the window?"

"I do not know." Edmund moved like a sleepwalker as he pulled the heavy brocade curtains aside, lifted the window and peered out into the dark. "There's nothing," he said. "Nothing I can see."

"We must hurry."

"Yes."

"Edmund." Anna's voice was like a razor. "If we are caught we will never get to England in time."

Edmund shook his head to clear it as the words penetrated; he breathed deeply and bent toward the shape of Stationmaster Punt, willing himself, forcing every move, driven by the strength of his wife without which, in those few dislocated minutes, both would have been lost. Taking the body of the stationmaster beneath its fat arms Edmund managed to lift it to its knees.

"My God, it's heavy," he cried.

Anna was beside him instantly. Together, each holding one limp arm, they hoisted the body higher, inching it. Strain distorted their faces. Their breath came in short, hard gasps. Somehow they managed to heave the body of Stationmaster Punt as high as the windowsill and then were forced to rest.

Gasping, Edmund stared at Anna, seeing the anxiety on her face, seeing horror also. There was blood on the floor as there had been blood on the arm of the Moonchild; there was a smear of it on the wall beneath the window. Edmund was absurdly grateful for the fact that Punt had been lying face downward; he did not know how he would have reacted to another torn and open throat.

"We cannot afford to delay," Anna said, the courage in her voice marked. "I cannot hold him much longer. My strength is going."

"We will lift again, together," Edmund said. "Now."

Anna pulled at one side of the heavy corpse, Edmund at the other. With infinite slowness, pushing and thrusting, tearing at the uniform, the looseness of the flesh beneath their fingers, they gradually moved the body until the head and shoulders were out of the window. And there it stuck. The mound of Stationmaster Punt's belly lodged in the window frame and once again the Blackstones were forced to pause, gasp for air, rest their aching muscles.

"We will never do it," said Edmund.

"We have to." Anna's strength continued.

"I can't."

"You must."

Anna's voice was within Edmund's ear, it rang in his head. The short, sharp, determined words forced him on. He heaved at the body, Anna with him, and together they moved it an inch or two farther. But once again it jammed, and Edmund paused, his breath ragged, his arms weak with effort.

Outside the darkness spun, the roar of the engine seemed closer, cold air flooded in. Anna realized their time must now be very short. "Come," she said, collecting all the strength she had left. "Try again."

"Yes," panted Edmund as he took hold of the body once more. He thrust against it, he strained, he sweated; his hair was unkempt. As the body began to move again, there was a sudden loud knocking on the door and the Blackstones realized that the guard had arrived for their tickets. "My God," Edmund said.

"Edmund." Anna's voice rose. She too was near panic. "We are undone. Quickly."

Without thinking and with more strength than he imagined himself capable of, Edmund bent and put his shoulder beneath the massive stationmaster's crotch and, straining with all his might, hoisted, hurled, catapulted the body through the window as the knocking was resumed and the compartment suddenly filled with dense black smoke.

"Shut the window," cried Edmund, reeling back. "We are in a tunnel."

"Open the door," said Anna. "There is the guard."

Recovering, Edmund slammed the window down and brushed the hair out of his eyes. Anna, composing herself as best she could, opened the compartment door and smiled at the guard. For a few seconds all three stood uncertainly.

"Ah," said Anna to the guard, "you have come for the tickets, I imagine?"

"Yes, madam." The guard coughed in the smoky atmosphere. "You've left the window open, I see."

"Correct," replied Edmund. "We had not realized there was a tunnel coming up." He controlled his breathing. "It was quite a tussle getting it closed again."

"I see." The guard looked at them both discreetly but a trifle strangely. "I would not have thought the night was clement enough for the window to be open, if you don't mind my saying so, sir."

"It was because I felt faint," said Anna and seated herself, spreading her skirts to hide the patch of blood on the floor. "A momentary thing, it has passed."

"I am sorry to hear you are unwell, madam. Is there something I could get you? Smelling salts, perhaps?"

"Thank you, no," Anna replied and sighed. "I feel almost recovered."

"If there *is* anything?" continued the guard, as Edmund handed him the tickets, which he checked carefully and returned. "If there is anything, madam, do not hesitate to ring."

"I shall."

As the guard left and shut the door, Edmund and Anna Blackstone felt the sane world go with him. Normality ceased, dissolved, no longer contained them. A fierce insanity seemed to storm.

One moment they had been in mundane conversation with the guard; seconds before, on the point of collapse, they had pushed a corpse through a window—a corpse for which that creature which had been their son was responsible.

As the guard went, they were left exhausted. The door closed; wheels clicked; outside in the open dark the world continued as if the Blackstones were no longer part of it. Their agony failed to touch it. Their horror was their own.

"Oh, Edmund." Anna's cry cut the acrid air. "What have we become?"

"I do not know." Edmund closed his eyes. "I am no longer certain of reality."

"But these . . . things are actually happening."

"Of that there is no doubt. The railman was dead."

"And the coachman?" Anna asked quickly. "Was that the child also?"

"Yes. The casket opened."

"But how could that occur? Was the lock of no service whatsoever?"

"It seems not." Edmund breathed deeply, stilling his heart. "It sprang loose when the coach crashed. And the railman must have discovered it for himself."

"Then, my God, what can we do?"

"I do not know." Edmund's hands shook; he adjusted his cravat and smoothed his frock coat. "It seems that whatever is against us is completely undefeatable."

"That I do not believe." Anna's strength returned. "We shall succeed, Edmund. We shall bring Simon to his place of peace. Nothing will prevent that. Nothing. Despite what we have to do. Despite what we become. Despite what this whole, dreadful business turns us into."

Edmund sighed. "It may not have turned us into anything, Anna," he said softly. "It may merely have shown us what we are."

Anna Blackstone stared at her husband.

"It may have shown us how far we will go to guard those we love, even if they have altered beyond all recognition."

"And just how far need we go?"

"I am unsure of that," Edmund continued wearily. "Never before in our entire lives have we committed the slightest crime. But now..." He moved his hands uncertainly. "Now I think we might even commit murder if we thought it necessary to return Simon to Tonbridge, so much do we believe it has to be done."

"We *know* it has to be done."

"So..."

"But murder, no." Anna shook her head self-convincingly. "That I cannot accept."

Edmund sighed. "I hope to God you are right, Anna," he said softly.

"I know it, Edmund. Do not despair."

Edmund smiled sadly. "It is not despair so much as the full realization of what one is capable of," he said.

He sat slowly, beside but a little apart from Anna, aware of a great need for reassurance, release. They had lived too long with their tragedy, they had borne too much alone. Edmund turned his head stiffly and read the same need for deliverance on Anna's fine-boned face. They had done as much as they were capable of, more than they could ever have imagined, and now they needed a token, a sign, an indication that someone or something was on their side.

Edmund sighed. "Come, Anna," he said gently, giving her. what he could. "Let us go to bed."

Anna turned her head. "Will you come to me, Edmund?" she asked.

"Of course."

"It will not release us."

"Perhaps not." Edmund managed to smile. "But at least we shall know that we have each other."

Anna bit her lip and stood, her face a mixture of courage and frailty. Quickly she opened the door to the sleeping compartment and entered. After a few moments Edmund followed and began to undress. As he removed his shirt he noticed for the first time a drop of blood on the starched cuff and rapidly, almost violently, tore it from him, then turned down the light and climbed into the narrow sleeping bunk beside his wife.

OUTSIDE, the night-dark curled, mist formed in the hollows, the farmyards slept and cattle were warm in their barns.

CHAPTER NINE

ALSO on a train, rushing northward through the blanketing night, asleep and mildly rocking in his compartment, Inspector Leopold Fuchs lay serene.

His coach ride, earlier that day, from the mountain village to Munich had been almost as uncomfortable as that of the previous night, its single consolation being that now he knew how essential the journey was. He had urged the horses onward in the chill and darkening air, counting each long minute as the coach came down the valley and across the foothills to Munich.

When Fuchs arrived at his office, as he climbed the marble stairs in the Police Headquarters Building a constable approached with two messages.

"I thought you would want to see these immediately, sir," the constable said. "In fact, I have been waiting for you."

"You are too kind," said Fuchs, cold and weary, vividly conscious that he had not eaten for a long time. "Is it good news or bad?"

The constable frowned. "I am not sure, sir," he replied.

"You are right." Fuchs remarked philosophically. "At times they are one and the same."

He took the slips of paper and began to read. They were both from the Duty Officer, Kempten Police. The first told of a dead coach driver who had been located beside a stream at a crossing on the road leading upward to the village the Blackstones had fled. It described how the man had been found, but neglected to detail the cause of death. The second message, telephoned a few hours later, informed that a damaged coach had been investigated by a constable on his beat in the town of Kempten itself. The Duty Officer wondered if both events were connected.

"Interesting," Fuchs remarked. "I am surprised, however, that they should trouble me with their local accidents. It is not as if I did not have problems of my own."

"I am responsible for that," said the constable. "I spoke to Sergeant Obelgamma when he telephoned, and, as a result of his information, I asked all likely places for reports on anything unusual as far as traffic was concerned. I also asked them to let us know if they came across foreigners, well, traveling, sir."

"And this is all that came in?"

"No, sir, there were several messages about a Hungarian dancing team and one or two others which I did not think were relevant. I have not bothered you with them as I knew you would be in a hurry."

Fuchs smiled. "Have you ever thought of becoming a policeman, constable?" he asked mildly.

The constable blushed. "It was just, sir—well, your train leaves in less than twenty minutes," he stammered.

"You have done well," Fuchs said. "Now, tell me about the train."

WHEN the Northern Express left Munich Station at 10:34 that evening Fuchs was aboard; he had neither washed nor changed nor eaten but had gone almost immediately from Munich police headquarters to the station. As the train pulled out of the bustling rail terminal, Fuchs was already seated in the dining car, a large plate of bockwurst, sauerkraut and dumplings before him, a stein of lager by his side. He ate steadily for half an hour, pausing only to ask for more; when he completed the meal he sat back, loosened the bottom buttons of his waistcoat and belched discreetly.

"Excellent," he told the waiter. "Send my compliments to the chef."

Later, as he lay in his sleeper, turning the events of the day in his mind, Fuchs felt he had reason to be satisfied. It was clear from the doctor's confused mumblings and the reports on the coach that the Blackstones *had* gone to Kempten. There appeared to have been an accident en route in which the driver had met his death, although the Blackstones seemed to have succeeded in reaching the town itself. From there they would, presumably, catch a train to one of the Channel ports and from timetables he had been given at Munich police headquarters, Fuchs guessed they would catch a night express to either Cherbourg or Le Havre—it mattered little which. Fuchs merely hoped that whatever ferry they caught was overnight, for that would ensure their landing in England on New Year's Day, whereas he would be in Dover the evening before, even if it meant holding the ferry for him in Ostend.

However, if the Blackstones did land in Southampton on New Year's Eve, at much the same time Fuchs himself was in Dover, he would still have the advantage of distance. Tonbridge was a lot closer to Dover than to Southampton. It was almost certain he would be in Tonbridge before them, awaiting their arrival, their mysterious casket and their seemingly desperate need.

Fuchs was glad it had worked out this way—it avoided his having to alert others to the Blackstones' flight. Had he been forced to ask for aid he would have found explanations difficult and—in spite of, or even because of, his international reputation —might have had trouble passing on his conviction that the evidence he possessed was sufficient to indicate his belief in it.

In a strange way the pursuit had become a personal matter to him now. He was compelled by something more powerful than mere curiosity to discover exactly what the casket contained. He was in danger of becoming as obsessed as the English with their flight. He knew, however, that whoever confronted them would need to do it with understanding, a degree of pity, a knowledge of background. And Fuchs, himself, was the only person in Europe who was capable of such action. It pleased him, in a manner he did not fully understand, to know this; it was as if the role had been made for him, as if he were part of something already planned.

With these thoughts in mind, their curious mixture of pursuit and compassion, he lay rocking gently until sleep overtook him as the train hurried northward through the enveloping night. Everything was beginning to fall into place, even if some of the doctor's references remained obscure, unplaced. He still did not comprehend what was meant by "hoof" and "claws" or who the "guardian" was.

When gray dawn lifted over northwest Europe, as the pale, wintry light filtered over city and landscape, both trains were nearing their destinations.

Fuchs was up early, shaved, dressed and anticipating breakfast. He had slept well, and although his destination was some hours away, he felt confident about the rest of the journey. Everything was on schedule.

The Blackstones' night express, however, was not on time. After the delay at Troyes the train had fallen farther and farther behind and was now due in Le Havre some two and a half hours after the time the steamer would sail for Southampton.

At Paris, the night express guard had been informed of the fact that the ferry would depart without his passengers. It was regretted but the decision had already been taken. "We have passengers with reservations," he protested. "What will happen to them?"

"We are sorry," he was told. "But the steamship company

will not wait. You are considerably delayed as it is."

The guard shrugged. "You miss your points once and it happens all along the line," he said. "We lost time at Troyes and it got worse, not better."

"There is an extra ferry in the afternoon," the guard was informed. "Your passengers will make it comfortably."

"That is overnight, is it not?"

"That cannot be avoided. At this time of the year, you understand, the pressure is very great on the steamers. They must run as close to schedule as possible."

"What do I tell my passengers?"

"Apologize for the delay. Tell them special arrangements have been made for them to take the overnight. At no extra cost. There will be entertainment on board. After all, it is New Year's Eve."

The Blackstones were in their compartment when news of further delay reached them. They had expected something of the sort, it was clear the train was well behind schedule, but it was distressing to learn there would be even more time lost in Le Havre.

"I am very sorry," apologized the guard. "There is really nothing to be done."

"When will the next ferry leave?" Edmund asked crisply.

"There is an evening steamer, sir. It arrives in Southampton early tomorrow morning."

"That's a whole day behind."

"Well, not exactly, sir. You will, in fact, be only a night later, some twelve hours. But as the steamer is a special, sir, and as there will be a New Year's Eve dinner, we felt it might be acceptable."

"New Year's Eve." Anna shook her head in disbelief. "It seems greatly out of place."

"You do not seem to realize," Edmund informed the guard, a little tersely, "we are a bereaved couple." He looked at the casket sadly. "We have not made it public, but that is our son's coffin. We are taking him home for burial. Time is of the greatest importance."

The guard's face paled. "I am sorry, sir. I had not realized." His eyes never left the coffin. "Usually this, this sort of thing, well, travels in the luggage van." He moved his hands uneasily.

"In the *luggage van?*" exclaimed Anna.

"I merely said 'usually,' madam."

"We have all the necessary papers," Edmund informed the guard. "Does anyone wish to see them?"

"No, not at all, sir. That will not be necessary. It merely came as somewhat of a surprise." He looked at the casket once again as if it might explain itself. "However, I will see to it that you have no trouble with the Customs at Le Havre. And I am sure we can find somewhere suitable for you to rest for the few hours until boarding." He coughed uncertainly. "I do regret the delay, sir. But we will make you all as comfortable as possible."

"Very well," Edmund conceded. "I hope we *do* catch the night steamer, that's all."

"No doubt about it, sir, I assure you."

When the guard had gone, Edmund turned to Anna. "This delay bothers me," he said in a worried voice. "I wonder if the police are involved."

"It is possible." Anna spoke calmly. "The body of that coach-man must have been discovered by now. If not that of the rail-man also."

"Would they connect us with either, I wonder?"

"That I could not say," Anna replied. "Was the—was the coachman badly injured?"

Edmund nodded.

"Could it have been put down to the attack of some animal?"

Edmund turned his head away and did not reply.

THE Blackstones' train arrived at Le Havre near noon, and almost immediately they were escorted to a small, well-furnished waiting room where a fire burned cheerfully. The room was obviously reserved for nobility. On the walls hung portraits of European royalty, living and dead. Stiff features peered out of heavy gilt frames with aloofness and disdain, ignoring the English couple and their elaborate casket which had been delicately but obviously placed on a small japanned table with cabriol legs carried in especially for the occasion.

No other circumstances could have shown more that the railway company was determined to do its best for the Blackstones; nothing could have allayed their suspicions further. Both had dressed elaborately for the occasion, realizing that to don formal clothes was something of an irony when they considered their actions of the past few days, but the circumstances seemed to call for it; now that they had declared what the casket contained, it would have been less than expected of them not to dress appropriately. They wore a combination of white and black. Edmund's linen shone crisply, Anna's hands lay folded neatly in her bombazined lap; her tidy buttoned shoes protruded from beneath the hem of her draped black skirt, as she and Edmund waited for time to pass.

After a while the door of the small, cozy room opened and a steward entered wheeling an ormolu trolley which contained two bottles of champagne in coolers and, beneath a large silver server, smoked salmon sandwiches on fresh brown bread.

"This is with the steamship company's compliments," the steward said, his tone distinctly formal. "I understand this is not an occasion for celebration, sir, and madam, but it was felt you might care to refresh yourselves while you waited."

"That is most thoughtful," said Edmund gracefully.

Anna nodded and dropped her eyes to her folded hands. She sat very still while the steward quietly opened the champagne and waited patiently while Edmund approved it. The steward then poured two glasses, lifted the cover from the sandwiches and backed out of the room. As soon as he had gone, Anna let her breath out in little, beating gasps.

Edmund peered at her. "Are you all right?" he asked.

"Oh, yes," Anna said, controlling herself. "It is just that I have an appalling desire to laugh."

Edmund's face relaxed. "I understand," he said, his eyes going from the ormolu trolley to the ornate casket to Anna's black, and his own equally somber, suiting. "If only they knew."

Anna put her hand to her lips. "At times I feel we are acting an enormous charade," she said, her voice shaking.

"In a way we are," Edmund replied.

"Yet, it could not be otherwise."

"No, it could not." Edmund passed a glass of champagne to his wife. "We are performing in the manner expected. It enables others to accept our role. They see what they expect to see and are content."

"And us?" Anna lifted her glass and sipped delicately. "What do we expect?" The sudden, quick laughter had gone, leaving her face quiet. "What do *we* need to become content?"

"Dear God, I wish I knew."

Anna sighed. "Will we have other children, Edmund?" she asked very carefully.

"Yes." The response was immediate.

"Even after what has occurred?"

"More than ever after what has occurred."

Anna nodded. She took a sandwich but the food was tasteless in her mouth, the champagne flat. She knew, had anything occurred to break the delicacy of that moment, had there been any signal to shatter the frailty of her belief, she could not have continued further; but the room remained still, the fire burned steadily. Edmund was silent.

Later the steward came and inquired if there was anything they needed. Later still they were shepherded onto the steamer, shown their cabin, escorted inside it with care and attention.

As the boat moved away from the shore the Blackstones stood by a porthole watching the flat French coastline fade into the dark. The ship heaved beneath them and both knew that the next time they stepped ashore it would be onto the soil which would signify the end of their journey and the beginning of whatever lay ahead.

"We will be in England by morning," Anna said as the lights grew faint in the distance, "and Tonbridge by evening."

"It does seem unbelievable."

"Will it end there?"

Edmund took his wife's arm; he watched the coast of France recede and hoped whatever it was that plagued them would go with it, but knew it would not.

As the boat carrying the Blackstones slid out into the dark, cold, silent Channel, a packet bearing Inspector Leopold Fuchs steamed from Ostend to Dover. Fuchs had already been at sea some hours and was becoming accustomed to the gentle swell of the quiet water. He had passed through Ostend on schedule. The boat had left on time. He was already ahead of the Blackstones and would be in Tonbridge a half day before them, although this information was not yet his.

At Ostend there had only been one message awaiting Fuchs which was from neither Inspector Kearsley nor any railway man nor Sergeant Obelgamma. It was from the Munich constable who had telegraphed surrounding districts for information which had led to news of the dead coach driver and the damage to his vehicle. Now he told Fuchs that the body of a French stationmaster had been found at the mouth of a tunnel some miles north of Troyes.

"The idiot," Fuchs said aloud as he read the telegram. "He's been at his own stupid command again." He turned to the official who had handed him the message. "Is this all?" he asked. "Nothing more?"

"No, sir."

"God in Heaven," Fuchs muttered. He eyed the official. "If

you ever come across a Sergeant Obelgamma," he said, "please shoot him for me. On sight."

He walked away, leaving the confused official, and boarded the boat. Fuchs realized immediately what had occurred, saw in his mind's eye the bald, brisk little sergeant sending a cryptic message to someone as overzealous as himself. Fuchs angrily wished he had more information, or time to probe, but the ferry was waiting and there was no certainty that a telephone call, even if it did get through, would provide any further details.

Once aboard, he shrugged his heavy shoulders, stuffed his hands in his pockets and went below to the smoking room where he sat on a brassbound chair chained to the floor and ordered beer and schnapps and sat brooding.

The death of the Troyes stationmaster had undermined his earlier confidence. He found the death difficult to add to the few facts he already possessed; it seemed unrelated to the Blackstones and their flight. Had it not been for the fact that he had asked Obelgamma to alert such a man along the route, there would be nothing to connect it to the English at all. But there *was* a connection, the constable at Munich Police Headquarters had recognized it, yet why and how and under what circumstances Fuchs could not imagine. He took a long pull of his beer, drank all the schnapps, ordered more and tried to connect what he knew of the three deaths.

"Very well, then," he said aloud, ignoring the look from a man with pince-nez at the next table. "Say they were all murdered—why?" He drank more beer and wiped his moustaches. "What reasons do you have? Robbery? I doubt it. We know of nothing that's been stolen. But even if there was—a coachman and a stationmaster hundreds of miles apart?" He sighed and shook his head. "No, there is no logic."

He glanced around. The man with the pince-nez was staring at him openly. "It is all right," Fuchs assured him. "When

I am puzzled I often think aloud."

"Puzzled?" queried the other.

Fuchs turned his eyes away. "Why else do people kill each other?" he asked himself. "Passion?" He spoke aloud again. "Over such distances? No, that would be particularly un-English." He paused. "What was that the doctor said? Hooves and claws? Something about a guardian?" He turned an idea over in his mind, allowing it to grow. He sat very still, as if a solution might approach quietly. Something was there, something very close. The sense of mystery and doom he had known in the doctor's wrecked room returned; he heard the sullen voice and saw the breakage. He sat, waiting for the thought to form, take shape, but it escaped him, disappeared even before it began. "If I knew how the others had died," he said. "If they also were strangled, one could be more definite."

"I talk to my cats," the man at the next table said. "If that's any help."

Fuchs turned to the speaker. "I beg your pardon?" he said politely.

"I said, I talk to my cats. Aloud."

"So do I," replied Fuchs and stood. "But always about food. Never about murder."

With that, Inspector Fuchs drained his glass, stood and walked away leaving the man with the pince-nez staring after him, silently mouthing the word "murder." His face had paled considerably.

Fuchs walked about the deck for most of the remainder of the journey to Dover, asking himself questions in a quiet voice, moving about the packet dozens of times, but failing to find answers that were in any way satisfying. It was beyond touching, there was nothing in his experience he could refer to. Fuchs felt heavy, restless, unproductive.

When the packet arrived in Dover, Fuchs was one of the first ashore. Carrying his own case he walked briskly along the quay, through Customs, and was approaching a hansom cab when a voice called his name. He turned to see a tall, rather elegant English police inspector whom he recognized. The sight cheered Fuchs immensely.

"Kearsley," he said happily.

"I wouldn't have done it for anyone else except perhaps Mother," the tall Englishman replied. "Not for another German, certainly."

"What is that?"

"Given up my New Year's Eve to come down to this dank and Godforsaken place to meet you."

"That *is* very generous." Fuchs smiled broadly. "How can I thank you enough?"

"By taking me to the nearest public house and buying me a large Scotch."

Some fifteen minutes later Inspector Leopold Fuchs and Inspector Peter Kearsley were standing at the long wooden bar of the Rose and Crown, Fuchs with a pint of English bitter and Kearsley with Scotch whisky, talking to each other animatedly. They had worked together closely twice before, had come to admire each other. Like opposites, they complemented.

Kearsley lifted his glass and drank, savoring the flavor. "Well?" he asked languidly. "What brings you to England this time, you overweight old Kraut?"

Fuchs gulped with laughter, spilling beer. He shook his head, his eyes moist with pleasure. "There is no simple explanation, my friend," he replied genially, wiping his moustache with the back of his hand. "None that I know of."

"Care to give me a complicated one?"

"I would, if it were possible."

"You mean to say you don't know why you're here?"

Fuchs shrugged. "I am not really sure," he confessed.

"Very unlike you, Fuchs. Very unlike you indeed." Kearsley drank a little whisky, then added, "I've looked into these Blackstones of yours, by the way. Respectable as the Tower of London, it seems." His eyes searched the room. "There's a table over there," he observed. "Bring your drink and I'll tell you what I know of them." So saying, he pushed his way through the crowd.

Inspector Kearsley began by telling Fuchs that although there had been little time, his inquiries had been simple enough: Edmund Blackstone came from a respectable London family, well established as wine importers, financially sound. He had an uncle in the House of Commons, but Kearsley had been unable to discover any associated scandal. They were, as far as he knew, above ordinary suspicion. The wife, Anna, came from an equally respectable Midlands family and there was one son, Simon, who would now be about seven.

"He's dead," Fuchs interrupted.

"Very young to die," Kearsley observed. "Anything funny about his death?"

"Not that I know of," Fuchs replied. "If there was, it might help explain things. The child was ill with fever for two weeks and then, well, he just died."

"Happens every day."

"Of course." Fuchs took a long pull of beer and Kearsley closed his eyes.

"Don't know how you can drink that stuff," he said delicately. "Always tastes of copper to me."

Fuchs smiled and wiped froth from his moustache. "I thought it was what made England great," he replied.

"Perish the thought," remarked Kearsley and sipped a little Scotch. "So the child died naturally enough?"

"Yes, although that is when it all began."

"You will need to tell me a great deal more than that," Kearsley said.

"I can see I will."

"Can you also see my glass is empty?"

Fuchs laughed, got to his feet, went to the bar, put his head into the nearest glass-paneled, walnut-framed gentlemen's server, ordered the drinks and returned to the table where, beginning at the beginning, he told Kearsley most of what he knew about the Blackstones and their activities in the village.

"I found myself faced with two mysteries," he said. "One was the death of the governess and the other was why the Blackstones had fled with, presumably, the body of their child."

"A simple connection," Kearsley observed. "They were, or knew who was, responsible for the death of the Harris woman."

"Why should they take their child?"

"Not unusual to want him buried on home ground, you know."

"Of course not, but the undertaker could have arranged all that. Why should they remove the body from his care?"

"Hardly seems fair."

"That's what the undertaker thought."

"So, you don't think it's as simple as I suggested?"

"I do not."

"Mmmm, might have been too easy," Kearsley mused. "Anyone else in the village know anything?"

Fuchs hesitated; his conversation with the doctor was so irregular, so grotesque, he was reluctant to mention it. "The only other person they had anything to do with *was* the village doctor," he admitted finally. "He helped them get away. And he is now insane."

"Really? Only now?"

"When I saw him he needed to be sedated to speak with me at all. Then most of the time he talked of hooves and claws, matters which seemed irrelevant. I could make nothing out of it. He did, however, mention the *necessity* of taking the child home for burial." Fuchs paused. "And something about a guardian."

"This gets better and better," said Kearsley. "Tell me more."

Fuchs did. He told Kearsley what he knew of the Blackstones' journey to Kempten, and that there had been some sort of accident on the way. A coach driver had been reported dead and a damaged coach had been found in Kempten. He believed the Blackstones would have gone from Kempten to Basel and from there to one of the Channel ports, which would mean they should be in England either this evening or, at the latest, in the morning. Whatever the case, it was his intention to confront them in Tonbridge when they arrived.

"You seem sure they will arrive," said Kearsley.

Fuchs nodded. "That is the one thing I am certain about," he replied.

"Any more, old chap?"

"There is something more," Fuchs said. "Another body."

"Really? Who was it this time?"

"A stationmaster. At Troyes."

"They don't half get around, do they? Come along, tell me all."

Fuchs supplied what scant information he possessed about the death of Stationmaster Punt and admitted it was mere guesswork that linked the body north of Troyes with the flight of the English.

"I see." Kearsley finished his whisky and went himself to the bar to refill the glasses. Fuchs waited broodingly. "Odd, wouldn't you say?" remarked Kearsley on his return. "Not exactly one of those where you can blame the butler, if you know what I mean."

"Only too well."

"Fishy."

"Yes." Fuchs nodded. "As you would say, fishy."

"I'd say damned fishy, actually."

Fuchs sighed heavily. "I have nothing to go on," he said.

"Poor chap," remarked Kearsley amiably. "Sounds as if nanny hasn't fed you properly."

"I think you know what I mean."

"Oh, I do, old man. I do." Kearsley sat for a few moments, swirling whisky in his glass; when he finally spoke his voice was musing. "You don't think, by any chance, they've some sort of monster in that fancy trunk of theirs, do you, Fuchs?" he asked very carefully.

Fuchs felt the hair on the back of his neck prickle. A shiver ran along the line of his jaw. "Why do you say that?" he asked as evenly as he was able.

"Fashionable, isn't it, with that Dracula book about?" Kearsley's bantering tone was denied by his level gaze. "After all, they were not all that far from Transylvania, were they?"

"You are not making a joke, Kearsley," Fuchs said. "I know you better than that."

"All right then," Kearsley said. "Let's seriously consider your problem in that light."

"I have tried not to."

"Understandable," Kearsley conceded. "But let's, if only for the hell of it." He put his glass on the table and, as he made his points, counted them off on his fingers. "One, you've got the geography for it. Two, there are three seemingly quite unconnected deaths. Three, an eminently respectable English family is rushing about the Continent with a coffin under their arm and not a lily to show for it. Four, a mad doctor talks about hoof and claw, and things in the night. Five, there's no other reason you or I can think of. Good God, man, you've a handful of excuses for believing in, well, whatever you like to call it."

As Fuchs listened, his heavy face grew more and more solemn. In spite of his knowledge of the English inspector, he was uncertain where laughter began or ended. He did not know if there was any seriousness at all in Kearsley's theory. Yet, at the same time, he was aware of his own response, of the mood he had known in the doctor's wrecked room, of the awful truth reflected in the doomed man's eyes, of all the little moments since when facts had not fitted or answers had not seemed to belong.

"Well, my old friend," Kearsley went on. "What do you think of that?"

Fuchs shrugged. "Now you *are* making fun," he said gruffly.

"Yes and no."

"Sometimes, my friend," Fuchs said heavily, "I do not understand you."

"Ah." Kearsley's eyes lit. "I've touched your funny bone."

"God in Heaven, you have." Fuchs lifted his glass and attacked his beer; there was froth along his moustache. "I am confused," he said. "There have been times when your theory has tempted me. But—" he shook his head—"I cannot afford to theorize along those lines, I have no evidence to put in that direction." He managed a smile. "If I actually did find a monster it would be different, but until that time I must work within my own experience. I must manage with what I know."

"So must we all," replied Kearsley amiably. "I was only trying to help."

"No." Fuchs shook his head. "I *do* know you better than that. You wished to see if those same thoughts had entered my mind. Well, they have, but I have put them aside."

"Rather stoic of you, old man."

"We Germans are known for it." Fuchs lifted his glass again. "The English are the hedonists."

Kearsley smiled. "Only part of the time." He paused a little, then went on. "What are your plans?"

"I have arranged to stay the night here. In the morning I will go to Tonbridge."

"Care for me to accompany you?"

Fuchs smiled with gratitude. "That is generous of you," he said. "I know you would not make the offer unless you meant it, but no, I feel this is something I should do alone." His smile broadened. "After all, it is not as if they were dangerous."

Kearsley laughed. "You fat Kraut," he said. "Let me buy you another drink *and* give you a piece of advice. Don't go wandering about here this evening or someone will throw you into a fountain."

"They throw people in water on a night as cold as this?"

"Especially on a night as cold as this, and especially Germans. Now, are you sure you'll have another glass of this filthy liquid?"

"I am sure," said Fuchs, hugely grateful. "Thank you, yes."

Later Kearsley said, "If you need any help in Tonbridge there's a good sergeant down there called Scot. Mention my name and he'll do what he can." The bar was noisier now. A man in a striped waistcoat and a gray bowler was playing music-hall tunes on an off-key piano. In one corner a group of Scotsmen was beginning to sing. "Mind you, he'll have a hangover," Kearsley observed.

"Will all of this country have a hangover in the morning?" Fuchs asked, his heavy face growing flushed.

"New Year's Day is a time of interlocking hangovers and absenteeism," said Kearsley. "You might even find yourself included."

"In the first, perhaps, but not the second."

"You're a dogged chap, Fuchs," Kearsley said. "Remember the girl from Acton?"

Inspector Leopold Fuchs laughed and took hold of his pint; the conversation grew and washed around them. The singers in the corner had been joined by others. Somewhere a woman was beginning to weep. Amidst the babble Fuchs and Kearsley talked of things done, people they had known, experiences shared and unshared, until finally they were out in the street again, the whole world about them singing, dancing, holding hands, in circles. Fuchs had his huge arm about Kearsley's shoulders, hugging him.

"Thank you," he said. "It has helped me a lot to talk to you."

"Including my outrageous theories?"

"God in Heaven." Fuchs laughed loudly. "Especially those."

He wished Kearsley goodnight and walked a little unsteadily

across the road to the hotel where a room had been booked for him, took his keys, went to bed and slept like a child. Watching him go, Inspector Kearsley smiled. "Just about the nicest German I've ever met," he said and, avoiding as much of the crowd as he could, went his way. About him were the sounds of the old year being replaced with the new.

THERE were scenes of festivity also aboard the Channel ferry on which the Blackstones traveled through the changing night. A costume ball was being held in the dining salon, the floor had been cleared for dancers, and an orchestra played the latest ragtime. In many of the cabins were small parties, and at one of these, Edmund Blackstone found himself, a glass of champagne in hand, talking to a pretty, petite woman wearing a gently plunging dress of watered silk. From her powdered bosom an essence of violets rose; her honey-colored hair was entwined with seed pearls. She was Beryl Fletcher, wife of an acquaintance Edmund had met earlier that evening walking the cold and bracing deck.

After the Blackstones had settled aboard the ferry and had seen the lights of France die in the dark, Edmund said, "We have but one more night, my dear, after which we should be able to rest."

Anna put the tips of her fingers to her brow. "Thank God, tomorrow will see the end of it," she said.

The ship rolled gently westward and the Blackstones prepared to retire.

They sat for a short while in the small cabin suite willing time to pass, hearing the vague, floating sounds of music and occasional laughter until, growing restless, Edmund stretched, got to his feet and slowly walked the length of the cabin. He took a grape from a Meissen dish and chewed it thoughtfully, then went back to where he had been seated. Anna watched her husband carefully, seeing impatience and the need for relief.

"Why don't you take a turn round the deck?" she suggested. "The fresh air will do you good."

Edmund raised his eyebrows. "Would you mind?" he inquired.

"On the contrary. I should prefer it to seeing you move about so restlessly."

"You have no concern about being left alone?"

"None at all," Anna replied.

Taking a heavy coat, Edmund went up to the promenade deck and walked briskly about; the night was crisp, cold and windless, the sea mellow, the fresh air welcome. Edmund breathed deeply as he strode, enjoying movement and a sense of liberation; here were no officials herding him into cabins; here were no prying eyes of stable owners concerned with departures. He was anonymous for the first time since he could remember, and the feeling was heady. It comforted, it elated, it cloaked. Edmund walked the deck a dozen times, then paused by a railing, breathing the clean salt air. He gazed out over the sea-black night; somewhere in the distance there was a light.

"*Edmund Blackstone*," a voice at his elbow shouted suddenly. "I'll be damned."

Edmund went rigid with fear. Sudden terror overpowered him. Sharp as a razor it sliced security, shattered illusions of peace. Forcing himself, he turned to see a bulky, florid-faced man he dimly recognized.

"It *is* Edmund Blackstone," the speaker confirmed. "What an amazing coincidence." He held out a beefy hand. "Geoffrey Fletcher, remember?"

"Why, yes." Edmund's throat was dry. He swallowed. "Lyme Regis, was it not?"

"That's it." Geoffrey Fletcher came closer, stood by the railing; he had not yet dressed for dinner and he wore heavy tweeds and a soft hat. "Must be what, four, five years ago now, eh?"

Edmund nodded; his pulse was returning to normal, the chill across his shoulder blades had disappeared. "Five, I think," he said and cleared his throat again.

"Been across to the Continent, eh?" Geoffrey Fletcher inquired. "Skiing, something adventurous like that?"

"No," Edmund replied. "Nothing like that."

"Well, well, well." Fletcher's open, florid face beamed. "Fancy that. It was those ammonites, wasn't it? That what you call them? All looked the same to me." He laughed loudly. "Beryl thought they were snails, what?"

"Yes, that's right," Edmund admitted. "It was a dig at Lyme. And it *was* ammonites."

"Never forget a fossil," Fletcher laughed.

"Of course not." Edmund breathed deeply. The shock had left him. "You're obviously on your way back from France. That where you spent your time?"

"With the Frogs? Heavens, no," Fletcher said loudly. "The wife and I've been gone to Italy, of all places. She has a cousin or something there who paints. We're going to look him up but never did." He gave a hyperbolic shudder. "Dreadful people, the Eyties. And their food, good God, man, I hope you've never had to eat it."

Edmund smiled. "Well, once or twice," he conceded.

"Dreadful stuff." Fletcher shuddered again, paused, sniffed the air, then resumed. "Where was it you said you'd been, old man?"

Edmund hesitated. "We've, well, we spent a week or two in a small place in the mountains. Bavaria, in fact," he admitted.

"Damned cold, what?"

"Yes. We'd hoped to do a little tobogganing, but you are right, it was far too cold."

"Bad enough out here on a night like this." Fletcher chuckled. "Been working up a thirst?"

"I was, well, taking a stroll."

"Wife with you?"

"Yes," Edmund replied. "She's below."

"And that cheeky little feller of yours? Real little rascal, if I remember, what? Must be seven or eight by now?"

Edmund shivered; he had expected the question but even so found it painful, difficult to answer.

"What's he been up to then?" Geoffrey Fletcher persisted. "Mischief of some sort I'll be bound."

"Unfortunately he's dead," Edmund replied quietly. "He died just about a week ago, as a matter of fact."

"Oh, God. I *am* sorry." Fletcher's beefy hand grasped Edmund's shoulder. "Oh, how dreadful for you both. I am so sorry. Really I am. Trust me to open my big mouth and ask a question like that."

"It was a perfectly normal question."

"Oh, dear, wait till Beryl hears about it. She was very fond of the little chap as I remember. Very fond indeed."

"Yes, well . . . " Edmund left the sentence unfinished.

"Ghastly business."

"We are over the worst of it."

"Yes, of course, of course." Fletcher shook his head heavily. "What a dreadful thing to happen." He patted Edmund's shoulder clumsily. "Listen, old man, don't think this is out of place. Was going to invite you anyway. But we're having a few people along to the cabin a little later. New Year's Eve and all that. Well, you and your wife just have to come along."

"That is thoughtful," Edmund replied formally. "But, under the circumstances, I think we must refuse."

"Don't be silly, old man." Fletcher was easier, now that the conversational ground had shifted. "Do you good, both of you. Cheer you up, if you know what I mean."

"You are very kind," Edmund murmured. Turning his eyes from the overenthusiastic face, he looked out to sea. The light he had seen on the horizon was gone; somewhere music was being played. "However, I do feel we must refuse."

"Last thing on earth you should do," Fletcher persisted. "Got to shake these things off, you know." He held up a hand as if in explanation. "Got a daughter of my own, twelve years old, you may remember. Know exactly how you must feel and all that. But you've got to get out and about, old man. I insist."

Edmund turned and stared at Fletcher's florid face; it looked greenish under the ship's lighting. "You insist?" he questioned.

"Absolutely," Fletcher continued. Taking a card from a pocket he rapidly scribbled a number on the back of it. "Now, here's where we are. You and your wife, Anne, isn't it Anne? just come along whenever you like. Needn't stay for any length of time. Just come along and say hello. Have a drink for the New Year. Do you the world of good, believe me."

"Really..." began Edmund, as Fletcher thrust the paste-board into his hand, but his voice died. For some reason he could not bring himself to snub the man's enthusiasm; the cheerful English voice was curiously appealing. "We'll see..." he ended lamely.

"That's the chap. Brush the cobwebs off. That sort of thing."

"I said, *We'll see*," Edmund stated, but even as he emphasized the words, knew he had conceded. "I shall speak to Anna about it," he added lamely.

"That's the chap." Fletcher patted Edmund's shoulder, looked about the deck and declared, "Well, old man, it has been good talking to you. Now see that you turn up, mind." He chuckled. "If you don't, we might just have to come along and drag you out."

"I wouldn't do that."

"Let's hope we don't have to." Fletcher waved his hand, walked away, pausing only long enough to call, "Don't you let us down now," before he was gone.

Left alone, Edmund shivered in the cold night air, aware he had conceded, yet not being quite sure how. Later, when he went below and attempted to explain the occurrence to Anna, he found himself incapable of doing so.

"You thought they were dreadful enough at Lyme, Edmund,"

Anna reminded him. "I can't imagine what you're doing with them here."

"I am not doing anything with them," Edmund replied. "I refused his damned invitation several times but it made absolutely no difference."

"Why did you not merely say no?"

Edmund shrugged helplessly. "I was unable to," he admitted. "It would have sounded churlish."

"Dear Edmund." Anna's voice was maternal. "You never could be rude to someone who was being pleasant."

"It is not that. The fellow actually threatened to come along and drag, yes, drag was the word he used, drag us away to his wretched gathering."

"In that case you had better go along."

"What would you do?"

"I shall wait for you," Anna replied. "You do not intend being late, I trust?"

"I do not intend going."

"I think you do," Anna observed.

So it was that Edmund Blackstone found himself in an overcrowded stateroom, a glass of champagne in hand, talking to Beryl Fletcher. Edmund had changed into evening wear for the occasion and as he stood beneath chandeliers rocking smoothly in the ship's movement, amid the elegance of ladies and the assurance of men, watching white-jacketed waiters glide briskly, seeing the glint of brasswork and the gleam of silver, he felt he had returned to a world from which he had long been absent. About him others laughed, talked, drank, smoked, picked at hors d'oeuvres, celebrated their transition from one year to the other. A woman with a lorgnette nodded and Edmund returned the greeting, neither knowing who she was nor greatly caring. He found it strangely restful to be surrounded by such normality, such elementary preoccupation with meaningless detail, such trivia.

Upon his arrival, Geoffrey Fletcher had greeted him cheerfully. "I knew you'd come, old man," he said. "Got to get back into the world, you know." Fletcher peered over Edmund's shoulder. "Didn't bring the little woman, I see," he accused.

"She would rather remain in the cabin."

"That's no way to spend New Year's Eve," Fletcher said loudly. "Couldn't you persuade her?"

"I think she'd prefer to be left alone."

"Really?" Fletcher laughed and clapped Edmund on the back. "We'll have to see what can be done about that."

Fletcher led Edmund across the room, made introductions, pressed a drink into his hand, saw that he ate something and handed him over to his wife, and Edmund passed a bemused half hour listening to Beryl Fletcher chat endlessly and frivolously about anything at all that came to mind. Her only moment of seriousness was when Edmund arrived; then she took his hand, her eyes softened and she whispered her regret at the death of his son.

Edmund nodded solemnly, replied in kind, and after a minute or two of embarrassed stiffness the conversation turned, another subject was selected, and Edmund relaxed to the sound of Beryl's banal but comforting normality. So it was with a feeling of shock, some time later, that he lifted his head to see Anna standing by the door being effusively ushered in by Geoffrey Fletcher.

"Excuse me," Edmund said immediately. "My wife has arrived." He was seized by a sensation so eerie it was physical; he felt his hand grip the glass more tightly, felt his lips stiffen. All the activity in the room was suddenly no more than a charade, a masquerade, a performance which lacked reality. None of the men with their cigars and glasses, none of the women with their skirts and smiles, were related to the horror the Blackstones knew. Edmund could not believe he had allowed himself to be seduced so readily, nor that Anna could possibly have left the cabin unless some new disaster had occurred. "I must speak to her immediately," he said.

"She's here? Oh, good," Beryl said merrily. "I'm so pleased."

"She intended to remain in her cabin." Edmund's voice shook. Then seeing the bright expression on Beryl's face he added, "Did you know she was coming?"

"I had certainly hoped so," Beryl said cheerfully. "When you arrived alone, Geoffrey thought he might be able to work something." She smiled with tiny mischief. "He was determined to get you both along. And when Geoffrey's determined he seldom fails."

"I must go to her." Edmund left Beryl, who, with a little giggle, followed as he pushed across the crowded room to Anna. She stood, her face drawn and anxious, half-talking to Fletcher, half-searching for her husband. When she saw Edmund, relief flooded and she held out an eager hand. "Oh, Edmund," she said, "I'm so glad you are all right."

"*Me, all right?*" Edmund frowned. "I don't understand."

Geoffrey Fletcher's chuckle interrupted. "I'm afraid it's all my fault, old man," he said heartily. "I take all the blame for going and bringing Anne along. But I just couldn't leave her sitting there all on her lonesome, you know."

Edmund's face paled with anger. "What did you tell her?" he demanded.

"He told me I was needed." Anna stared at Geoffrey Fletcher with distaste. "He was very careful not to be specific but he distinctly gave me the impression that you were ill."

"You fool." Edmund's angry face glared at Fletcher. "What right do you imagine you have to behave like this?"

"No, don't get on your high horse," Geoffrey said cheerfully, success elating him. "I merely told her, well, that you might need her, that's all." He laughed and pointed at Edmund's angry face. "And by the look of you, I'd say I was right. Wouldn't you, old gel?" he asked, turning to his wife, who nodded her agreement.

"*Is* everything all right?" Edmund asked Anna quickly. "There is no other reason for your being here?"

"None at all. I was told you needed assistance."

"The crass fool."

"Talking about me, old man?" Fletcher said happily. He laughed and touched Anna's arm. "Now let me get you a little something to drink, my dear."

"Nothing, thank you," Anna replied. "I must return to the cabin."

"So must I," said Edmund.

"Now, now, now." Geoffrey Fletcher put an arm on each of them. "What's all this?" He smiled broadly. "Takes all my ingenuity to get you along and now you're off without even toasting the New Year." He shook his head sadly. "That is no way to be. In fact, I shan't allow it." He beckoned a steward. "Champagne for both these good people," he said. "And be quick about it, my man."

"Good God." Edmund's anger made him slightly ridiculous amid the smiling faces, the conversation, the warmth. "Was there any need to go to those lengths?"

"If I hadn't, old man," said Fletcher, "the lovely Anne would not be here at all. Would she now?"

"That is hardly the point. And her name is Anna," Edmund said icily.

"Exactly the point," continued Fletcher imperturbably as the steward arrived with champagne. Taking a glass, he handed it, with a small bow, to Anna. "There you are, my dear. I insist you have at least that before you go."

"Very well," Anna murmured, background, breeding, education not permitting her to act otherwise. "I shall take just this."

"That's better." Fletcher raised his glass. "The best to you both for a great and auspicious New Year." He drank, laughed and added, "Which I have no doubt it will be."

It was some moments more before Edmund was able to speak to Anna alone. Then he edged closer and whispered, "Is everything really all right?"

"I imagine so," Anna replied. "When that dreadful man arrived with his story of you needing me I made him wait a moment while I checked that both the locks on the casket were in place. Also, I secured the cabin door myself. The key is in my handbag."

Edmund sighed. "You have done well, Anna," he said. "But we must not remain here."

They were unable to escape readily. Geoffrey Fletcher and the laughing Beryl erected a constant barrier between the Blackstones and their exit. It became a game with them. Their determination grew as the minutes passed, until Edmund, white-faced and thin-lipped, said, "I am sorry, but we really must go."

"I understand, old man," Fletcher said, beckoning another steward. "Just one for the road, or should I say the deck?"

"No, thank you."

"Why the tearing hurry, old chap? Nothing to worry about, is there?"

"What do you mean?" Edmund asked, too quickly.

"Precisely that. Nothing to go wrong, what? Understand how you feel with all these people about. Feel the same way myself, but there's no real need to rush back to that cabin of yours, is there?"

"Well, no." Edmund caught Anna's worried look. "Of course not, it's merely that . . . "

"In that case, have one more. Just one, I promise, then I'll let you go."

Geoffrey Fletcher clicked his fingers and a waiter appeared with champagne. While the man attended to the Blackstones, Fletcher took his wife momentarily aside. "Listen, old gel," he said, "they do seem a touch overanxious about that son of theirs, what? Why don't we send the daughter along for a bit? Sit with the little feller, take a watch, that sort of thing. Sarah won't mind, she used to be very fond of the little chap, eh?" He winked confidentially at his wife.

"That's such a kind thought, Geoffrey," Beryl agreed.

"Send the girl along then, eh? And give her a key? Saw Anne lock their door, but all these cabin locks are much the same, if you want my opinion. One of ours should do the trick."

Beryl Fletcher smiled, lifted her pearl-entwined head and kissed her husband gently. "I'll do that right away," she said and disappeared.

As the Blackstones uneasily remained in the Fletchers' stateroom, waiting their moment of escape, Sarah Fletcher stood staring at the elaborate casket which contained the Moonchild. She had gone to the Blackstones' cabin immediately she had been asked, aware of a new responsibility, fascinated by the mystery of her task, but, in spite of her father's confidence, the lock on the cabin door had not responded to the key she carried. Sarah Fletcher tried several times without success. It fitted easily enough but failed to turn and the child was about to retrace her steps to the stateroom when a white-coated steward, carrying a tray of caviar, appeared.

"Having trouble, miss?" he inquired.

"Yes I am," Sarah replied. "I think Papa's given me the wrong key."

"Never mind." The steward took a ring of keys from his pocket with a free hand and opened the Blackstones' door. "There you are."

"Thank you." Sarah Fletcher looked up with round eyes.

"Not at all. Anything for a lady." The steward made a small mocking bow and started down the corridor. "A happy New Year to you, miss," he called.

"Happy New Year," Sarah Fletcher replied and entered the cabin.

In the dim interior her eyes went directly to the coffin with its heavily carved woodwork, glint of rhinestone, dull bloom of malachite; she was deeply awed by the knowledge that it contained unshared secrets, undreamed-of surprises.

Sarah Fletcher had never seen a dead body. Death was one of the mysteries that still required explanation. There had been a kitten once which had died, and a dog she had seen from a carriage window lying prone by the side of the roadway, but never a human being. On one occasion she had gone with her parents to the funeral of a friend, and the solemnity, the darkness, the overpowering ritual of the process had absorbed her. She had wondered what the body looked like in its long, black box but could imagine nothing at all. The flowers, the dress, the hushed voices, the pervading, heavy music told her clearly that death was an important state, that a body must be greatly respected to engender such theater. So now, as she stood at the casket, she wondered if she dare lift the lid of the beautiful box and peep inside.

It would do no harm, she reasoned. No one need ever know. It wasn't even as if the body were that of a stranger. She had known Simon, had played with him on the pebbled beach; heard his laughter. It was right that she should take a final look at what was left of her memories.

Very slowly, her heart beating rapidly, Sarah Fletcher moved a little closer to the casket. Her mouth opened with curiosity, the pink tip of her tongue peeped from between her lips. She was a plumpish child with her father's open, round face, and she stared at the casket as if it contained every secret she had ever wanted to know.

It has a silver clasp, she noted. And it didn't seem to be very hard to open. She could lift it instantly. In a moment.

Tentatively, as if teasing, as if she had not quite made up her mind and was waiting to see what first contact would offer, Sarah Fletcher reached out and with one fingertip traced the lines of carving from the lid of the casket, down one side to the base; she allowed the finger to touch a glinting rhinestone, let it rest a moment on cool green malachite; her face was vivid with concentration, her tongue licked her inquisitive lips. Slowly she came closer, opened her hand and placed it flat on the side of the casket, her concentration, her exquisite fear so charged that a shiver ran through her and she gasped audibly.

There, she said to herself. Nothing's happened. It can't be as bad as they want me to believe. It won't hurt to open it, just a little. It won't hurt anyone to have a tiny look.

She placed both hands on the casket and brought them slowly together, running them delicately over the carved surface until they came to rest, one on either side of the silver clasp. Then Sarah Fletcher began to play with the clasp, teasing it open, toying with its parts, so that should it come undone in her hands she might consider herself less blameful.

I wonder how he looks, she thought. Her hands teased and pushed, pulled and idled, until the silver clasp lay free and open and she imagined all that remained between her and the secrets she was so desperate to discover was the simple lifting of the lid. She stared at it hesitantly for a long time. Finally she reached forward, and, with the same infinite slowness, the same indirectness, she played with the lid.

In the Fletchers' crowded stateroom, between walls of conversation, waves of laughter, bright smiles on ready faces, Anna Blackstone suddenly said to her husband, "I must go immediately, Edmund. I cannot stay a moment longer." There was genuine fear in her voice.

"What has distressed you?"

Anna shook her head. "I have this dreadful premonition something awful is about to happen." Her face had paled and her hand trembled.

"What is it?" Edmund took her hands; they were cold. He peered at her face; it was almost gray. "Anna, are you ill?"

"I do not know." Anna's voice dropped to a harsh whisper. "Take me away from here at once."

"Of course."

Edmund gripped Anna's elbow and began to thread through

the crowd, pushing past a back, easing by a shoulder, smiling stiffly as he interrupted conversations, once muttering an apology as a glass jolted and champagne spilled, all the time aware of Anna's growing panic.

"Do you feel faint?" Edmund asked.

"Yes, but I am unsure why." Anna shuddered. "I merely know I must return to the cabin immediately."

"Has it something to do with Simon?"

"I am dreadfully afraid it may."

Edmund pressed forward, but it seemed to take an infinitely long time to reach the stateroom door. There were more people than he thought possible; the festive crowd was thick, unmovable. Finally, as they were about to exit, the florid face of Geoffrey Fletcher appeared, smiling, before them.

"Hello," he said loudly. "Going without saying goodbye?"

"I am afraid we must," replied Edmund.

"Wouldn't think of letting you." Fletcher lifted his head and peered about the room. "Where's Beryl, I wonder?" he said. "She'd feel awful, letting you slip away."

"I am sorry." Edmund's voice was tight. He felt Anna's pain, she shivered like a trapped animal. "Please . . . "

"Wouldn't think of it."

"I did say *Please*." Edmund's voice was like a rasp, his eyes were cold. "Now, get out of my way."

"I say—" Fletcher's heavy face sagged—"that's no way . . . "

"If you don't get out of my way I shall knock you down," said Edmund. "Do I make myself clear?"

"Blackstone?" Fletcher sounded uncertain. "What *is* this all about?"

"You would not understand."

"At least do me the courtesy of an explanation."

"Oh, shut up, you idiot," Edmund said, his temper snapping. "Move yourself, immediately."

Fletcher did, his eyes round with surprise, his jaw hanging. He stared stupidly at the backs of Edmund and Anna Blackstone hurrying down the corridor. "Well, I'll be damned," he said as his wife arrived.

"What is the matter, Geoffrey?" Beryl asked. "Have the Blackstones gone?"

"They certainly have." Fletcher ran a hand over his face. "Had some sort of tiff, I shouldn't be surprised."

"The poor people, it must be such a strain."

"I am sure it must."

"Never mind, come along." She lifted her pearled head. "We've other guests to attend to."

"Coming, old gel." Fletcher, rebuffed by the departing backs, the sound of heels echoing down the long corridor, said, "I shall draw their attention to this next time I see them. Just you see if I don't."

Hurriedly, moving with an urgency she did not understand, Anna followed the course of the corridors toward their cabin. She knew only of an overwhelming sense of doom, of disaster, of the need to leave the crowded stateroom and return to where she had come from, immediately, compulsively.

"Anna?" Edmund questioned, hurrying beside her. "What possesses you?"

Anna shook her head vigorously; her face was set, molded. Edmund had never seen it so determined. "I do not know what it is," she said. "I only know I must return immediately." She lifted her skirts to facilitate progress, obsessed by the need for haste.

"Are you *sure* it's Simon?"

Anna bustled forward. "I cannot say, Edmund," she said as she moved. "If I could I should tell you. Please do not delay me." Her voice was on the edge of control.

Edmund said nothing further but walked swiftly by Anna's side. They turned a corner, passed a steward carrying an ice bucket, who was forced to pause, lean away from them, as they swept by. They climbed broad wooden stairs with inlaid panelwork to the deck above. They strode down a further corridor toward their cabin, looking at the numbers they passed, straining to reach their destination a second or two sooner until, finally, they arrived at their cabin door, where, without pause or hesitation, Anna threw it open.

"Stop," she cried as she entered, not knowing why or to whom. "Stop that immediately."

Sarah Fletcher screamed.

With both inquisitive hands on the casket, the clasp undone, her heart pounding with excitement, Sarah Fletcher was about to discover the secret lock. She had tested the weight of the lid and found it unmovable; she had pushed at it with increasing force until she realized the silver clasp was not all that held it in place; so slowly, inch by inch, her seeking hands had explored the details of the casket, remembering stories she had read, tales she had been told of magic clasps and secret openings. With each little failure, with each passing second, her excitement had grown, and when her hands reached the rose in the center of the casket she knew instinctively that she had found what she was looking for. Now, when she was on the point of opening the casket completely and discovering its ultimate secret, the door behind her was flung wide and a voice she did not know called harshly for her to stop. The shock was too great. She screamed, turned, her face white with fear, and burst into tears.

"Who are you?" Anna demanded.

"Sarah Fletcher." The child was terrified. "Papa sent me . . ."

"You stupid little creature," Anna cried, moving forward like a storm. "Have you opened this?"

The girl wailed and shook her head. "I couldn't," she sobbed.

"Thank God for that," Anna said harshly, putting the silver clasp into place. "You'll never know how lucky you were."

"I . . . I was only looking after it."

"Who let you in?"

"Papa. He . . . he gave me a key." Sarah's sobbing heaved, her face collapsed. "I want . . . to . . . go home."

"And so you shall, my dear," said Edmund, taking a handkerchief from his pocket and wiping the child's tears. "I shall see you home at once." His voice was gentle with relief.

"I want . . ." Sarah's chest heaved with sobs. "I want . . . Papa."

"You shall have him," Edmund assured her. "Come with me."

He took the child by the hand and led her toward the Fletchers' stateroom. Sarah paused once to look back with longing and dread at the casket which had fascinated, and the face which had terrified; then she accompanied Edmund along the endless corridors, sobbing relentlessly, the handkerchief pressed to her swollen face. Only when they were within sight and sound of the Fletchers' stateroom did her manner alter. Her sobbing increased, rose to a frenzy and, leaving Edmund, she ran a ragged path towards her parents' cabin and burst in, howling as if possessed. Edmund paused, saw her enter, then turned and went back to Anna, the casket and the doom it contained.

When he returned he found Anna seated stiff, rigid with fear; her face was pinched, drawn back along the cheekbones; she held her hands together as if afraid to move them apart.

"Anna?" Edmund went to her. "The child is unharmed. There is nothing to fear."

"There is everything to fear. It was so close."

Edmund took his wife's hands; they were like ice. "But she is safe. She discovered nothing." His words attempted comfort.

"She would have." Anna's lips barely moved. "They, all of them, will in time." She gripped Edmund by the wrists suddenly. "Don't you see, Edmund? Do you not understand? They will *all* discover a way to open the casket because . . . Simon, or whatever it is he has become, wishes it, guides them." She shivered. "There is a dreadful force within that casket, Edmund. I felt it the whole length of the ship."

"Anna?" Edmund's eyes were fearful. "How could that possibly be?"

"I do not know, but for the first time *I* felt its terrible power."

"Anna . . . ?"

"Hold me." Anna stood unsteadily and extended her arms. "Hold me please."

Immediately, almost roughly, Edmund clasped her, holding her, sharing the desperation, saying nothing, for there was nothing to say; keeping her as the steamer churned onward through the changing night, the drifting sounds of music, laughter, the faint crashing of the sea.

CHAPTER TEN

THE following morning, New Year's Day, the Blackstones
awoke to the sound of foghorns, the creak of ropes, the slapping
of water against the sides of the ship. The air was rich with the
oily smell of port water. They had slept, crushed together, clinging through the long, rocking night, and now, pale, drained with
anxiety, they lifted their faces and peered through the gloom
of an English early-winter morning.

The sight cheered them. The sound of Southampton dockside
voices rising above the hurly-burly of activity, the familiar dis-
plays of commercial signs, were welcoming aspects of home, like
furniture known from childhood. Thos. Cook & Sons seemed as
old friends.

The steamer was already at berth, linked to the soil they were
seeking, bound to the earth they had toiled to reach. Edmund
stood by a porthole and filled his lungs with the smoky, used
industrial air, and it lifted him. "Come along, Anna," he said,
mustering heart. "We have much to do this day." He turned
hopefully to Anna, seeking response.

"I am with you, Edmund," Anna replied. She took a deep
breath. "Let us begin."

"I shall start with breakfast," said Edmund briskly. "Something very English."

Anna smiled a small, brave smile. "God bless you, Edmund," she said softly.

They sat down to kidneys and bacon, crisp toast, marmalade and tea. Only once during the meal did they allow the courage they had summoned to falter and permit the terror they held in so tight a rein to stand clearly between them.

"You have not been further troubled by the . . . ?" Edmund hesitated, picked up a cup. "By the—force—you felt last evening?"

Anna turned her face away. "I have not been further troubled, as you say," she replied carefully. "But I feel it still, Edmund, in a manner I have not been aware of before."

Edmund sipped tea. "We are both becoming overwrought," he said evasively. "The strain has been immense."

Anna nodded slightly, unconvinced.

"You, in particular . . . "

"Perhaps you are right." Anna's voice was brittle. It was clear she wished to close the matter, resume the pose they had both adopted on sight of the land they sought. "It cannot be anything more than that."

"I trust not." Edmund replaced the cup on its saucer; the noise seemed unnaturally loud. "We are so close to success."

"I hope so," Anna replied. "With all my heart, I hope so."

Edmund Blackstone glanced at the shuttered face of his wife and was silent. Outside, beyond the ship's side, herring gulls cried their guttural cries and dived for jetsam.

After breakfast Edmund contacted the chief purser, who advised that there were two trains available for Tonbridge that morning, both of which required changing to a branch line at Woking. One left at 8:07 and the other at 10:13. Edmund decided to take the second, which would bring them to their destination about four in the afternoon. Presuming they were in Tonbridge before dark, there seemed no cause for concern; once there, they had several days in which to locate the place for burial and arrange for it to be effected.

Later, a porter was sent for, who unloaded the luggage. Formally dressed as befitting a couple returning the body of their son to its native soil, the Blackstones watched hands bear the casket from the cabin, down the gangplank, onto the dock.

A horse-drawn carriage took them to Southampton Station where they boarded the train effortlessly, without disturbance. They could have been as they appeared: a well-endowed, middle-class couple with an elaborate casket over which they took inordinate care, which, considering its rareness and beauty, caused no wonder. Having passed through English Customs, Edmund felt no obligation to further declare the contents of the handsome box—the less known about it in Tonbridge the better. Once in the town, that which had to be done could be taken care of as quietly and as smoothly as possible.

From their railway compartment the Blackstones watched the flat, winter-brown Hampshire countryside pass, saw black rooks, stark against a leaden sky, flung from their trees by engine noise. The trees themselves, leafless and bare against tailored grassland, held the hollow sky with slender branches. Smoke rose from chimneys and a solitary plowman wended his harsh way.

"I am beginning to feel confident," Edmund confessed as the train steamed through Basingstoke. "I believe we shall surmount our difficulties after all."

Anna's glance flickered toward her husband. "Have you thought of what we must do when we arrive at Tonbridge?" she asked.

"Well, not exactly." Edmund raised his eyes to the paneled ceiling. "Simon was born in the house in Willow Street. It is to there he will be returned."

"Will that be difficult?"

"I believe not," Edmund replied cautiously, wishing to avoid further strain. He noted the rings below Anna's eyes, the taut flesh of her face: something was happening to her, something new that he did not understand. "If there are problems, I believe we shall overcome them, so long as we retain our faith."

Anna relaxed a little. "You are right, Edmund," she conceded. "We must continue to believe that what we are doing will succeed."

"It will."

Anna sighed and turned her eyes to the passing landscape. "It was an ordinary enough birth," she recalled quietly. "Doctor Paley was in attendance. Why it should have turned out this way I shall never understand." She fell quiet, her voice faded, and she sat as a statue watching the countryside pass.

In this sober frame of mind they changed trains at Woking and traveled the remainder of their journey through thickening English dusk. They passed graying shapes of hedgerows, clusters of houses: some with smoke spiraling from chimneys, others with light peeping between curtains. At Tonbridge the train steamed slowly into the station. Hills rose soft and pastel in the cold, misty winter air; the shape of the yellow Norman castle bulked out of the burgeoning dark; lights streamed down hillsides. In the gentle, rustling, numbed and cushioned sounds of evening, the Blackstones felt a surge of substance, as if the object of the long and painful journey was now to be fulfilled.

"Oh, Edmund," said Anna as they left the compartment. "We are at last here, are we not? We are at last home?"

"We are, my dear." Edmund watched porters bear luggage: the casket, the cases, their pieces from the carriage. "It may seem unbelievable, but we are finally in Tonbridge."

So saying, he took her arm and together they walked the length of the platform, past yellow brick booking offices and waiting rooms, toward the grimy stone exit where the heavily built, moustached and somber figure of Inspector Leopold Fuchs in his tall hat and black cape waited beneath the yellow glow of a station lamp.

INSPECTOR Fuchs had recognized the Blackstones immediately. Their air of anxiety, their concern with their luggage told him at once who they were. As he watched them descend, hold each other and begin to walk toward him, he recognized their vulnerability.

When they drew abreast, Fuchs stepped forward. "Do I have the honor of addressing Mr. and Mrs. Blackstone?" he asked politely, his English faintly accented, precise.

Edmund stopped, white-faced. He felt Anna's fingers grip; his heart turned painfully. "I beg your pardon?" he managed to say.

"You are Mr. Blackstone?"

"Edmund Blackstone, yes."

"I am Inspector Leopold Fuchs of the Munich Municipal Police," Fuchs explained as gently as he could. "I am afraid I must ask you some questions."

Edmund stood still with shock. Anna gave a little cry, like a defeated child. Her knees shook, her jaw trembled. Edmund, feeling her strength ebbing, willed control as he examined the heavy, solemn face of Inspector Fuchs and wondered what lay behind the man's words, what threat his unknown mind contained.

"I deeply regret any inconvenience I may cause," Fuchs continued. "But if I am correct, you have arrived from Le Havre this morning? You have come overnight from Germany?"

"That is correct," confirmed Edmund, keeping his voice steady. "What do you want with us?"

"The truth." Fuchs smiled gently. "It is all I ever ask for."

"Do you have any reason to suspect we might withhold it?"

Fuchs's smile remained. "No, Mr. Blackstone, I do not." He glanced from the Blackstones' anxious faces to the knot of porters standing patiently, waiting for further instructions. "I have spoken to the stationmaster here," he continued. "He has kindly permitted me the use of his office." He indicated the porters. "Perhaps, if you were to tell them to wait, we could continue our conversation where it would be a little more private. And a little warmer." As he spoke, he felt the Blackstones' pain and knew he was right not to involve others. The local police were unaware of his visit.

"Very well." Anna sounded defeated. "Let us go inside."

"One moment," challenged Edmund. "*Why* do you wish to question us?"

Inspector Fuchs's eyes were sad. "I had hoped you might be more cooperative," he said slowly.

"In what sense?"

"In every sense." Fuchs's gaze was steady. "For I believe you know what questions I am forced to ask."

"Is it about Simon?" whispered Anna. "Is that what this is all about?"

"Was that your son's name?"

"Yes."

"Do you have the body with you?"

"Yes." Anna's eyes went to the casket. "We have brought it all the way from Bavaria." Her breath caught. "It was essential. Do you realize that?"

"I know little," replied Fuchs. "Hardly a thing. When I spoke to Dr. Kabel, he was not a well man."

"Dr. Kabel?" queried Edmund.

"The doctor from the village."

"How strange." Edmund's voice was almost idle. "I never knew his name." About them was the final bustle of departing passengers. The porters clung to the luggage. Hillsides were smoothed with dusk, houses were beginning to live with light. The evening air was becoming heavy with the smell of chimney smoke. Shapes moved in and out of doorways. Edmund studied the scene as if he might never see any of it again and needed to imprint each detail on his memory. He breathed out slowly. "Very well," he said. "Let us go to the stationmaster's office, where you may ask your questions."

"Thank you," said Fuchs. "That is considerate."

"We do not really have any choice."

The stationmaster's office was small. There was a littered desk, shelves filled with papers. In one corner a small fire burned, and Fuchs took up a position with his back to it. The luggage, including the casket, was placed on the floor. The Blackstones sat on bentwood chairs. They stared at Fuchs and waited.

Inspector Leopold Fuchs examined the Blackstones for what seemed an unusually long time. Now that they were finally before him, figures of flesh and shape, color and variety, no longer shadows flitting across Europe, he was unsure where to begin. Their anxiety was evident, their vulnerability clear. The manner in which they sat was resigned, patient, defeated. They were like prisoners. For the first time in his long career Inspector Fuchs disliked what he had to do.

"Well?" It was Edmund who began. "Now that you have us here, what is it you wish?"

"I will begin by informing you that I have four deaths to account for." Fuchs' voice was even, polite, friendly. "That, you might say, is the basis of my inquiry."

There was a small, pitted silence. "Four?" Edmund questioned. "I know of only three." His eyes went to Anna.

"Your son also died," Fuchs pointed out.

Edmund's whole body stiffened. "We are not unaware of the fact," he said tersely. "What purpose does that information serve?"

"Try to understand," Fuchs continued. "My knowledge is scanty, almost impossible to fit together. There was no thread to follow. No logic. And always there is a semblance of logic somewhere, however twisted it might be." He shrugged, looking at them both. "You must have some idea of what it was like, coming from the outside?"

Edmund sat very still. "There is no sense to any of it," he said softly. "What is it you *do* know? Tell us. It could not be more grotesque than what has actually happened."

Fuchs cleared his throat and related the facts as he knew them. As they listened, the Blackstones remained unmoved, blank, unresponsive. Their expressions gave Fuchs nothing. Both appeared saturated; they had heard it all before.

Fuchs paused, studying them, probing. What he needed was something to unlock the Blackstones' silence, some key to their numb, leaden isolation. Apart from Edmund's one oblique admission they had given nothing away.

"That is almost as much as I know," Fuchs said, after a moment. "What can you add to it?"

Edmund Blackstone shrugged slightly, glanced at Anna's defeated face. "There is nothing to add. The details as you express them are accurate." His voice was distant, remote, uncommitted.

Inspector Fuchs nodded. He breathed deeply and quite suddenly altered his manner, put aside politeness, added challenge to his words.

"Whatever you might or might not tell me," he said abruptly, "whatever your version turns out to be, I can only construe as most callous your abandoning of your servant's body without the slightest concern for care or burial." He watched the effect of his words.

"That is untrue." Anna responded. "We did what we could."

"Really?"

"Quiet, Anna." Edmund's face was stiff. "He would not understand. That earlier act of kindness of his was only one of his methods. Likewise this brusqueness is merely to provoke."

Fuchs, silent, stood and listened. Some corridor was open, some door had been unlocked.

"He is a police inspector," Edmund continued bluntly. "He has an official job to attend to. How can you expect him to understand what has happened to us? Dear God, we do not even understand it ourselves."

"Oh, Edmund." Anna sounded as if they were alone. "I am so tired, so weary of all this. We have neither rested nor relaxed since I cannot remember when. And now, just when we are so close to what we have come for, we are frustrated. I do not think I can stand much more."

Fuchs lifted his head so that his gaze went past the Black-stones. He was close and he knew it. When he spoke he addressed the littered shelves behind them. "What *has* happened to your son?" he asked and felt an electricity in the air. The shock of his question crackled. "*What actually occurred?*"

"What do you mean?" said Edmund.

"What I ask," Fuchs stated. "No more."

Edmund stared at the tall figure gazing seemingly at nothing.

"Well?" Fuchs persisted. "Answer my question."

"He died," Edmund replied. "You know that as well as I do."

"As *well* as you?"

"Yes." Edmund's voice was cold as night air. "If you have spoken to the doctor, he will have told you what happened to Simon."

Fuchs lowered his eyes; he looked squarely at Edmund. "When I spoke to Dr. Kabel," he said, "the man had lost his reason. He acted, in fact, like someone *possessed. He was raving mad.*" Again Fuchs felt the electricity his words generated.

"*Possessed?*" Edmund breathed the word, to absorb, to control its significance. "Do you mean what you say?"

"The man was raving," Fuchs continued ruthlessly. "He was completely insane. He had destroyed his rooms, terrorized his servant, torn his books to shreds. He was as possessed as any man I have ever seen."

Anna whimpered as the short, harsh sentences fell. "Poor man," she whispered. "Poor, poor man." Her voice hung with pity.

"When I was finally able to talk with him he spoke of things I did not understand," Fuchs added. "He referred to a mystery which made no sense to me. He talked of hoof and claw. Guardians." Fuchs's eyes were hard. "Does *that* convey anything to you?"

Edmund looked like a shell. "What else did he tell you?" The force had gone from his voice.

"From what I could gather, he believed you had some sort of

mission to undertake concerning the body of your son. He spoke of taking the child home for burial and was obsessed with the urgency of getting it back to England." Fuchs disliked what he was doing, the anguish he caused, the deadly stillness in the room, but he sensed effectiveness. He was near to what he had come to discover. "However, it was difficult to comprehend the doctor," he continued. "The man was almost beyond assistance."

"Oh, my God," whimpered Anna. "He had done nothing but help us. He was in no way to blame."

"To blame for what?"

"For what happened." Anna was hushed, crippled, still; she spoke as if in a confessional. "It was not his fault he became involved. The old woman sent us to him, that was all."

"You are now talking of the same mysteries," Fuchs said. "I do not understand."

"Nor do we," said Edmund and recognized Anna and himself for what they might seem to have become: hunted, fugitive, callous. The moment filled him with despair. "Neither of us understands," he said simply. "Our actions have been based on the belief that they were necessary. No more than that."

"Please explain them."

"All we have done?"

"Everything," said Fuchs.

For a long moment the room was crystallized, stilled with the unspoken force of words yet to be uttered. Then Edmund breathed deeply, preparing for the ordeal. "Have you ever heard the term 'Moonchild'?" he asked. His voice rasped suddenly, filling the barrier between himself and the inspector, exposing them both.

"Moonchild?"

"That is what my husband said." Anna's face was lifted; there was nothing to hide from now. *"It is the term the doctor used."*

Inspector Fuchs felt the hair on the back of his neck respond like a dog's, in fear, in caution; along the line of his jaw ran the cold tremor of impending evil. Deliberately he turned away from the Blackstones and examined a piece of paper on the desk beside him, to consciously still the beating of his heart, to create a small hiatus in his emotions. The paper his hand had turned was a report of new rail work being carried out in Tonbridge, of houses which were to be removed to make way for a new rail station, of destruction and the earth-moving equipment necessary. The words made no sense to Inspector Fuchs, they blurred and ran together; their meaning seemed no part of the charged room, of the sense of evil, of the resurrection of the nightmare he had tried to avoid. Fuchs shivered. He was suddenly afraid.

"Well?" Edmund's voice was relentless. "Have you heard of a Moonchild before?"

Slowly Fuchs returned his gaze to the Blackstones. He shook his head.

"Would you care for me to expound on the condition?" Edmund continued in the same biting tone. "After all, a German inspector of police should know all there is about such creatures. There is no knowing when the information might prove invaluable."

Fuchs held both hands before him and closed his eyes. "Please," he urged. "Do not attempt to punish me for all that has happened to you. I am only doing what is required of me. I am not responsible for your sufferings."

Edmund swallowed and looked away. The plea the German inspector made was for them all, for each contained in the stationmaster's shabby office.

"Listen to me, both of you." Fuchs cleared his throat. "Slowly I am beginning to . . . comprehend." He breathed deeply, absorbing what he could, piece by piece. "Tell me, what did the doctor mean when he spoke of bringing the . . . child home? Of burying it in the place where it was born?" His look was for assistance, a lead into darkness. "It *is* what he said, no? He did speak of taking your son back to where he was born?"

"That is what must be done to put a Moonchild to rest," Edmund answered, his voice empty now, bleak. "It is not what a

Moonchild does, you understand. That is a different matter." There was no venom left, no search for reparation, merely a relentlessly sustained injury. "They are worlds apart."

"What is the difference?"

"The knowledge may not assist your official investigations."

"Tell me nevertheless."

Edmund Blackstone shivered. "We have been told that Simon must be buried exactly on the spot on which he was born. He must be buried there as quickly as possible. Before his seventh birthday, it seems."

"When is that?"

"January the seventh. Unless you delay us, we have time in which to conduct the burial."

"I see." Inspector Fuchs touched his moustache. "And the location of the exact position for this burial?"

"I know where he was born." Edmund's mind raced; he saw the ends of corridors, the shutting of blinds. "We had a house by the river, not far from here."

"And you would bury him beneath it?"

Edmund nodded with more confidence than he felt; nothing would defeat his purpose at this stage. Whatever barriers the German inspector raised would be overcome. "I do not see why not. It should not prove impossible." The challenge recharged him.

Anna's eyes went to Fuchs; beneath his heavy official surface she detected a willingness to help. "What will you do with us?" she asked levelly.

Inspector Fuchs chewed the ends of his moustache. "What is it you have to do exactly?" he asked. "Apart from burying your son?" His head went to one side, questioning.

"Nothing. That is all we ever needed to do."

Fuchs nodded. "I take it, from what Mr. Blackstone has told me, your son requires a special burial. It is a matter of some ritual, no?" His eyes remained on Anna, reserving Edmund, keeping him remote.

"Yes," Anna replied, her voice strained. "That is so."

"I see." Fuchs hesitated. "And I gather your son has undergone some sort of alteration? Is that correct?"

"He has undergone a *monstrous* alteration." Edmund's voice shredded, the words chilled Fuchs; he was aware of a new fear: a simple basic hatred of the dark.

"How?" he asked and felt his lips frame the words.

"There would appear no answer to that."

"But . . . it has occurred?"

"More fearfully than anything you could possibly imagine. More horribly than anything you have ever encountered." Edmund's eyes burned. "Does that answer your questions, Inspector? *Does that solve your mystery?*"

Fuchs held his response as if it were a glass of liquid he was compelled to carry unspilled. He breathed deeply. "Are you suggesting that what has happened to your son, or whatever it is he has become, is in some way responsible for the deaths of the others?" His words were received so calmly that in one clear instant Fuchs realized the Blackstones were beyond any shock they might contain. His inquiry held no horror. "Do you really want me to believe that what you call a Moonchild caused the deaths of your governess, a coachman and a stationmaster from Troyes?" Fuchs felt himself beginning to sweat.

"That is correct," Edmund's voice was even. "Simon, our son, killed all three."

"After he, himself, was dead?"

"Yes." Beside him Edmund felt Anna tremble. What they had been forced themselves to believe became a new horror when admitted to a stranger. It was their final exposure. "Simon died and became a Moonchild." Edmund held himself steady. "Or he died because he was a Moonchild. No one seems to know. As a Moonchild, he killed. He is possessed, you understand? He is not responsible for his actions, however evil those actions might be."

"God in Heaven." Fuchs felt the need to cross himself. "That is diabolical."

"What our son has become is undoubtedly the work of the devil."

"You are sure?"

"Certain."

"Do you realize how enormous this is?" Fuchs felt sweat roll beneath his arms. "What you are asking me to accept is . . . hideous."

"You have no choice but to accept it," Edmund continued, strengthed by confession. "You may search for the rest of your life but will find no other explanation for the three deaths. No other exists, there is no alternative. Simon killed those unfortunate people. That is what happened."

Fuchs pressed his heavy hands together; their knuckles whitened. Acceptance was more difficult than he imagined. In spite of what he had heard, seen, reasoned, the admission of a creature such as a Moonchild in his own time, his area of responsibility, was insane, impudent, outrageous. He could hear the shallow rasp of his own breath.

"It is true," Anna confirmed quietly.

"Are there others?" Fuchs asked, to lessen the immediacy. "More deaths than the three I know of?"

"No." Edmund's statement was clear. "There are no others."

"Are you sure?"

"The circumstances of each was quite unique. There could not have been others."

Avoiding the casket, the Blackstones, Inspector Fuchs walked to a grimy window. Pale, last evening light filtered the dying landscape. "If I were to accept what you have told me," he said slowly, "what evidence could you offer? What proof do you have?" Outside, a train went past—it seemed irrelevant, part of a world he had left.

Neither of the Blackstones replied. For a few raw moments the untidy office was silent. Skin scraped without sound; blood flowed cold and quiet. Then Fuchs turned from the grimy window and walked to the center of the room. "What *exactly* does that box contain?" he asked bluntly, pointing to the casket with the toe of his boot.

"The body of our son."

"Is that all?"

Anna's voice rose. *"That is more than enough."* Her words sent new ice through the room.

Fuchs shivered. "Would it assist me to examine it?" he asked, moving unconsciously away.

"It would kill you." Anna's voice pitched sharper. "Do you not yet understand?" Quickly she took up a position by the casket, protecting, shielding it like a bird before a nest. "What is in here is a monster. It is evil. It will kill you or anyone who opens the lid." Her hands came up in defense. "Don't you see, you stupid man, there is the *greatest danger in this casket.*"

"Madam, I am an inspector of police." Fuchs cleared his throat. "I require evidence. I need proof to persuade others. Understand me, I do not work alone."

Edmund went to Anna. "Could you not make your examination of the coachman and the railman? If you saw what had happened to them would that not be enough?"

Inspector Fuchs shook his head. "Not nearly enough," he said. "Nor is there anyone else I can question. The doctor who knew of your son's condition is mad. There is no other."

"There was the old woman."

"Where would we find her?"

"In the village."

"If she is as much a part of this as you wish me to believe," Fuchs said steadily, "she may not even exist at all."

"This is merciless." Anna buried her head in Edmund's shoulder. "It is without pity."

Fuchs sighed heavily. "Believe me, I wish to help. But, you

understand, I am not responsible for the law or what it insists must be done." He raised his hands in their gesture of appeal. "If, for example, I were to allow you to bury whatever that box contains, it would only be dug up again. If I have not seen what is in it, if I am not a witness, it will only be a matter of time before it is disinterred. And that, believe me, would be infinitely worse."

"Do *you* believe our story?"

Fuchs shrugged. "Enough," he said.

"Then would it not be sufficient," Edmund continued, "for you to report that the casket contained something so evil it had to be buried immediately?"

"You do not understand the bureaucratic process, Mr. Blackstone," the Inspector said wearily. "Reports would be needed. Questions would be asked. Descriptions would be required. Others, more cynical than myself, would need to be convinced." His hands moved eloquently, he felt less afraid on his own ground. "How could this possibly be achieved if all I was armed with, in the way of persuasion, was a secondhand belief?"

"You are sure?"

"I could not be more positive." Fuchs's mind was clear. He would allow them to continue *if* they supplied the evidence he needed. "Listen, they say that if you put a pearl in a glass of vinegar it will dissolve. That is one of the tests for a pearl. The only danger is that you lose the pearl before you know it is real. What you are doing is giving me a glass of vinegar and telling me it *contains* a pearl." He smiled knowingly. "It is not enough. You, Mr. Blackstone, who have some scientific background, know as well as I it is not enough."

"I cannot permit it. The consequences would be horrific."

"Whatever the consequences, you cannot prevent it," said Fuchs. "If need be, I will call the local constabulary and have you forcibly detained. I would regret such an action, it would benefit neither of us. But I am determined to do it if I have to."

"You idiot." Anna's voice filled the room once more. "Edmund has not told you, but light is deadly. Once a Moonchild is exposed to light you are doomed."

"What is this?" Fuchs bristled.

"It *begins* when there is light."

"I do not understand." He stared at the woman. "Please explain."

"What Anna says is true," said Edmund. "The Moonchild, despite its name, is a creature of darkness. In the dark, apparently, it may lie dormant. But when exposed to light, any light, it rises and will not rest until it has taken a life." The calmness of his explanation surprised him. "I do not understand any of it but I have every reason to believe that the creature's activities are triggered by light. Some sort of cycle is begun which ends in death. It has occurred three times and I am convinced it will happen again."

Inspector Leopold Fuchs put his head to one side as if balancing all he had heard, then shook it firmly. "I am sorry, Mr. Blackstone. Until this moment you had me almost convinced. But this last condition is too extreme. For what you are telling me is that the only way in which I may examine the contents of your box is in darkness, where I will not be able to see anything at all. Forgive me for doubting you, but I insist on opening that casket immediately." He shrugged massively, putting all doubt aside.

Slowly, despairingly, the Blackstones moved out of his way.

Inspector Fuchs stared down at the casket, fascinated in a new way, now it had come to this. The ornateness of the piece was charming, the rhinestones, the malachite, the heavy-petaled rose elegant. "Is this clasp, the silver one, all that keeps it closed?" he asked, and the words were dry in his mouth.

"There is one other, concealed," Edmund informed Fuchs woodenly. "It is opened by depressing the core of that rose in the center and turning it to the left."

"There are no others inside?"

"None. The lid hinges back."

"Interesting," Fuchs heard himself continue as if the voice were not his own, were part of another's conversation. "Silver is the metal of the moon, did you know that?"

"No."

"Why is . . . it called a *Moonchild?*"

"It is a lost creature." Edmund watched the heavy inspector delay the opening, flirt with fear, excitement. "It was born on a lost day related to a Callipic, a Greek, a calendar."

"Curious . . ."

"Please . . ." Anna whispered, shouted, cursed. Those outside, forgotten on the darkening platform, heard and turned and shifted their feet. "You stupid, damned man, open it. Go ahead, lift the lid. Do not continue with your ridiculous questions."

"Forgive my delay," said Fuchs almost humbly. His moment had come. He reached forward, twisted the core of the rose, heard the muffled clicking of the internal lock, then placed his hands on the silver clasp. "But, you understand, the decision to actually open this is immense."

"Don't." Anna turned. "Forgive me."

"I must."

"Dear God. What a waste."

Swiftly, willing himself not only to begin the action but to carry it through, Inspector Fuchs undid the silver clasp, took the lid in both hands and in one single fluid movement—so that from the second he slipped the clasp until the lid was actually open, flung back, there was neither pause nor hesitation nor delay. He lifted it and gazed into the purple-dark interior of the casket and at the Moonchild there.

Anna emitted a short, harsh cry of anguish and lament; she could not bear to see what the casket contained. She turned, her hands to her head.

"God in Heaven," gasped Fuchs. "It *is* a monster." The sight of the Moonchild froze him. He remained still, stiffened, his hands on the upright lid. "God in absolute Heaven."

Of the three only Edmund retained any presence of mind. He felt Anna turn, heard her wail; saw Fuchs stand rigid, stiff with terror. Quickly, acting from an instinct older than he knew, he brushed Fuchs roughly aside and, his own eyes averted, incapable of gazing upon what remained of Simon, the distortion of his son, grasped the lid and slammed it shut, and twisting the rose, shot the secret lock into place. Rapidly he secured the heavy clasp.

"Are you satisfied?" he spat at Fuchs, turning to comfort Anna. "Have you seen what you wanted to see?"

Fuchs had. In the brief instant of the raised lid, in that second before it was torn from him, he had seen all he ever needed to see of the Moonchild. One glance was enough to register the monstrously deformed arm, huge, twisted, bulging with muscle, forcing the remainder of the body to one side, crushing it against the casket—indicating that it was only a matter of time before the casket was too small to contain the beast, before the creature burst free of its coffin and was loose, springing from the purple velvet like the demon it was. The moment had been long enough for Fuchs to see the hand and the nails and the claw, the darkness of the foreign flesh, the inhuman hair it grew. He had seen also the golden-crowned face of the innocent child, its eyes closed, untouched by alteration, lying seemingly asleep, but grafted to, part of, the hideous arm and its satanic claw. Fuchs shuddered like a man in fever and raised a hand to his face. It was wet, covered with sweat. He closed his eyes; the arm of the Moonchild burned against the lids, it was an image nothing could destroy.

"Well, Herr Inspector Fuchs?" demanded Edmund, holding Anna's head against his chest. "What further evidence do you need?" The words flayed. The voice was iron.

"Nothing." Fuchs replied in no more than a whisper. "I have witnessed enough."

"Then you will not prohibit our progress?"

"On the contrary. I will give you all the assistance I can."

"Dear God," said Anna. "At last."

"It was the arm," said Fuchs, wrapping his own arm about himself. "Why did you not tell me of that change?"

"What difference would it have made?"

Fuchs trembled slightly; it was his question and he knew the answer. "I am truly sorry. How you must have suffered." He was like a man who had been sentenced and finally realized what death might mean.

"Do you mean what you say?" Anna asked. Fuchs's face was pale, his moustache a black band against the whiteness of frightened skin. "You really will help us?"

"All I am able."

"Then let us begin," said Edmund briskly, shaking off the seal of fear. "There is much to be done."

But even as he spoke, there was a change in the station-master's office. It began with a quiet, almost unheard, rattling: wood being knocked with a steady, monotonous rhythm which grew, spread suddenly, filled. The Blackstones, Inspector Fuchs, turned, stared at the casket. It shook, heaved, thudded on the floor as though alive. As if the Moonchild, having glimpsed light, then having had the source removed, was active, enraged, determined to emerge and fulfill its evil, but was bound by the confines of the heavy, wooden coffin, frustrated by the locks which secured it. All watched aghast as the casket shook with fury, raised dust, thudded on the floor.

"Edmund . . ."

"Remain still."

"Simon . . . is trying to escape."

"Whatever it is, it is not Simon."

"Do something."

"There is nothing to be done. Either the locks will hold or not."

"And if not?" Fuchs spoke. "What then?"

"Pray they hold."

The violence within the casket increased, lifted it bodily from the floor. The woodwork seemed to bulge with the force inside, to swell with the pressure fighting for release. A rhinestone burst suddenly free and rolled across the floor to Anna's feet; she gave a small cry and leaped aside. The room was thick with fury. For a moment it was about to explode. Then slowly, infinitely, with deadening relief, the intensity inside the casket subsided, became subdued, retreated as it had begun, withdrew into silence. It stilled, and all three watching allowed their breath release. The coffin ceased its vibrant motion and the three horrified spectators felt the corseting band of fear slacken. Finally the casket was quiet, it issued neither sound nor movement. For a time, at least, the great power it contained was dormant, restrained, silent.

"God in Heaven," Fuchs whispered. "What force."

"It was the light," said Edmund. "It *must* remain in darkness."

Inspector Fuchs nodded. "The sooner it is placed in the ground the better." He wiped perspiration from his forehead.

"That is all we have been trying to do."

Inspector Fuchs shook his head briskly, like a heavy dog, and became businesslike. Whatever doubts he had held, whatever reservations bound him, were physically shaken aside. There was work to be done and, of the three, he was best equipped to do it. Years of training, a nose for method, an ability to pursue were now to be focussed on locating the birthplace of Simon Blackstone and burying the Moonchild there.

"Very well." Fuchs's voice was new, the look in his eye alert. "Let us determine the place of burial immediately. Tomorrow we will take the casket there."

With Inspector Fuchs assuming command, they with their luggage, went to the George Hotel, Tonbridge, an old coaching house, where Edmund Blackstone had already booked rooms and where Fuchs was able to find accommodation for the night.

"Good evening, Mr. Blackstone," the booking clerk said as Edmund signed the register. "Nice to see you again, sir."

Edmund smiled politely.

"Been away for a while, have you sir?"

Edmund nodded. "That is correct," he replied.

"Used to live round here, if I remember correctly," continued the booking clerk, a garrulous man with hair parted in the middle.

"We did, as a matter of fact," Edmund acknowledged. "Willow Lane, along by the river."

"Now I recall." The booking clerk beamed, then his face clouded. "You wouldn't know the area now, sir. Wouldn't recognize an inch of it."

"I beg your pardon?"

"All pulled down now. Leveled it is. Razed to the ground."

"I do not understand." Edmund glanced at Anna and Fuchs. They were listening. "Would you make yourself clear?"

"It's the new railway station they're building, sir. And the marshalling yards. Taken the whole of it, they have. Knocked the lot down."

Edmund leaned over the reception desk, his face pale, his voice stiff. "Do you mean to tell me that the houses in Willow Lane have been destroyed?" he asked slowly.

"Every last one of them, sir. I'd have thought the place might be a little damp for what they want it for. But, no. They've taken the lot and already have started with their large machines." The booking clerk shook his middle parting in distress. "Looks like a cornfield, sir, it does. A regular quagmire."

"Are all the houses down?"

"Not one left standing."

"And the roads, the signposts?"

"Couldn't tell one end from the other now. As I say, looks like a field. Play football there if you wanted to."

"My God, man," said Edmund rudely, as if the booking clerk were personally to blame, "do you mean to tell me the area is unrecognizable?"

"Quite, sir." The man was a trifle piqued by Edmund's manner. "If you doubt my word, sir, you may look for yourself."

"I believe you." Edmund Blackstone turned, his face gray, his eyes fatigued. "Did you hear that?" he asked the others. "The house where Simon was born is gone." He held out a hand to Anna, who looked as if she might faint.

"We are lost, Anna. Without a reference we have no hope of finding the place we seek."

"Let me make a suggestion." Inspector Fuchs wiped his moustache with the back of his hand. "If this were Germany, there would be an office for municipal surveying in the town. There we would find plans of the street you lived in, and also the lot where the house stood."

Relief softened Edmund's face.

"Of course, it may now be closed." Fuchs recalled a piece of paper in the stationmaster's office, something he had turned and almost read. "I will make use of the telephone to call a local sergeant here whose name I was given. Scot, I think it was."

As Fuchs went to make his call, Anna turned to her husband. "I feel as if I am in the middle of a whirlwind. Everything is happening with such speed."

"I understand." Edmund breathed out slowly. "I too am bewildered by the turn of events."

"Thank God for the German inspector."

"Yes," agreed Edmund Blackstone. "Thank God for him."

Inspector Fuchs returned, his heavy face pleased. "I think we will succeed," he said loudly. "I have spoken to a Sergeant Scot. He will make arrangements for us to study the plans we need. He suggested we meet him in the morning but I felt it would be better to make our study tonight. Do you not agree?"

"I do," said Edmund. "The sooner the better."

"Then I suggest we have dinner, and afterward keep our appointment."

"We shall arrange to dine in our rooms." Edmund hesitated a moment, then added, "Would you care to join us there?"

"I should be delighted." Fuchs smiled. "You will, I imagine, have your *luggage* with you?"

"At all times," Edmund confirmed. "In fact, we will not leave it unguarded a second. Anna will remain with it while we make our examination of the town plans."

They parted and went to their rooms, arranging to meet later. Whatever the Blackstones faced seemed lessened now they had Fuchs to share it with. Assistance was at hand when they needed it most. The fact that they received help at all was superseded only by the unexpectedness of its source. They were beginning to trust the heavyset German and the smile that lay beneath his handlebar moustache.

They had come to the turning point in their fateful journey.

PART III

THE BURIAL

CHAPTER ELEVEN

Beneath traditionally low ceilings the rooms reserved for the Blackstones in the George Hotel were spacious, comfortable. The gentleness of the decor, the coziness of the beamed, secure ceilings gave the Blackstones a sense of respite. The achievement of the journey to Tonbridge had fulfilled a major part of their task. Progress gave them faith.

When Inspector Leopold Fuchs arrived to dine he noted the subtle change in their bearing. "If you do not mind my asking," he inquired when settled, a glass of sherry in his hand, his feet pointed toward the fire, "how does your . . . suffering seem, now that it appears to be mostly over?" He smiled to lessen the clumsiness of his words.

"It has been horribly unreal," Anna replied simply. Her eyes went to her husband.

"That is undoubtedly true," Edmund confirmed. "There have been occasions when I was unable to actually believe we committed the acts that were necessary."

"Such as?"

A shiver ran through Edmund. "Such as pushing the railman's body onto the line. One cannot conceive of it in cold blood."

"And what of—that?" Fuchs indicated the casket to one side of the gaslit room. Its sheen was heightened by the light, the rhinestones glowed, the malachite bloomed; it looked like a sleek, well-fed animal. "How close do you feel to what it contains?"

"What it is, is no longer part of us," Edmund replied.

"I cannot imagine it as my son," Anna said and lowered her eyes. Hope was dead, she knew that. Yet somewhere, lost, remote, distant, wandered a half-prayer that what Simon had become would re-form, be once again their lively child. "I mean," she lifted her head, gazed into the firelight, "Simon will never return."

"He cannot," said Edmund steadily.

"There was a time when I thought otherwise," said Anna. "I did believe the ghastly process might be reversed." She sighed inwardly. "Otherwise I might never have been able to do what I did."

"When did you finally lose hope?" asked Fuchs.

"When I saved that child." Anna's eyes consulted Edmund. "The Fletcher girl. When the choice lay between her and what . . . was in the casket. Then I realized I could do no more for the . . . creature."

"Do I know of this instance?" queried Fuchs.

"I should not imagine so," said Edmund. "No one was attacked, thanks to Anna's intervention."

"It was on the steamer," Anna explained. "The daughter of an acquaintance was, unbeknown to us, actually with the casket. When I returned she was about to open it." Anna shuddered. "It was a hideous moment."

"A strange one, also," said Edmund. "Anna seemed to know something dreadful was about to happen."

"That is true." The memory subdued Anna. "Although I shall never know why."

"Yet you responded?" Fuchs queried.

"I did, without hesitation."

"I am surprised you left it alone?"

"We had not intended to," Anna replied. "Perhaps that is why I was drawn back in time."

"Curious." Fuchs eyed the English couple.

"We shall never have this explained," Edmund said. "Of that I am absolutely sure."

Inspector Fuchs put his head to one side, thoughtfully. "Did Dr. Kabel attempt any sort of explanation?" he asked.

Edmund shook his head. "Nothing that convinced. He expressed some witch's tale of vengeful creatures. A piece of ancient astrology. A missing day from an antique calendar. There was no explanation, just an assortment of bizarre detail." It seemed very distant now.

"That is all?" Fuchs asked carefully. "He said nothing about a guardian?"

Edmund shook his head.

"Why do you ask?" Anna questioned.

Fuchs shrugged. "It was the last thing he talked about. Just before the drug took its final effect he said something about— what was it now? Not being able to warn you. Not telling you who the guardian was." He stroked his moustache thoughtfully. "Does that mean nothing?"

"Not a thing," said Edmund. He looked at his wife, questioningly.

Anna's eyes went to the fireplace, the leaping flames, the coals. She shivered but did not reply.

Edmund coughed. "He did not add to the remark?" he queried.

"No." Fuchs watched them, suddenly uneasy. Part of the mystery remained. "He was capable of nothing further."

"The poor, poor man." Anna Blackstone gazed at the fire: the leaping flames were hope; the brightness of the burning wood, living. "I feel such pity for him."

There was silence as they sat, stilled for the moment, moved by something not understood.

AFTER they had dined, Edmund Blackstone and Inspector Fuchs left the hotel to keep their appointment with Sergeant Scot in the Norman castle where the Municipal Office functioned.

Outside the air was dank, it swam about them heavy with river mist. In the yellow glow of streetlights the two were eerie, nebulous. When they arrived at the heavy oak door of the castle, Sergeant Scot was waiting. He was a brisk man with reddish hair. He had already spoken to the town surveyor, who was in his office expecting them.

The Survey Office, an oak-paneled room with pigeonholes to store maps, contained a wide baize-covered table in its center where the town surveyor had already spread several charts covering the region where the Blackstones had lived.

"This is the earliest we have," he said, after initial greetings had been exchanged. "It is historical, really, pre-Norman in fact, but you might be interested."

"Thoughtful of you," said Edmund Blackstone. "It was the more recent material we were after, actually."

The town surveyor nodded, was about to roll the ancient map and put it away when Fuchs stopped him. "Please, just a moment," he said crisply.

The town surveyor nodded. Used to the indecisiveness of laymen, he relaid the map on the table. Inspector Fuchs bent over it, scanning details. Then he lifted his head and called softly to Edmund. "Take a look at this, Mr. Blackstone. I think you will find it quite interesting." His voice was carefully controlled.

"What is it?" Edmund's finger traced a position on the map. "This does not even begin to resemble the town as it is today."

"Look closely." Fuchs pointed to a section beside the river. "Is this not, more or less, where your house used to stand?"

Edmund peered. "More or less," he admitted. "Willow Lane

did follow that bend of the stream. It used to run..." He stopped abruptly; the words ceased as if cut with a knife.

"You do see what I mean?" Fuchs probed.

Edmund breathed out slowly. "Only too well." His face had paled. He stood very still.

For a few moments there was complete silence while both men gazed at the ancient map; then the town surveyor coughed. "So, that pre-Norman survey is of some use after all?" he questioned, asking for more.

"It is most interesting," said Fuchs, beginning to reroll the map. "It shows there was an Anglo-Saxon burial ground down by the river." He smiled to avoid further questions. "I would not say it helps us specifically but it is always interesting to see what the ground was used for at any earlier period. Is that not so, Mr. Blackstone?"

Edmund swallowed, recovering. "Yes, of course, but do you think it has anything to do with...anything?" he asked as casually as he could.

"I hope so," Fuchs replied confidently.

What Inspector Fuchs had pointed out to Edmund Blackstone was a series of mounds and hillocks which formed twin circles to one side of the river. In their common center lay a larger mound, and it was here on almost the precise spot, as far as they were able to determine, that the Blackstone house had stood: built above the ancient ground where in a time better known to the old woman with the burning eyes and the doctor in the shadow of his room, someone or something of supreme importance had been buried. The central point was the focus of an ancient graveyard. It was here that Simon Blackstone had been born. It was here that the Moonchild must be returned to earth, be buried in the center of the circles.

Edmund wet his lips and stared at Fuchs as the heavy man carefully rolled the map and returned it to the town surveyor. "It is a sign, is it not?" He felt the weight of the words on his tongue.

"I believe it is." Fuchs replied confidently.

Edmund Blackstone and Inspector Fuchs then turned their attention to a more recent chart the town surveyor slid toward them; on it Willow Street was clearly marked and the lot on which the Blackstone house had stood was indicated; the bend in the river was in evidence and the Norman castle distinct.

"Do you mind if I make a tracing of this?" Edmund inquired. "By taking bearings from the castle and lining them up with the river I should be able to pinpoint the spot I am looking for."

"Not at all." The town surveyor supplied Edmund with paper, pins and an indelible pencil. "I see you've done a little map work, eh?"

Edmund nodded, laying the tracing paper over the section he needed. "I have made a study of paleontology. That often requires the use of cartography." He began following the outlines on the map.

The town surveyor watched Edmund complete his tracing, then he rerolled the map. "Is that all you require?" he asked. "Nothing more we can help you with?"

"That is all, thank you."

"Well." The town surveyor smiled broadly. "I do hope you find what you are looking for, Mr. Blackstone."

"Thanks to your splendid records, I am sure we shall." Edmund carefully folded his tracing.

"Any time at all." The town surveyor was like a schoolboy whose butterfly collection had been praised. "Just call if there is anything more you need."

Shaking hands with the town surveyor, Edmund Blackstone and Inspector Fuchs left the Survey Office; Sergeant Scot accompanied them. Slowly they walked down the hill toward the George Hotel, Edmund and Fuchs deep in thought, the sergeant tramping beside. The air was thicker now, river-mist had risen. Men in boots, coats buttoned to the throat, shadowy shapes in numbers, swirled in the fog. A thin, drizzling rain had begun to fall. The scene was dim, ghostlike, as if everything was slightly out of focus.

When they reached the George Hotel Sergeant Scot asked Inspector Fuchs if there was anything further required.

Fuchs paused, thought a moment, then said, "Yes. In the morning I will need a rig of some sort. A small carriage." As he spoke, rain dripped from his moustache.

"At what time, sir?"

"Six, I think. If that could be arranged."

"Of course, sir," Sergeant Scot assured him. "I shall have a rig and a driver outside the hotel at six A.M. Sharp."

"No driver."

"I beg your pardon, sir?"

"A driver will not be necessary," Inspector Fuchs informed him. "Either Mr. Blackstone or I will take the reins. All I require is the rig."

"Very good, sir." Sergeant Scot became quiet; like the town surveyor, he felt excluded. He looked at the large German inspector and wondered what lay beneath the request. "You will need no further assistance from us then, I take it, sir?"

"You take it correctly, Sergeant." Fuchs smiled, held out a large hand. "Thank you for all your help. I regret I am unable to supply you with more information, but believe me, it is impossible."

Sergeant Scot shook the inspector's hand, then saluted. "Not at all, sir," he replied and disappeared into the swirling, misty, glossy dark.

Inspector Fuchs watched the figure vanish in the wet blanket of mist. "It *is* quite impossible. No one can be told what we are doing here." His voice was sympathetic.

"Not now, perhaps," said Edmund. "But later?"

Fuchs wiped drizzle from his moustache. "That is something I have carefully avoided considering," he said slowly. "Reports will be needed, of course. My superiors and some of your countrymen will wish to be informed about my journey and what the findings have been. But God in Heaven knows how I shall tell them." He shrugged heavily.

"What if you said nothing at all?"

"Quite out of the question."

"Why?"

Inspector Fuchs smiled and took Edmund's arm. "How little you understand the bureaucratic process, Mr. Blackstone. How little you know my world. Come in out of this annoying rain and I will try to explain those ties which, at times, bind me hand and foot." He led Edmund into the hotel.

"I have an uncle in the House of Commons," Edmund said, inside the lobby. "Is there anything he could do?"

Fuchs raised his eyebrows. "What would you tell him?" he asked.

Edmund thought. "I would say you had joined us here at our invitation. That, when we left the village, we insisted on being further informed about the death of Miss Harris. That you followed to bring the results of your investigations first hand. It is quite possible he will accept that."

"What information did I bring?"

"Your investigation disclosed nothing. Poor Edith was the victim of some unknown attacker. However, you intend to question certain other guests who had been in the hotel at the time and if your findings are in any way conclusive you will be in touch with us at once."

"And the other deaths?" Fuchs asked, intrigued, amused. "The coachman and the stationmaster?"

"Unrelated as far as you were concerned."

"And the burial we are about to conduct?"

"Who would know of it?"

Fuchs smiled. "It is all pure fiction, Mr. Blackstone. It does not hold a drop of proverbial water."

"It might be enough?" Edmund persisted. "If a member of Parliament were convinced, I believe your report would satisfy a lot of people in this country. If not your own."

Fuchs wondered. Inspector Peter Kearsley would be dubious but would say nothing. It was his manner to trust colleagues. "Let me think about it, Mr. Blackstone," Fuchs said. "Although I must say that for a man little versed in red tape you seem to know a great deal about pacifying its demands." His eyes were faintly critical.

"I know that politicians live by plausible explanations," Edmund replied. "Now, shall we go upstairs and see how Anna fared?"

When they entered the low-beamed Tudor rooms they found Anna Blackstone seated, staring emptily into the dying, softly flickering flames. The casket remained where it had been placed: unopened, sleekly reflecting firelight.

Anna looked up as they approached. "Did you succeed in finding what was needed?" she asked.

"We did," replied Edmund. "What is more, I have a copy of the map. Locating the position should prove little hardship."

"I am glad of that." Anna returned her gaze to the fire. "We will begin quite early, I imagine."

"There is a carriage arriving at six," Fuchs replied. "We must complete what we have to do before workmen arrive on the site."

Anna Blackstone watched the flames and sighed—a deep, desolate emptying which captured them all. Edmund glanced at Fuchs, who stood pensive, then he moved closer to Anna and peered at her face, sadly limned by firelight.

"Anna?" he asked gently. "Why do you sound so despondent? Now, when everything seems about to succeed?"

"Does it really appear so?"

"Of course it does. We have the location and the transport." His voice was encouraging. "And I am sure there will be workman's tools on the site we can use if necessary." Taking his wife's hands in his own he continued, "Inspector Fuchs and I may have to roll up our sleeves and engage in a little hard labor, but I doubt if that will do us any harm." He paused, wondering.

"There is no real need for you to attend, if you prefer not to."

"Nothing will keep me away." Anna straightened.

"Then, why are you so downcast?"

Anna stared at the fire: the little flames, the red coals, the gray ashes formed patterns which had no meaning. "I do not know, Edmund. But I do feel melancholy." Her voice spun thin and whispery.

"What has occurred to make you so?"

"Nothing. All has been quiet here. There has been nothing specific to make me feel the way I do."

"What can it then be?"

"I lack faith, Edmund, and that is the truth." Anna Blackstone's hands clenched. "I have no conviction that once we have carried out the burial all will suddenly become peaceful once more. I cannot, for the life of me, imagine such an occurrence."

"Why not?" Edmund asked. The journey lay behind them, the organization was complete. All they had striven for was to be achieved in the morning. With the assistance of Inspector Fuchs there appeared no further cause for concern. "We have done what we were told to do. Nothing remains save placing the casket in the earth itself."

Anna's eyes were dark coals. "Have you no reservations, Edmund? Does not your scientific mind raise doubts?"

"What sort of doubts, my dear?"

"Doubts of *really* achieving permanent peace. Doubts that once that...*thing*...is buried it will remain there. Doubts that it will not continue to haunt us for the rest of our lives."

"Why should that be?"

"Oh, don't be so simple, Edmund." Anna's eyes sparked angrily. "Why should it have happened in the first place? Why should we believe anything will ever be normal again?"

Edmund Blackstone released his wife's hands slowly. There was a change in Anna. Something deep, dark, different had occurred in the time she had remained in the low-beamed room with the coffin sleekly glowing in the firelight.

"Anna?" Edmund questioned softly. "What is with you?"

"Do you not feel it yourself?"

"I do not."

"Oh, Edmund, I am consumed with a fearful sense of disaster."

There was silence. Anna, bleak-faced, gazed into the coals. Edmund, concerned, uncertain, stared at her. Inspector Fuchs, who had remained squarely in the middle of the room between the firelight and the casket, now stepped forward and spoke crisply.

"Could you define exactly when this feeling of despair first overtook you, Mrs. Blackstone?"

"I am unsure," Anna replied. "It happened slowly, in the time that you were gone."

"How did you occupy your time while we were absent?"

"I remained seated, here. Staring into the fire, watching the flames."

"Nothing more?"

"That is all," she replied in a withered voice.

"Please think," Fuchs demanded. "Was there no other action you undertook?"

Anna lifted her face, looked at the heavy figure of the inspector, who stared uncompromisingly back. There were deep lines in her countenance, lines which Edmund had not seen since they left the little Bavarian village. There was a lost quality about her he had not observed since their journey to Tonbridge had begun. "Are these questions really necessary?" Edmund asked Fuchs.

Anna sighed then, deeply, a sound of total expiration. "I do know what Inspector Fuchs is talking about, Edmund. He is right, it does have something to do with the casket." She closed her eyes and shivered.

"He has not mentioned the casket."

"Nevertheless, that is what he means."

"What occurred?"

"I sat close to it for a while." Anna shrank in her chair, hid in its shelter. "I put my arms about it, thinking of what it used to contain."

"Is that all?"

"Yes, Edmund. That is all."

"Then you have no need for concern." Edmund turned to Fuchs, who stood still, confident; he had heard what he expected to hear. "That is a normal enough thing to do."

Fuchs alone understood the full power of the creature in the coffin. What had begun as a vague notion, a bizarre explanation for a series of events that appeared to have no other cause, was confirmed. In the untidiness of the stationmaster's Tonbridge office, among the irrelevant litter of schedules and the one sane related piece of handwritten paper detailing earthworks on a site they were yet to visit, he had actually confronted the monster, the half-child, half-demon. He had seen the mutation, and it had shattered all the safe beliefs he had ever held, thrust before him a sight so grotesque, so frightening, he would never be the same again. The thunder in the casket after it had been closed, the violence of the charge attempting to escape, had converted him to a cause he did not comprehend. He knew the creature in the casket personally now. The confrontation was his, the challenge his own, the knowledge of the evil an almost private possession. Now he stood massively in the shadowed room and spoke with an objectivity the others did not possess. "Normality has nothing to do with it. We are dealing with forces more corrupt than you could possibly imagine."

"We have seen what it can do," Edmund protested. "The people it killed."

"All you have seen has been with the eyes of parents." Fuchs was positive. "Never with the objectivity of an outsider. You still do not really appreciate the full power of that creature you swirled upward, as the flames drew on new fuel. When the waiter returned, he placed a bottle of Glen Grant on a side table together with the glasses; carefully he poured a small measure into each and, picking up a cut-glass water jug, looked inquiringly toward Fuchs.

"Water, sir?" he asked dubiously, displaying his concern with foreigners. "Did you say?"

"Under no circumstances." Fuchs held out a hand for his glass. "And bring the table closer," he added. "Within reach."

When the waiter had gone, Fuchs lifted his drink in a small but positive toast. "Here is to our success in the morning." His voice was gently confident.

Edmund responded with a small tilt of his glass. Anna did not move; her eyes remained on the firelight.

Inspector Fuchs drank a little whisky and smiled with satisfaction; he held his glass to the flames and watched them dance through the spirits. "Please do not be offended by my intention," he said, "but I shall spend the night here, in this room, just to make sure nothing unforeseen happens to our charge." His voice was clear, polite, courteous but completely, utterly unyielding.

Abruptly the Blackstones turned their heads: here was the policeman at work. "Why do you consider that necessary?" Edmund asked.

"For the best reasons in the world," Fuchs replied. "And the worst."

"Do you not trust us?" Edmund rose and walked a step or two away. "Is that what you mean?"

"It is not a matter of trust so much as a matter of susceptibility. I am not as vulnerable as you."

Edmund Blackstone swirled whisky, watched its movement. "Perhaps you are right." Tiredness had crept into his voice. "I have never been sure of any of this, save the deaths and the overpowering sense of horror. So, I must confess I do not understand the influence the being in the casket has on me, or Anna."

He stared fixedly into his glass as if it were the only point of reality in the room. "I would be less than honest if I denied our frailty."

"You are wise to recognize it." Fuchs turned his inquiring face to Anna. "Do you not agree, Mrs. Blackstone?"

"Edmund speaks for us both," Anna replied levelly. "For I too am lost when it comes to knowing how strong or weak we have been." Her eyes softened. "But I must say this, I do firmly believe we would not have been able to continue had it not been for your presence."

Inspector Fuchs felt his throat tighten. "Thank you for that, Mrs. Blackstone." Through his eyes the fire misted; he was strangely moved. "I know how difficult it must be for you to accept such a thought. And to utter it." His voice blurred.

The room stilled once more. Firelight grew as each new log was added and reduced to ash; the level of Glen Grant lowered as Fuchs refilled his glass and that of Edmund Blackstone. They waited—the Blackstones, Inspector Fuchs, the Moonchild—for morning, when in the dim and misty rising dark they would begin their final journey.

In the end Anna rose, bid Inspector Fuchs goodnight, and retired to bed. Edmund was about to follow when he turned to Fuchs and asked, "This matter the doctor raised . . ." He swallowed. "About a guardian . . . Do you think it could be Anna?"

Fuchs blinked. "I do not know," he answered honestly.

"It is possible."

"Yes," Fuchs replied. "It is possible. Although neither of us knows what it means."

Edmund nodded soberly. He opened his mouth to make another remark but turned suddenly and left the room. Fuchs watched his departure, then shrugged and settled more comfortably into the chair where he remained, bearlike, gazing at the curling fire, sipping whisky, wondering who and what the guardian was and when the name would be disclosed.

He thought he could feel its presence.

CHAPTER TWELVE

THE night passed slowly. Edmund and Anna Blackstone slept fitfully, murmuring vague doubts, turning as the hours passed and the long night unfolded. Inspector Fuchs dozed in his chair, waking every now and then to add more wood to the fire, to glance at the dormant casket licked by flame, to grunt and move into a new position until he became aware of another day.

Outside there was a freshness of breeze, the beginnings of new woodsmoke, a symphony of birds. Fuchs heaved himself from his chair and peered at his half hunter in the pale light of the fire: it showed five thirty. He walked to a window and pulled back a curtain. The darkness swirled mistily, rubbing against the pane, light drizzle sprinkled, cold made its presence felt through the glass. It was a gloomy day; wet, bleak, unyielding.

Inspector Fuchs grunted. "God in Heaven," he said softly. "It has been manufactured for the occasion."

After turning up the gaslight Fuchs went to the bedroom door and knocked gently; from within he heard the muffled voice of Edmund in reply. Fuchs yawned massively, then shuddered as the spasm subsided. He buttoned his waistcoat and felt ready for whatever the day held in its cold, damp, uncompromising arms. He put on his cape and his hat.

Some minutes later Edmund Blackstone appeared followed by Anna. Both had dressed formally, wore black from head to toe.

Edmund, in frock coat, carried a black silk hat. Anna's throat was muffled in black fox; her black dress covered her solemnly, her bonnet and veil masked her. In the pale, yellow glow of gaslight they appeared impressive, dignified, designed for the occasion. Their faces complemented their dress: they were stiff, white, ironed of emotion. Fuchs greeted them silently, then turned away. There was a lump in his throat and he was unsure of the cause.

"Well," he said in a moment, going to the window and gazing at the emptying dark, "the carriage should be downstairs by now." Indicating the casket he added, "I suggest, Mr. Blackstone, you and I carry that between us."

"Of course." Edmund tugged at a glove. "Perhaps, Anna, you might go ahead."

Anna Blackstone preceded the small procession out of the suite, into the corridor; Edmund and Fuchs followed, the casket between them. It swayed gently as they bore it, reflecting from woodwork and rhinestone the light as it passed.

Downstairs, before the main entrance, shadowy between pilasters, stood a small, black rig with two horses in harness; steam plumed from their nostrils, their hides were polished with rain. Beside them was a uniformed constable, water dripping from his cape.

"Are you Inspector Fooks?" the constable inquired of Edmund.

Edmund shook his head. "That is the man you're looking for." He nodded at the German.

"Then, this is the carriage you ordered, sir," the constable told Fuchs. "I understand a driver wasn't wanted."

"You understand correctly. If you would be kind enough to help by placing this casket on the floor of the carriage, that will be all.

"It will fit in the boot, sir," the constable pointed out. "There is quite enough room."

"Place it inside, on the floor." Fuchs spoke as if he had not heard the remark. "Under a seat, if possible."

The constable blinked. "Very good, sir." He proceeded to do as asked. When he had completed the task he returned to Fuchs. "Will you be wanting anything further, sir?"

"No, thank you, Constable. That will be all."

The constable nodded, saluted, was gone.

After helping Anna into the rig Edmund Blackstone said to Inspector Fuchs, "I will drive, if you have no objection. It will be easier, as I am familiar with the route." So saying he climbed into the driver's seat.

Fuchs nodded, then entered the rig to sit with Anna.

Edmund took a last look about him, at the gloomy, rainy, early morning, then sighed heavily and clicked the reins. With a shuffle and a billowing of breath the horses began to proceed. The sound of their hooves on the cobbles was all that was to be heard in the town.

Tonbridge seemed deserted. Only the rig moved through the swirling, misty drizzle as Edmund guided the horses down to the foot of the town. They traveled by the station, its green iron-work dripping, along the bottom of the low, flat valley toward where Willow Street had once been, where the Blackstone house had stood, to the ground on which the Moonchild had been born. It was a short, slow journey. Edmund felt his way carefully through the semidark, half-forgotten streets, past corners just remembered, between houses almost unknown in the early drizzle.

Edmund Blackstone traveled a wasteland of buried memory, he shivered as the horses moved fitfully over the wet cobble-stones. They disliked the footing, were uneasy in the meager light, regretted the lost warmth of their stables and the fodder there. As the rig approached the river it passed a group of plane trees where the sudden noise of the horses' hooves woke a flock of pigeons which darted, as if shot, from the trees. The beating of their wings cracked the morning. At the sound the horses shied, reared, thrust against their reins. Edmund swore and stood, drawing their heads, holding. Inside the coach Inspector Fuchs was aware of the whites of Anna's eyes as she clung to a strap in the half-dark and resisted an impulse to scream. Outside, Edmund lowered his voice and spoke more softly; the horses responded, they stilled and balanced. Anna breathed more easily. Fuchs was ready. The rig was stable. It continued.

Finally they approached the torn and open ground where the earthmovers had leveled and new work was about to begin.

At the edge of the site Edmund halted. The horses stopped between stacks of timber, pale gray in the morning; a mountain of bricks, blood-red in the wet light. Edmund peered over their polished hides to recognize nothing. Building material was strewn everywhere, the ground was directionless, there was nothing to guide him. To his right he knew the river lay; somewhere above and to the left was the castle, but in the lusterless morning he was unable to determine where he was exactly, or where Willow Street had been. The site of his former house was lost to him completely. Everything was dead.

"Good morning, sir." A man's voice at Edmund's elbow broke the silence with such sudden shock that Edmund spun in the driver's seat, half-turning, half-leaping at the sound. His heart lurched, the muscles in his cheeks stiffened. "Was there something you required, sir?" the voice continued. "Perhaps I could assist."

Steeling himself, Edmund peered down in the direction of the sound. Standing by the rig, almost at its side, was a small man wearing a long black overcoat and a tall black hat. His face was thin, wizened, his eyes narrow; on his top lip, vivid as a scar, was a great, red, harelike weal. It stood crimson against the whiteness of the thin, pinched face.

"I am the watchman, sir." The man's voice was faintly lisping. "I am in charge here until the foreman arrives."

"My God." Edmund turned fear to anger. "You scared me almost to death."

"I regret that, sir," the man replied politely. "Perhaps you did not see me approach."

"Where did you come from?"

"I have been here all the time, sir."

Edmund stared through the drizzle at the man in black. There was something totally contained about him. He possessed an unshakable quality. His remoteness suggested he might have arrived without having made the effort to approach. Edmund shivered, a coldness ran along his spine which had nothing to do with rain or dawn. It was as if an old fear had been reborn, something from another time. Edmund gripped the reins tightly. The horses stamped the ground uneasily. The rig moved, the door opened, and Edmund heard with relief the sound of Inspector Fuchs.

"What is this?" Fuchs asked. "Do we have company?"

"This man tells me he is a watchman."

"That is correct, sir." The man turned his pinched face to Fuchs. "I am *the* watchman. I am in charge of this place until the foreman arrives." The formula was the same.

Fuchs cleared his throat. "You are not by any chance . . . the guardian?" he asked very carefully.

"No, sir, I am the watchman." The man in black was positive. "Can I be of any assistance?"

"That depends," said Inspector Fuchs, seeing the scar, the remoteness. "We are here on a sort of . . . mission."

"Is that right, sir?"

"It is undoubtedly right. I am an inspector of police from Munich, Germany."

"I have heard of the place." The watchman's tone was steadily polite. "You are a long way from home, if you don't mind my saying so."

"Correct," said Fuchs and coughed. He plunged his hands

deep into his pockets. "This is Mr. Blackstone." Fuchs's chin pointed to Edmund, seated with the reins in his hands. "He once owned a dwelling in this area before it was taken over by the rail company. We were, ah, trying to locate the exact spot on which the house stood."

"Really, sir." The man with the hare lip nodded soberly. "That could prove rather difficult, now."

"We have a map," Fuchs explained. "With it we should find what we are looking for."

The watchman was thoughtful. "Where was the house, sir? When it was here, that is?" he asked.

"Willow Street," Edmund said, climbing down from the rig. "It ran by the river somewhere over there." His hand indicated, through drizzle and gloom, the line of trees where the sluggish river ran. "Near a bend in the river."

"I know it well," the man said. "Perhaps I could show you where it used to be."

Edmund Blackstone shrugged, there appeared to be no way of excluding the watchman; he was here and gave the impression of remaining. "That would be most kind of you." Edmund opened the door of the rig. "Both my wife and I would be grateful for that service." Anna stepped from the carriage and drew her breath in sharply. She stared at the man in horror. "Who is this man? What is he doing here?" she asked in a harsh whisper.

"He calls himself the watchman," Edmund explained. "He says he will help us locate the lot on which the house used to stand."

"Why?"

"He seems to know where it is." Edmund took Anna's elbow. "Are you shaken still?" he asked. "Did the horses, when they shied, disturb you?"

"Only a little."

"Then . . . ?"

"It is nothing," Anna said quickly, almost abruptly. She took her arm away, pulled her coat more tightly about her. "Forgive me," she added immediately. "I had not expected anyone else."

"I have been here a long time, madam." The watchman spoke as if the words had been addressed to him. "I know every inch of this ground." He smiled, stretching the weal on his lip. "Almost as if it was my own, you might say."

Anna shuddered. Edmund shifted his feet uneasily. The air was foreign. The land had turned. Edmund glanced at Fuchs, who stood massively in the wet, rain dripping from his moustache; his eyes were like small beacons.

The Inspector spoke. "Very well," he said to the watchman. "If you know where we are bound, please be good enough to show us the way." His gaze was level.

"It will be my pleasure, sir." The watchman turned to the rig. "Will you want to bring that with you now, sir?" he asked politely. "Or would you prefer to return for it later?"

"What do you mean?" Edmund's voice was tight.

"This gentleman from Germany said you were on a mission." Nothing about the watchman moved. "In that case it occurred to me you might need your carriage. That is all, sir."

Edmund Blackstone turned to Fuchs, who merely shrugged. "There is no need for the rig immediately," Fuchs told the watchman.

"As you wish, gentlemen." The watchman began to move through piles of building materials, huts, machinery. The workplace was quiet. On the level earth, dwellings, securities, hearths, were making way for a greater machinery. The watchman led through the beginning and ending of different architectures. Beneath his feet was mostly mud. Here and there a line of bricks had been laid as pavement; duckboards had been placed over puddles. There were pools of slush, quagmire. The walking was slow, clumsy, uncomfortable. Anna Blackstone picked her way carefully, lifting her skirts. Edmund and Fuchs trudged steadily, the stoutness of their boots giving them a little more protection. All three were confused, lost in the alien landscape, the towers of material, the brutal, basic mud. Only the watchman was at home. He followed a path which wound and turned, twisted and doubled, with steadiness and determination. "We will be there in a minute or two, gentlemen," he said after a while. "What is it you are looking for, exactly? If you don't mind my asking, that is."

"The house I used to own on Willow Street." In the lifting light Edmund looked over the wasteland. "When people still lived on this ground."

"What number Willow Street was it?"

"Twelve."

"Ah." The watchman's voice remembered clearly. "A narrow, three-storied place, if I am correct, sir?"

"That is right."

"With a gazebo on the western side?"

"Why, yes. It was so." Edmund stared at the watchman, seeing more of the face now the dawn was closer: the narrow eyes, the thin bone of the nose, the pointed face; and above all, gleaming, wet, florid, the scar on the lip. Edmund was forced to clear his throat. "Did you know the house?" he asked.

"Well, sir," the watchman replied politely. "I know most of the places about here. Those that exist now. And those that used to be."

Anna Blackstone peered around her husband's shoulder. "You seem to know a great deal about us," she challenged.

The man in black continued to stand there. His feet squelched mud. He gazed but did not reply.

"Why is that?"

"It is not a matter of knowing, madam," the watchman answered with his gentle lisp. "But a man in my position keeps his eyes open, uses his memory. If you understand my meaning."

"I understand nothing," Anna replied. "Least of all what you expect from us."

"Expect, madam? Not a thing. I am merely trying to be of some assistance. It is part of the job, so to speak."

"There is something incomprehensible about all of this."

Anger entered Anna's voice. "It is far from clear why you are here at all."

"I am the watchman, madam. It is my duty to look after things until the foreman comes."

"So you have said."

"There is no other reply to give." The man in black's lisped words filtered through the rain.

"Oh, my God." Anna Blackstone faced her husband. "We cannot pretend any longer, Edmund. This man, who has set himself about us, must be told what it is we have to do."

Edmund nodded. The moment had come. If this was to be the end of the Moonchild a termination must be made. "Our purpose here is more complex than it might seem," Edmund told the watchman. "If you were to show us where the house stood, we will proceed. In the meantime, I ask your patience."

The watchman's lip moved slightly, the hare mark spread. "You are not, now, far from the spot you are seeking. You can take my word for that." He turned toward the river and walked into the lifting light, over mud, tramping the barren landscape.

Immediately Edmund followed through the rain, his step as determined as the footing would allow.

Anna hesitated, then went also, lifting her skirts, as if by clearing them from the mire she were freeing herself of the dark demands within. "Please God," she whispered, "let this be done as quickly as possible." She followed in the direction her husband had taken, behind the little man in black and his determined stride.

Fuchs went with them. The tiny procession proceeded past brick and timber, machine and hand tool, through elements of creation and destruction, toward the final site.

Presently the watchman stopped. He had come to a space a little more open, exposed. It lay between a tower of red brick and a mountain of gravel, where a huge and monolithic earth machine stood beside a hole. In the drizzling rain, the watchman turned to Edmund Blackstone. "There is where you used to live, sir. Number twelve Willow Street stood right here." His lisp seemed softer in the open ground.

Edmund peered about, seeking some sign, some small aspect of recognition. "Are you sure it was this very spot?" His concern was manifest.

"You are standing where the gazebo used to be." The watchman's voice was confident. "Look, sir. There is the bend in the river."

"You are certain?"

"I am positive."

Anna moved a pace or two closer. "There is nothing familiar about any of this, Edmund. All is totally unknown." Her voice was filled with doubt.

Inspector Fuchs peered through the wet. "Do you have your map, Mr. Blackstone?" he asked sensibly.

"Yes, of course." Edmund reached into an inside pocket and produced the tracing he had made the previous evening. Opening it, he held it against the landmarks he could see. Immediately rain spattered on the tracing paper, the indelible pencil began to run. The hard lines he had drawn softened, blurred, soaked into the paper. Edmund lifted his head bleakly. "It is useless. I cannot make out anything."

"I assure you, sir," the man with the harelip persisted, "this is the place you are looking for."

"How can you be so sure?"

"I have been here since the beginning. I knew all this before any of the changes were made." He gazed about him. "This was Willow Street, sir. It was here you had your house. Believe me, I am certain."

"Very well." Edmund Blackstone crumpled the wet tracing and dropped it in the mud. "If you are certain, our journey is over."

"I am glad to hear that, sir," the little man said. "It is satisfying to know a job is complete."

"It is," replied Edmund, searching for words. The declaration was yet to be made. "As the German inspector had already told you, we have come on a mission. There is, in fact, something special that must be done here."

"Really, sir? What would that be, if I might ask?"

"I shall tell you in a moment." Edmund extended his time. "First, *I must be certain* there is no doubt about this being the site we are seeking."

"There is none, sir. As I said, you are standing where the gazebo used to be."

Edmund peered: behind him was the pile of bricks, the gravel; before him stood the earthmoving machine and the hole it had dug. "In that case, the bedroom would have been just about there," he said, his eyes on the hole.

"I beg your pardon, sir."

"I am attempting to recreate a plan of the house."

"That should not be too difficult, sir." The man in black moved closer. "If I remember correctly, this is where the drawing room used to be. There was a window, was there not? With a view of the river?"

"That is correct." Edmund allowed the house to be recalled by the softly lisped words. "The bedroom we seek was almost in the same position on the floor above." Slowly, like a dreamer, he moved through the memory of the neat, paneled dining room. Above, he saw the master bedroom which he and Anna had shared. To one side, across the hall, had been Simon's bedroom. It was clear now, it was about him: the shell of the dwelling reconstructed. There was the birth, the business of women, the coming and going of a tall, bearded doctor.

The eerie cycle swirled: conceived, born, to be interred above and below the same piece of earth, there to remain encaged, held by whatever links chained the Moonchild to that ground. Edmund Blackstone looked at the hole the earth machine had dug. It was deep, deeper than he could discern in the early light, some six feet by four, carved from wet clay. Edmund shivered, accepting the coincidence, if that was the name it went by.

"What is this?" he asked the watchman.

"It is a hole, sir," the man in black said simply, as if speaking to a child. "The machine dug it yesterday."

"For what purpose?" Edmund ignored the facility of the reply. "Do you know that also?"

The watchman moved his shoulders, his harelip spread in a tiny smile. "Well, sir, you know what workmen are like. They dig it up today and fill it in tomorrow. No one ever seems to know why. It's just one of those things, if you understand my meaning." There was a light in the narrow eyes, a knowledge older than Tonbridge.

"It has no special function?"

"That depends, sir."

"On what?"

"On what it is used for." The watchman's shoulders moved again in their gentle, easing shrug. There was no insolence, no disrespect, only a certainty, an understanding of use. "It is what it becomes, sir."

"Edmund," Anna called, lifting a hand, "what is all this?" She turned to Fuchs, ignoring Edmund even before his reply had begun. "Why have we put ourselves in the hands of this stranger?"

"I am not certain we are putting ourselves in his hands," Fuchs answered. His breath fumed, cocooning his words. "Nor am I convinced he is a stranger. We are here to complete a task. He also is here. Who is to say we are not bound in the same direction?"

Anna Blackstone pressed her hands tightly together: she recalled pain, a long slow unrelieved process. There was a huge, desperate, brutal cry as the child slid free and the waiting hands took it. She sensed the house about her: there was the dim, drowning after-darkness when her cry had been replaced by that of the child; the faces blurring to show the tiny, pink, squalling thing.

Now, in the mud, she broke.

Her vision clouded. She stared at the hole lying black and open, gaping like a wound in the earth. Darkness rose and swam upward, her knees softened, she heard Fuchs's voice and was aware of Edmund's movements.

"No," she heard herself whisper, speak, scream: the finality of the event blanketing. "Not in there. Not in that awful place."

"Anna." Edmund stared at her whiteness. His eyes met Fuchs's. "She is overcome."

"She has borne too much," Fuchs replied, supporting the woman. "Leave her with me. Get the rig and the casket. Let us be done."

Edmund Blackstone stood, turned, looked. The man in black had not moved; his shape by the hole remained unaltered. "We must begin," Edmund said to them all. "We must do what we came for."

"No," said Anna. "Yes."

The watchman inclined his head very slightly. "What is that exactly, sir? If you do not mind my saying so, nothing has been requested." His narrow eyes were steady.

"Do you not know?"

"*Know*, sir?"

"Why we are here?"

"How could that be? Nothing has been stated."

"We have come to bury our son." Edmund's voice was raised, lifted, thrown. "He is to be interred here, on this spot. In the place where the hole has been dug. Do you understand?"

"Where is he now, sir?"

"In the carriage." It had been a confession with neither absolution nor pity asked. He had given and received nothing. "It is in the rig in which we came."

"Shall I fetch it for you, sir?"

"No." It was Anna. "He must not touch it. Edmund, do not allow him to."

"He must," Edmund said, his voice dropping. "There is no alternative."

"Please." Anna's cry became a plea. "Do not permit it, Edmund. If he does it will be the end."

"The end is necessary." Edmund's eyes went to Fuchs. "Is that not also your opinion?"

Inspector Fuchs nodded his heavy head. The man in black was as much a part of it as the shrunken doctor crying in his shredded room. It was complete.

"If I might comment," the man in black said softly, left whole by the voices about him, "you do not have any choice, gentlemen. I, alone, am capable of locating the carriage and guiding the horses to this place."

His simple truth finalized. Anna's head sank to Fuchs's arm. In the inspector's chest a doomed silence grew. There was no answer. The instant belonged to the watchman. Only he knew where the carriage stood. Only he was capable of fetching it to this place where the house with the gazebo had looked upon the winding river and the hole in the wet clay yawned.

"I will collect it now, sir," the watchman continued. "It will not take me long. I shall be right back."

"I will accompany you," Edmund called.

"That would only make me slower, sir. I know this place so well I shall travel faster alone."

"No."

"*Yes*, sir. If you don't mind my saying so."

With that, the small figure on the far side of the hole disappeared in the rising light. He turned, stepped to one side soundlessly and was gone. The dawn swallowed him; the tight, black shape vanished.

Edmund's face, when he turned to Anna, to Fuchs, was strangely bland. Accepting, he shrugged. Anna made an attempt to recover; she moved from Inspector Fuchs and pressed her face with her hands. Then she closed her eyes and replaced a hand on the inspector's arm, uncertain now how much she was involved, not knowing what tore her. Inspector Leopold Fuchs waited.

"Who is that man?" Anna whispered, knowing there would be no answer. "What *does* he want with us?"

"I imagine we will discover," replied Fuchs: an empty answer to a lifeless question. "It will be explained."

"No." Anna's sudden strength lifted her voice. Her face appealed to both men. "Nothing will be explained. We will never know why that man is here as we never knew why the old woman understood what Simon would become."

"He is assisting." Edmund's voice was softly balanced. "That is what is important now. He has gone to fetch the carriage."

"Will he return?"

"He will return. He is part of it now." Edmund's reply was confident. "There will be a confrontation, and we will witness it." The murky light was lifting, the trees at the bend of the river were becoming stately through the rain. "It could not be any other way. Nothing else would be acceptable."

"This is not an excursion of scientists looking for fossils." Anna accused in the voice of another. "There may never be any conclusion of the kind you speak of. There may not be a series of neat reports to conveniently file away. None, do you understand, none." The rain was a fine veil between them. "*It may not end here.*"

"It will, Anna. Believe it."

"Be still, Mrs. Blackstone. Be still." Inspector Fuchs stood, his hands ready to support. "I too am convinced the watchman will return. There would have been no point in his going, otherwise."

"There would have been every point."

"To leave us here, lost? No." Fuchs shook his heavy head.

"There is a pattern in all of this, somewhere. There is a design everywhere." The words were not ponderous nor the voice pompous. "You will see."

"You are both fools." Anna's voice rose, growled, and both men recognized the source. It came out of malachite and gemstone; from an elaborately carved wooden box polished to a sleekness. A little light had entered. A clasp had been swiftly replaced. "Don't you understand? This should not be the end."

"Hold her," said Edmund as Fuchs took Anna by the arms. "She is not herself." More he would not admit but moved a pace closer and waited as Fuchs held Anna Blackstone in his bearlike arms. She neither fought nor struggled, merely opened her mouth in wordless sound and stared at her husband through an alien eye. "Anna?" Edmund's voice was close and distant. "Please, it must be done."

So they were: transfixed, welded, until the drizzle was broken and the early light fractured by the whinny of a horse and the slow sucking of the rig approaching through mud. All twisted in anticipation; the heads lifted, the eyes strained. It was the moment they needed and dreaded in the same place in their hearts.

The rig came round the side of a pile of wet brick and halted massively before them. The horses were easy in the reins, the woodwork handsome in the drizzle; the little man in the driver's seat was controlled, absolute, defined.

"Here we are, gentlemen." In the silence his softly lisped words seemed unusually loud. "I came as fast as I could."

Edmund Blackstone approached. Fuchs and Anna remained. "Is the casket inside?" Edmund asked as he watched the man in black secure the reins and climb lightly to the ground.

"It is, sir."

"Then let us remove it at once."

"Very good, sir." The watchman reached for the door. Anna Blackstone stared, her eyes wild, her voice silent as Fuchs held her torment. "Just as you wish, sir."

Edmund Blackstone and the man in black removed the elaborate casket from the rig, taking it cautiously: opening the carriage door with care and standing for a moment gazing at the bejeweled woodwork, pausing at the glint of rhinestones and the dull bloom of malachite. For the first time since he had approached, the watchman displayed something other than disinterest. His eyes flickered quickly over the woodwork, taking in detail, absorbing polish and gleam. He drew breath sharply as if recognizing something familiar. Then he moved as Edmund moved, in parallel. A hand from each side reaching, they took the handles and lifted the casket free of the coach and turned with it clockwise toward the hole into which it would be cast. The drizzle drifted endlessly. The morning light grew fuller.

"Well, sir?" The watchman's narrow eyes were bright. "Do we put it in the hole now? Just as it is, if you understand my meaning?"

"The hole *is* to be used, you say?"

"Oh, yes, sir. There was never any doubt about that."

"Then let us begin." Edmund looked to right and left. The morning would commence soon, workmen would arrive, the watchman would be replaced by the foreman. "The sooner it is done the better."

"Very good, sir. Just as you say."

They took the steps which brought them to the edge of the hole, its mouth wide, yawning, receptive. Its base was cloaked in darkness. Anna Blackstone and Leopold Fuchs watched.

At the edge of the hole Edmund Blackstone and the watchman paused, the casket slung between them, and considered what lay next.

"We will need a rope," Edmund's mind was clear. "Something to lower it with."

"There are many, sir," the watchman replied. "I shall fetch one immediately."

They placed the casket in the mud, setting it beside the gap. The watchman once more disappeared into the mounds of construction and returned, almost in the same instant, a coil of white Manila in his hand. "There you are, sir." Placing the rope on the casket he looked at Edmund with his bright and narrow eyes.

"Excellent." Edmund stood a moment, examining the casket in terms of engineering. "If we double the rope and slip it between the handles," he said, "that should function quite adequately."

"Edmund." Anna's voice came in a long, low whisper. "*Please.*"

"It will be quite all right, my dear." Edmund's eyes were on the casket. "Do not concern yourself unduly."

"You do not understand."

"Of course I do. It will take but a moment."

The man in black stepped a fraction closer. "If I might make a suggestion, sir." His head was inclined, his harelip vivid. "Once we have lowered this below, might it not be a good idea to use the equipment to cover it? If you understand my meaning, that is."

"I'm afraid I don't, exactly."

"The digging machine to your left, sir. It would assist us greatly."

Edmund's eyes went to the monstrous machine, huge in the wet morning, sitting in the primeval mud like a beast: dormant, uninvolved, massively present. "That?" he asked, astounded, curious. "Would it, in fact, be possible?" He walked to the creature, black and green in the silent light.

"I think it could be arranged, sir." The watchman was at Edmund's side. "It is one of the very newest models, you understand." His voice was clearly proud. "Worked by electricity, sir. Very easy to start, as they say."

"It does not have a steam engine?"

"No, sir. They say it is the coming thing, if you understand my meaning."

"I understand you only too well." There was a fresh enthusiasm about Edmund now; there were unexpected aids. "With it we will be able to do what we have to do in practically no time at all."

"Precisely, sir. Exactly what I had in mind."

"Well done." Edmund clapped the man on the shoulder. "Let us start the engine immediately."

"Very good, sir." The watchman made his way to the far side of the machine and climbed into the cabin. After a moment or two there was a low, purring sound as the earthmover came to life. The crane on the front of the machine lifted, turned, seemed to sniff the early air like a beast awakening, then it swung slowly until it faced the gash in the wet clay. Its shovel-nose vibrated gently as its almost-silent engine purred. There was the sound of engaging gears and the machine crept forward until it was beside the hole. There it stopped, waiting, trembling with power, ready to do whatever it was asked. Bringing it to life had made it a servant, giving it movement had ensured an acceptance of will. "Is that about the right position, sir?" came the voice of the watchman. "Will it serve us there?"

"Yes," Edmund called. "It is perfect."

While the watchman descended, leaving the machine with life, Edmund turned to Anna and Fuchs. They stood like stone on the far side of the hole—she silent now, void; her eyes black holes in her face; her mouth a thin, tired line. There would be nothing further from her; what would pass was beyond her interference.

"Anna?" Edmund questioned softly. "Can you be left?"

Anna Blackstone remained untouched.

"Anna?" The voice lifted, repeating. "We will need assistance. Are you capable of remaining alone?"

"She is capable of nothing," Inspector Fuchs replied for them both. "She is dangerously near collapse."

"Dear God." Edmund came closer, round the gash in the earth. "I had thought her recovered."

"She will not recover until the casket is safely away." Fuchs supported the woman. "Do it quickly, before it is too late."

"I shall need your help. If you and I lower the casket the watchman can work the machine."

"Is that essential?"

"If we are to be quick."

"God in Heaven." Fuchs peered at Anna's gaunt face, at the eyes distended and the cheeks hollow. Moving her of a piece, as he might a doll or a child, he took her to the pile of bricks and placed her against them, leaning. Her blackness clung to their blood-red wetness. The whiteness of her face was a personal signature. "Mrs. Blackstone," Fuchs said calmly, authoritatively. "You are to remain here until it is over. Do you understand?"

Anna's eyes reached his. She nodded slowly, dumbly, like a patient in hypnosis.

"You must stay."

Again the numb and lifeless nod.

"Let us get on with it," Edmund addressed Fuchs, moving with him to the hole. The ground sucked at their boots, the rain was a constant pressure. On the far side of the gash, as if positioned eternally, the man in black stood patiently, ready to do whatever might be asked, prepared to act without question or demand,

"Are you ready?" Edmund called and seeing the almost inanimate response, added, "Please be so good as to enter your machine. We will need its power immediately."

"Very good, sir. Just give me the word when you are ready."

As the watchman returned to the machine, as he went through rain and climbed upward, as Inspector Fuchs, pale now, sweating despite the creeping damp, as Edmund Blackstone, tense, no longer played with artifacts, indulging in games, as Anna Blackstone, numb and silent, supported by bricks, watched hollow-eyed: *the casket began to tremble in the mud.*

It commenced by rocking steadily as the manic force within issued a final, desperate attempt to escape. It began quietly, its movement cushioned by mud, so that at first no one noticed the activity. Then the rocking increased, thrust back and forth, built motion until slowly, relentlessly, it began to edge away from the hole.

Anna Blackstone was the first to see the movement; she stared in dumbfounded terror as the casket, like a live, blind animal, urged itself from the cut in the earth, instinctively tried to leave that one place which for it was death, eternity, impotence. Anna Blackstone watched the primitive journey with only her eyes alive; her mouth was closed and silent.

Above, the man with the harelip sat unseeing in the cabin of his monster, his hands on levers, holding in readiness the throbbing life the machine contained.

Then Inspector Fuchs saw the movement of the casket. It caught the corner of his eye and he turned, horrified by the steady beating of the force within, the pressure which caused the woodwork to bend, bulge with power.

"God in Heaven," he called and sprang toward it. "We must hurry."

Edmund turned at the sound, the movement. "Fuchs," he called, not knowing why, following the heavy German.

"Did you call, sir?" came the voice of the watchman. "Are we ready to go, did you say?"

"No," Edmund shouted, moving. Fuchs was already by the casket, his hands reaching to still the force. "Wait."

Inspector Fuchs touched the casket and felt the shock. Like electricity it stung. His muscles jarred, his fingers curled. Like electricity it clung, bonded. As his hands came into contact with the casket, as they held the carved woodwork, sought grip on the embedded stones, Fuchs felt the charge inside the coffin respond. It clung to him as though seeking a form on which to adhere, to complete a process already begun but cut short, postponed when a lid slammed shut and locks resetted. Fuchs held and was himself retained. The hunter and the prey were one, indivisible, indistinguishable.

Edmund approached.

Fuchs turned his head. "Do not come any closer, Mr. Black-stone." He spoke formally, as if he had all the time he needed.

"Has it revived? As it did yesterday?"

"It has." Fuchs's face was calm. "I can manage alone."

"What has happened?"

"I have it. Let us put it away."

Edmund took the rope, doubled it, extended the ends. "It must go through the handles," he said, his mouth dry suddenly as he faced the rhythmic casket steadily beating the mud. The hands of Fuchs were bound to it so that he too moved as the force came, went, lifted, subsided. Edmund saw knowledge in the German's face, resignation, acceptance. "Can you not re-lease it?" he asked purposelessly.

"At the moment, no."

"Allow me . . ."

"Do not come nearer. Do not lay a hand upon it." As In-spector Fuchs's voice rose, he stood upright, surged, his force bearing the coffin's own. He came erect, lifted the pulsing Moon-child, raised himself and the casket, stood with the heartbeat of the monster in his hands as his foot slipped and he fell, calling, "I am all that is necessary."

Anna's cry wrung the musty air.

Edmund sprang, but too late.

Inspector Fuchs fell, tumbling backward into the hole in the clay, pulling the casket inward to his chest. His hat flew up and his cloak opened and his great round head with its heavy mous-tache disappeared into the grayness of the gash in the earth: he and the coffin were bound. His huge hands crushed the heavy-petaled rose carved on the polished woodwork.

"Fuchs?" cried Edmund from the side of the hole, peering. "Are you hurt?"

There was no voice from the depths, nothing save the hollow sound of splashing in the heaviness of mud.

Anna Blackstone began to shake, doll-like, spastic. The force was all within the casket now. Bursting, it had left her to return to itself and its victim.

"When you are ready, sir," called the watchman. "The machine has the power to proceed."

"Fuchs." The cry rose steeply. Edmund's eyes grew used to the gray light below; he saw the shape of Fuchs in the sludge, gripping. The casket was open now, burst. Fuchs's hands had released the rose lock. The silver clasp had sprung loose in the fall. And from the plush interior the long-nailed, alien, dark-fleshed claw of the Moonchild was beginning to emerge. "God," Edmund said in prayer and whisper. "The devil."

"Do not hesitate," Fuchs called. "Begin with the machine."

"We must get you out."

"It is too late for that."

"Fuchs." Again the pitiful cry of name as if a miracle might be called. "I will lower the rope."

"God in Heaven. Do what you are told." Inspector Fuchs grunted the words. He held the tremendous force of the casket with all his power, knowing that what little time was left to him was almost gone. Light came from the creature now, from within the casket he saw its glow. It began to fill, polish the inside of the cavern with a cold, brilliant patina. The twisted claw extended. Fuchs saw clearly now the ancient muscle, the darkened flesh, the coarse animal hair which grew on this extension of the child's body. He hoped the earth would come down and darkness invade before he was exposed to the full malignancy of the force, for he sensed the change was almost complete: that which had begun with the hand would have overtaken the whole. He wished to be spared it. Death was inevitable. While he regretted his inability to survive, somehow he was able to accept that the process begun in the stationmaster's office must necessarily be completed. Dying was more difficult than death itself. His arms were tiring, his breathing fire. He twisted, using his weight upon the casket to press against the gap from which the hand extended. It was clawing at him now, feeling for life. The rough nails tore at the fabric of his suit; the charged arm thrust. "Quick," he called: a hollow rising from the grave. "I cannot hold much longer."

"Fuchs. I will get help."

"There is none."

"You will die."

"I am dead already. I have been in contact."

"I cannot." Edmund stood stricken. In the invading light he watched the forces struggle in the mud below: the claw he loathed and the face he had come to love, the bulging of the casket, the huge arms encasing jewelry and scrollwork. And filling now, devouring, a distant, sour, earthen smell Fuchs had known in the doctor's shredded rooms: as if someone had lived there too long. Fuchs's eyes rolled upward, pleading, the line of his mouth begged. He knew now who the guardian was: himself; the keeper. "No," Edmund shouted. "I cannot bring myself."

"You must, Edmund. You must." Anna left the brickwork and approached gaunt and mud-stained, her hands reaching. "He understands."

"What?"

"More than you."

"It is beyond my determination."

"Then I must."

"Anna."

There were forces about Edmund Blackstone he would never comprehend. Beyond life, beyond death. The pattern was more complicated than he was capable of divining. Anna Blackstone halted on the far side of the gap. Her face was beaten. Her hands shook. Inspector Fuchs groaned as he struggled with the coffin and the Moonchild claw. A nail slashed across the inspector's cheek below the eye, above the black moustache, causing a line of red to flow into the mud. From the casket the light increased, filling the hole as if it were a liquid, rising to the level of the ground above. Every part of the casket and that which emerged was visible in the glow of its own creation. Inspector Fuchs heaved and the casket shuddered. His eyes turned upward to the twin figures in black above and cried for mercy.

"Help me."

"Did you call, sir?" came the thin, lisping voice of the watchman. "Are we ready to complete the mission, if you understand my meaning?"

Edmund saw light and heard thunder. There was cold and heat and the odor of decay. "Yes," said Edmund and there was the crashing of gears as the man with the harelip thrust his levers and the beast he sat in responded. Anna remained, wet, bedraggled, reprieved, on the edge of the hole.

The green-and-black earthmoving machine pushed its shovel-nose down toward the hole and seized the earth beside it. In one gigantic thrust it lifted a mound and dumped the soil into the gash in the clay, and in a single movement blackened the light which flooded, covered the casket, the arm and the bearlike figure of Inspector Leopold Fuchs.

Fuchs felt, saw, welcomed the descent of blackness. The weight of it released him, took the tiredness from his arms and the pain from within. He felt the force in the casket cease, the reaching claw wither. In that moment he saw himself liberated. He regretted there was not time to do more but knew he had done enough. The blackness descended, enveloped.

Above, the machine completed its task. In minutes it had replaced the wet earth, drummed the hole, erased it and its contents, destroyed the light the dark, the good the evil.

The machine's great nose moved carefully over the freshly replaced earth, sniffing for any further sign, determining that the task was complete. Then it lifted away, scanned the morning, retreated to its original position and was still.

"Fuchs." Edmund Blackstone released a long, shuddering sigh. It had happened quickly, there had been no time. He bent and touched the packed earth, lifted a little in his fingers, feeling for what he knew was no longer there. It was gone. The Moonchild was buried, its guardian with it. "My God, Fuchs. Forgive me."

"Edmund."

Edmund lifted his eyes and saw the shape of Anna.

"Edmund, I am myself again."

Edmund stood and was held as the watchman walked lightly over the muddy ground, rain upon him glistening.

"Well, sir? Is that what you came for?" The soft, polite lisping voice was detached. "Is there anything more, if you don't mind my asking?"

"What shall we do?" Edmund whispered.

"Do, sir?" The thin face tilted, the narrow eyes were faintly curious. "Why, I thought you had done all there was to do, if you understand my meaning."

"The German . . . the inspector." The words seared the lining of Edmund's mouth. "He is beneath. Buried."

"Really, sir?" The man in black raised his eyebrows. "Rather unfortunate, if you don't mind my saying so. Was there nothing that could be done?"

"Nothing."

Anna lifted her head. It was over. It was complete. Her eyes went to Edmund as his dazed expression began to re-form. "The inspector knew. He realized there was no alternative."

The watchman blinked. "He did give the impression of a gentleman who knew his business," he said politely.

Anna Blackstone looked away. The morning was opening. Early mist hung white and shrouded over the river-trees, curled about them bleaching. The sky was leaden above, but everywhere was the freshness of a new day, the sense of something beginning. The rain was clearing. There was new light on the leaves.

Edmund Blackstone drew in a lungful of the damp, earth-smelling air. There was no longer anything to do. He knew emptiness: his son had gone. The journey was over and the Moonchild returned. A friend was lost. He looked about and was surprised by the familiarity of the surroundings.

Beside, the watchman stood patiently, his blackness positive, his inevitability accepted. "If there is nothing further, sir," he said after a moment or two, "perhaps I could show you the way out again?"

"What will happen?"

"Happen, sir?" The head tilted. "Very little, I should say."

"Will questions be asked?"

"I very much doubt it, sir, if you understand my meaning. Matters are constantly changing, as you know. A hole was empty and a hole was filled. Nothing more than that, sir. I very much doubt if anyone will even notice it, if you don't mind my saying so."

"You do not question any of it?"

The narrow eyes glistened "It is not my function, sir," the polite voice replied.

"You were not expecting any of this?"

Again the lift in the almost disinterested eyes, again the wet, red scar showed life. "Well, sir, a good watchman expects anything. Anything at all, if you understand my meaning?" His mouth closed, the conversation was over.

There was a sadness in the landscape, a sense of grief the early light and the misted willows seemed to compound. Wet, red brick and turned earth; the green-and-black machine; stacked timber, gravel, hardware; a damp invading source of sorrow which reached the bone. All felt it, even the watchman, for he turned suddenly, pulling his coat tighter, and looked toward the rig. The horses stood in the mud, the whites of their eyes distinct.

"I feel we should go now, sir," the man in black requested. "The foreman will be here soon. Then it becomes his responsibility, you understand."

Edmund Blackstone nodded, reluctant to depart, unwilling to remain. Anna's hand on his arm told him she shared the dilemma. Fuchs was present: his heavy build and the black moustache, the level eyes and the gently accented English pervaded the construction site, patently lost through the mounded factors. There would be no returning.

"You do understand what I mean, sir?"

Edmund turned; beside him Anna's fine-boned face was stronger. Simon Blackstone was at rest, the Moonchild home. The earth had received as the flesh had given. Edmund and Anna Blackstone followed the small black figure of the watchman on his way to the rig. High above, a curling rook folded the leaden cloud.